A Certain Th

Amazon Customer

Seafaring Masterpiece ★★★★★

Cracking tale in the Hornblower genre. Unputdownable. If a period seafaring adventure is your preference. You can't do better than this. Can't wait for the next in the series!

Great read! ★★★★★

As seafaring books go this is a very good read and I would recommend it to a friend. Once you've picked it up you can't put it down. Looking forward to the next book.

Irish Sea Saga ★★★★★

An excellent book that was so hard to put down. Interestingly set in the Irish Sea between the wars with France, yet cleverly involving the French. Highly recommended.

Best Napoleonic war story I have read ★★★★★

Very good story and good likable people. I want to read more from this author. Good story well put together. Next one please!!!

A very Readable Book ★★★★★

Very much in the Hornblower tradition but well put together, which kept the action coming. I recommend the book wholeheartedly.

A book that was difficult to put down ★★★★★

Superb read, the story flowed smoothly from start to finish, would recommend it, it is a fine work of fiction.

Merriman and company ★★★★★

A plot involving the Irish, Welsh and French and add a bit of pre-war espionage and you might have a story. Give it to Roger Burnage and that is what you have.

Mystery and naval mayhem add further intrigue, throw in government and the secret service and you certainly want to read a little just to find out of this what it is about, and you are hooked.

Don't worry there are another six more to read

Could not put it down ★★★★★

Being from the Wirral and knowing the area very well - mind you the 1960's not the 1700's although the sea hasn't changed much - I was captured from the first chapter. I have sailed many of the areas mentioned and have even dangled my hand in the water at Parkgate although it is mainly vegetation now.
I am so pleased I was as it is a wonderful read and I am in love with Helen.

A gripping read ★★★★★

A gripping read that I struggled to put down. Entertaining and while I'm no expert seemed to be very well researched. I'll be reading the next book in the series.

Great naval historical yarn ★★★★★

Merriman is in a league with other naval heroes such as Kydd written by Stockwin. Hornblower and others. Once started you will not be able to read quickly enough. Great story.

Great read ★★★★★

Great series read the lot and thoroughly enjoy them.

Britannia Rules The Waves ☆☆☆☆☆

To all who appreciate a rousing tale of British seamen, this book is for you. Intrigue, spies, rebels and the British Navy. Who could ask for more. Well, me for one. I'm ready for the next one. Enough authenticity to leave the smell of ocean spray and tar in the nostrils.

Excellent read! ☆☆☆☆☆

Excellent read. The characters were believable, the story was exciting. The book is based on some letters found behind a fireplace and the author stuck what was documented in the letters. He has faithfully recounted what was in the letters. I now wish he would let his imagination take flight and create some adventures for a thoroughly likable character.

If you like sea stories, this book is for you ☆☆☆☆☆

This book kept me turning pages well into the night. Excellent writing about an action-packed story. Would love to read the next book in the story of Captain Merriman.

New sheriff in town ☆☆☆☆☆

This book is excellent, historical and give us a run for the money to all previously known authors. A great read.

The Merriman Chronicles

A Certain Threat

By Roger Burnage

Copyright Information

The Merriman Chronicles

Book 1

A Certain Threat

Copyright © 2012 by Roger Burnage

All rights reserved

With the exception of certain well known historical figures, the characters in this book have no relation or resemblance to any person living or dead

This book and all "The Merriman Chronicles" are works of fiction

Roger Burnage grew up in the village of Lymm, a civil parish in Warrington, Cheshire. National service with the RAF took him to Ceylon - Sri Lanka as it is now known – where he worked as a radio mechanic on large transmitters but never once flew in an aeroplane.

After release from service Roger went to work as a draughtsman at Vickers in Manchester, eventually becoming a sales engineer and travelled abroad to Scandinavia and India. It is during this period that he started to read the Hornblower novels by C. S. Forester which sparked his interest in this genre.

Roger eventually settled in North Wales to build a business and raise a family. The thoughts of writing for himself were never far from his mind. Retirement finally gave him the opportunity.

"I have always enjoyed reading history and historical novels and it was the finding of simple mistakes in some of them that encouraged me to write for myself. I find great pleasure from both writing and doing the historical research needed. The Merriman series is the result, with seven novels completed and more still in the planning stage".

The Merriman Chronicles – Books in the series

James Abel Merriman (1768 – 1843)

A Certain Threat

The Threat in the West Indies

Merriman and the French Invasion

The Threat in the East

The Threat in the Baltic

The Threat in the Americas

The Threat in the Adriatic

Edward James Merriman (1853 - 1928)

The Fateful Voyage

Contents

Foreword – Author's notes 1
Prologue 3
The Doctor and his daughter 6
Home on the Estate 17
Merriman's Court Martial 25
Magistrates and smugglers 39
A chance meeting in Chester 53
A Revenue ship is taken 62
Welshman Owen joins the smugglers 67
The Doctor operates on Merriman 77
Merriman reports to the Admiralty 89
News of French Agents 97
A new Command 108
Duties of the ship *Aphrodite* 114
A visit to the Custom House 128
French Spies & Irish Allies 139
The Viceroy of Ireland 146
Patrolling the Irish Sea 153
Wounded and rescued 163
The Cutter recaptured 179
A traitor to be hanged 193
A warning to the Captain of the *Dorset* 197
Successful operation 206

Welshman Owen returns	216
French Agent Moreau	230
Prisoners interrogated	233
Sirene attacks the *Dorset*	242
The Viceroy delivered to Dublin	249
Terrible weather and the search for *Sirene*	255
Trial and execution	269
The Lawyer flees	276
War with France Now certain	280

Foreword – Author's notes

In the spring of 1998, workmen demolishing an old nursing home in the country to the north-west of Chester, discovered bundles of old papers concealed behind a bricked up fireplace.

One of the men with more perspicacity than his fellows, rescued the papers from the bonfires of rubbish and gave them to his employer, a builder, who, knowing of my interest in such things, passed them on to me. The discovered papers were mostly in a very bad state due to the effects of dampness, mildew and the depredations of vermin over the years, and many of the oldest bundles were totally illegible. Another obvious problem was that the papers had been written by different people and some of the handwriting was not of the best. Sorting the papers into chronological order took many months of part time effort, indeed I gave up on the job for weeks and months at a time, but as I progressed with the work I realised that it was a history of the Merriman family from the late 18th century to the early years of the 20th century.

The first clearly decipherable writings referred to a certain James Abel Merriman, a naval officer at the time of the Napoleonic wars, and revealed some startling facts about French activities in and around Ireland and the Irish Sea at that time. I quickly realised that I had in my hands the material for a novel or novels about a little known part of our history.

Other papers showed that beside those serving in the navy, other members of the family were connected with the 22nd Regiment of Foot, the Cheshire Regiment. Intriguingly, a family tree was among the papers in one of the later bundles. Armed with that and from research in local archives, church records etc., it appeared that the last direct male heir of the family, Albert George Merriman was killed in France in 1916 and the last descendant, his unmarried sister Amy Elizabeth, a nurse, was also killed in France in 1917.

I have written several novels about members of the Merriman family whose members served their country and sometimes died for it and I have collected them under the heading "The Merriman Chronicles". This novel, the first, is "A CERTAIN THREAT".

Prologue

In the pale light of dawn the sea was the colour of old pewter and the sullen grey clouds emptied their contents in a steady downpour that had not ceased for several hours. As the rain eased, a stray gleam of pale sunshine broke through the clouds, illuminating a small boat moving sluggishly with the waves, urged on by the wind and flooding tide.

The boat was partly filled with water which surged backwards and forwards over the three people lying inside. Only one of these appeared to be alive. He was young, little more than a boy, wearing white breeches and a blue coat, both torn and horribly stained.

Suddenly the boat lifted and crashed down onto a sandbank causing the water inside to surge forward and splash into his face and mouth. The boy coughed, the movement causing a ripple of agony through his shoulder and chest. Weakly he tried to lift himself up to see where the boat was, but fell back against the thwart with a groan. Blood ran down his chest as the wound in his shoulder opened anew. He raised his head slowly and his eyes moving along the boat saw the two bodies half covered in water.

At once he remembered……….. the shouts and screams, the Welshman Aled, picking him up and jumping over the side, another seaman there too, swimming, climbing into the boat, the musket fire, the seaman killed even as he cut the painter to free the boat, The ball in his own shoulder and Aled shot down, dying in front of him as the boat whirled away into the darkness. He stared at the bodies with tears pricking his eyes as he thought about how kind the Welshman had been to him, a raw newcomer to the service.

He was only thirteen and he was sure he was going to die. Half lying, half sitting, leaning against the thwart, in the icy water *sloshing about in the bottom of the boat, he was aware of this with a vague sort of resentment and detached interest as though he was somebody else. His head dropped and he stared miserably at his clothing. He had been so proud of that blue coat with the brass buttons when his mother sewed them on.*

He could feel the boat bumping on the sand beneath him but he was lost in his own little world of pain and misery.

The next thing he knew, rough hands were lifting him, wrapping him, and the neck of a bottle was thrust into his mouth. The fiery spirit burned a path down his throat, he coughed, cried out and then he passed into darkness.

The Doctor and his daughter

The year 1792

Merriman wakened, cursing fluently when the coach lurched violently as a wheel dropped into a hole in the appalling road, causing his left arm and bandaged hand to bang sharply on the window frame. "God damn it to hell, can't the damned coachman keep out of the bloody holes------ Your pardon Ma'am," this last as he realized where he was and that the lovely dark haired and bright eyed young lady seated on the opposite side of the coach, swathed in a voluminous travelling cloak, was looking at him with something like a smile of amusement on her face. He flushed with annoyance and turned to the window vowing not to fall asleep again, thus giving others the opportunity to show pity or sympathy.

Despite the appalling state of the road the coachman managed to encourage his horses to maintain a reasonable speed, the old mud splashed coach bouncing and rattling as it hit the worst parts of the road or moving more smoothly on the better stretches, although better was only a relative word for it. The horses were more often than not up to their fetlocks in squishy mud, the result of the heavy rain of the last few days on to the poorly maintained road surface. Indeed it was only fit to be called a road where the turnpike trusts took the trouble to repair it which usually only happened close to the various towns and villages along the way.

The day was cold with no rain at present with but a small, pale, weak sun glimpsed briefly through the mist enveloping the countryside and which did little to help. Although the heavy frost of the early morning had mostly disappeared the air was still cold enough due to a biting easterly wind to make the breath of horses and passengers alike look like the steam from a boiling kettle. The passengers on the roof of the coach were the worst off and could only sit and shiver and huddle into their coats and scarves, cling desperately to the handrails and hope not to fall off when the coach swayed, lurched and bounced on its through braces which passed for springs. Inside, the passengers were at least sheltered from the wind and rain by the leather window blinds and in their coats and blankets managed to keep tolerably warm, some even managing to doze off on the smoother parts of their journey.

Merriman, looking out unseeingly at the passing scenery where the remnants of the late September frost lay in the hollows shaded from the weak sun and the trees were no more than black outlines, let his mind drift back over the past few weeks. The arrival of the flagship at Portsmouth, the surgeon fussing over his arm and hand, the constant pain, the fear of losing his hand and the dark despair at the realization that he had lost his ship *Conflict*, even though he had been cleared at the subsequent court martial at Gibraltar.

Unthinkingly he clenched his bandaged hand, the pain in his arm making him gasp aloud and the sweat to gather on his forehead.

"Are you unwell Sir, may we be of some assistance?"

Merriman came out of his reverie to find the lady and the elderly gentleman seated next to her leaning forward, looking anxiously at him. "Thank you Ma'am, I shall be myself directly, just a small twinge, no more." He lapsed into embarrassed silence again. The coach began to pick up speed again on a down slope and the jolting and rattling were enough to ensure that he would not drop off to sleep again.

The young lady regarded him with interest. She saw a dark haired young man of perhaps twenty-two or twenty-three years, dressed in naval uniform. His face and one visible hand were deeply tanned, so that it was clear that he had been in the tropics, but the darkness of the features was enlivened by his bright blue eyes. The face was interesting, severe and brooding as it was at present, she felt that the serious expression was but a facade to hide the real person beneath. Merriman was aware that he was still the subject of the young lady's attention which annoyed him and he looked about him with a little more interest at the passengers enduring the journey with him.

Beside the lady and gentleman opposite, to whom he had already spoken, there sat next to him a gentleman of sober appearance dressed all in black except for his cravat and tie-wig. His large, well rounded paunch and several wobbling chins indicated that he was no stranger to good living, confirmed by the food stains on the front of his waistcoat. He was trying to read what appeared to be a legal document. Beyond him, a smallish little man, with a wizened face and beady eyes, which gave him a sly and furtive look, peered from time to time into the depths of a large black leather bag which he carried clutched tightly on his knee. He too was soberly dressed.

Merriman took one look at this character's unprepossessing appearance and made an immediate judgement, saying to himself, "*I wouldn't trust that one further than I could see him.*"

In the opposite corner was a young man dressed in full regimentals, scarlet coat with buff and gold facings and buff vest and breeches, obviously an officer, fast asleep in spite of the rattling and bouncing, snoring gently, his wig twisted askew revealing a short growth of blonde almost white hair.

With a sigh, the fat man next to Merriman folded the document and passed it to the little man who carefully placed it in the black bag.

"Impossible to read Sir " he said addressing the elderly gentleman opposite to him, "As we are likely to spend some time together in this contraption before we reach our destination, it occurs to me that the time might pass more agreeably if we each knew who the others are.

"Permit me to introduce myself; my name is Jeremiah Robinson, attorney at law and this person beside me is my clerk Beadle, a man of discretion, having a prodigious memory for suits and torts, precedents and punishments, faces and names, documents, wills and all cases of law. In short, my right arm as it were." During this recital of his virtues the little man bobbed his head and smiled slyly.

"We reside in the city of Chester and I shall be heartily pleased to be back there. Too much hustle and bustle in London Sir, too much hustle and bustle. And now Sir, whom do I have the pleasure of addressing?"

The elderly man, as slim as the lawyer was fat replied "Doctor William Simpson Sir, at your service, returning home after some twenty four years in India in the employ of The East India Company, or John Company as it is commonly called." He indicated the young lady next to him, "May I present my daughter Helen, my only child."

The lawyer inclined his head, "Your servant Ma'am. A pleasure to make your acquaintance. And you Sir, it is obvious from your uniform that you are part of our glorious navy. May we know more?"

"Merriman Sir, James Merriman, Lieutenant in His Majesty's navy. As you see, nursing a small hurt received in a trifling skirmish with corsairs off the coast of Africa."

"Upon my soul" said the doctor, "I am sure that you must have many interesting tales to tell of your experiences. We've all heard about the heroic deeds of our navy but certainly you will be able to give us more details than are conveyed in the dispatches."

Merriman shook his head, "I fear that I am but a poor raconteur Sir, a sailor who might know the handling of ships in a gale or in a naval action against the enemy but one who has difficulty in finding adequate words to describe these things, especially with a lady present. But you Sir, surely you will have many strange stories to relate about your time in India. I for one would be glad to hear them."

There was a general murmur of agreement. "Well, yes I do have," replied the doctor "and I would be pleased to tell you but not whilst this infernal contraption is bouncing around so."

"If I may join in?" All heads turned towards the young army officer who sat up and straightened his wig. "I must apologize for falling asleep in your company, but it was late before I saw my bed last night and with the early start this morning, dashed if I could keep my eyes open. Captain Robert Saville, en route by way of Chester, to rejoin my regiment, the 22nd of Foot, in Ireland."

The conversation became a little more general, even Mr. Beadle chancing the odd timid remark, but as the journey continued, the talking became less frequent and each passenger retired into their own small world of discomfort and boredom, which lasted until darkness was almost upon them and the coach rattled under the archway and into the yard of the Crown Inn at Oxford.

All was then hustle and bustle, with ostlers and stable hands un-harnessing the sweating, steaming, stamping horses and servants dashing to and fro carrying the passengers' luggage into the inn, chivvied on by the innkeeper. That personage, a large jovial man almost completely bald and of prodigious girth was there to welcome the weary travelers. "Welcome,

welcome, come inside, come inside, there's a grand fire to warm you and my wife will show you to your rooms, take care with that lady's travelling case Tom you clumsy oaf, or you'll find yourself in trouble my lad!"

He appeared to say all this and more without once drawing breath. As they descended from the comparative warmth of the inside of the coach, the passengers stretched aching muscles and hurried into the inn. Merriman looked up at the half frozen passengers climbing down from the top of the coach to see his man Owen helping the servants with the baggage.

"Inside with you man, smartly now, and get yourself warm. A hot toddy will do us both good." "Aye – aye Sir, just the thing" replied the shivering man, following Merriman inside into a large room with a low ceiling where the other passengers were gathered in front of a roaring, crackling and welcoming log fire, reveling in the warmth whilst the landlord dispensed hot drinks and urged the servants to help the ladies and gentlemen with their coats, chattering all the while about the dreadful weather and the terrible state of the roads.

Later that evening, well fed and warm, Merriman relaxed in front of the fire. The doctor and his daughter had retired to their rooms, pleading fatigue from the journey. The lawyer and his clerk were in a corner, their heads close together, discussing in whispers several documents spread on the table in front of them. Owen had disappeared into the kitchens where no doubt he was trying to make himself popular with the serving girls.

The soldier had joined a group of men round a large table in one corner where a game of cards was in progress. One of the men, a tall, lean, hawk faced individual, was obviously of quality, but the other three appeared to be rougher types although perhaps a little better dressed than one might expect. One of these three was a large, fat man with a pock marked face wearing a grey coat and breeches. The table was illuminated by a lantern suspended from one of the beams overhead which did little more than give the players enough light to see their cards and which cast heavy shadows beneath the table. Watching the men, Merriman saw one of them pass a card to the fat man on his right who surreptitiously slid it into his cuff. It was obvious that the others had not seen this, so Merriman rose to his feet and casually approached the table as a spectator might do.

That the soldier and the hawk-faced man were losing was clear from the small pile of coins before each of them and the larger pile in front of the fat man.

"Come Sir, must we wait all night for you to play?" said one of the ruffians with a sly grin at his fellows.

The soldier cursed, "Damn me, it's no use, you have the better of me again" and he threw down his cards with something like despair. The fat man placed his cards on the table and reached forward for the coins in the center of the table with a smile of triumph on his face, which instantly disappeared when he felt the muzzle of Merriman's pocket pistol pressed below his ear.

"I think Gentlemen, that you should all place your hands on the table or this little toy might go off" and for emphasis Merriman cocked the small double-barreled pistol.

He continued, speaking to the fat man, "You are an honest man and I'm your uncle. That's two lies at once."

"Damn me Mr. Merriman, what's this," cried the soldier as they all complied with Merriman's command including the hawk-faced man who smiled briefly, saying nothing.

"If you would feel in this fellow's cuff, I think that is all the explanation you will need."

Saville reached forward and felt in the cuff, pulling out three playing cards.

"By God! A cheat," he cried. "I thought his cards were too damned lucky. Quite plainly these three are together so I think this gentleman and I should share the pot."

The table went over with a crash as the fat man threw himself violently backwards. As he fell, Merriman caught a glimpse of a glittering blade in the man's hand and felt his pistol explode. The man screamed and fell away and then Saville was helping Merriman to his feet. One of the ruffians was cowering on the floor clutching his arm from which blood was falling in bright drops to the floor. The fat man and the third man had vanished as had the lawyer and his clerk.

"I'm vastly obliged to you Sir," declared the other gentleman, wiping a long blade on the coat of the man on the floor and then sliding it into his walking cane with a snap. "I'd been loosing steadily as had your friend, but could not see how they were cheating. Allow me to introduce myself. My name is Laurence Grahame, travelling independently to Chester as a guest of friends in that city."

Merriman bowed. "Lieutenant Merriman Sir. My friend, though I scarcely know him, is Captain Saville." He turned to the innkeeper who had appeared from somewhere and was wringing his hands and babbling some nonsense about villains using his respectable establishment to try and rob decent people.

"Pull yourself together man, for goodness sake, and throw out this wretched fellow who is bleeding all over your floor. Then whilst we sit by the fire and discuss these events, you can collect the money scattered about the floor and give it to these gentlemen. Then you can bring each of us a good measure of your best brandy, to my account."

The three of them settled down together and after the usual pleasantries the conversation turned to the subject of card cheats, general villains and highwaymen. Coaches were frequently stopped on the more lonely stretches of road by highwaymen looking for easy pickings from wealthy travelers.

"Of course such rogues must be desperate to do what they do, for they would be hanged if caught" remarked Mr. Grahame, "although I'm sure that some of them do it for pure devilry or the thrill of adventure".

"Such people are often given the choice between hanging or imprisonment or being pressed into the King's service", said Merriman. "Heaven knows the navy always needs more men, though I'm not sure that those who choose the navy realise what a hard life they are in for as the punishments at sea can be harsh for any wrong doing".

The conversation soon became more general with Merriman and Saville finding much in common to discuss. Grahame was more reserved though when the talk turned to politics and the possibilities of war with France he became quite eloquent.

The following morning, as the passengers gathered for breakfast, the doctor enquired about the shot he had heard the previous evening. "As there was no further disturbance I judged it wiser to stay upstairs after calming my daughter who was rather alarmed."

"Nonsense Father, I was not in the least alarmed. Indeed what you did was to stop me coming down to see what was going on."

There was excited discussion for a few moments while the lawyer explained what had happened, but the need to fortify themselves for the continuing journey ahead caused the hum of voices to be replaced by the rattle of cutlery and the scurrying footsteps of the servants bringing more steaming dishes to the table.

Merriman finished his meal, a modest one by the standards of the day, a naval officer's stomach not being used to such rich fare, to find the dark eyes of Miss Simpson fixed upon him. She was in no way embarrassed to be seen to be studying him, but having gained his attention immediately spoke. "I am pleased that you and these other gentlemen are none the worse for your adventure of last night Lieutenant, I'm only sorry that we missed all the excitement"

"Little enough excitement Ma'am, it was over in a very few moments, really nothing for you to concern yourself with," replied Merriman with a laugh.

"Maybe Sir, but I believe that if it were not for your actions these two gentlemen would have lost money to those fellows."

"Indeed you are right Ma'am," broke in Captain Saville, "I was losing heavily to the rogues, nearly all my allowance in fact. If the Lieutenant here had not such sharp eyes I would be in the difficult position of asking my father for more. *He* wouldn't be pleased I assure you."

"There you are then" said the young lady, "Mr. Merriman has amply displayed the qualities we have come to expect from our naval heroes."

"Nothing heroic about it" mumbled Merriman, "I took the fellows by surprise, and to quote the proverb, 'A man surprised is half beaten'".

"Come Sir, you are too modest" she replied.

Merriman, beginning to tire of this repartee rose to his feet and with a muttered excuse he left the room, convinced that the woman was laughing at him.

Soon afterwards they all boarded the coach. The driver settled himself on his seat and gathered up the reins and his whip and at his shout the ostlers released their hold on the horses' bridles and jumped clear. At the crack of the whip over their heads the eager horses lunged forward and the coach was on its way.

Home on the Estate

Two days later the coach arrived in Chester and with a flourish of his whip the coachman turned the horses into the yard of the "Pied Bull" inn. The passengers alighted thankfully, straightening cramped backs and legs with relief.

A small crowd had gathered to welcome the travelers and Merriman saw his father at the back, somewhat aloof from the rest. A voice in his ear and a hand on his arm made him turn to find the soldier behind him. "I shall be in Chester for some time, quartered near the castle and I should be honoured if you were to allow me to entertain you to dinner one evening."

"I would be delighted Sir, I'll send a message to you when I'm settled. I'm sure you will be welcome to my father's house in return." With mutual expressions of goodwill, and a handclasp, the two friends parted.

Merriman pushed through the crowd suddenly realizing that the tall young fellow next to his father must be his younger brother Matthew, now nearly fourteen years old. As he embraced his father Merriman could not help but think how much older his father looked although the grasp of the hand was as strong and the great booming voice as powerful as ever it was when his father commanded one of His Majesty's frigates.

" 'Fore God, James, it is good to see you again after so long, what, five years is it? Your mother and sister are waiting at home, but young Matthew here has been beside himself with excitement for a week or more, ever since we heard that you were coming home, and he would waste no time in meeting you."

His father grasped him by the shoulders, looking keenly into his face. "Aye son, you've weathered some and you need feeding up a bit, but a few weeks of good home fare will soon put that right. Now then, who is this fellow? A sailor if I'm any judge."

Owen was standing behind Merriman trying to look inconspicuous, but with his great breadth of shoulder and his air of confidence and competence it was no easy matter and his tarpaulin jacket and other clothing and the pigtail he affected marked him as a seaman to anyone.

"This is Owen, Father, topmast hand in *Conflict*. Somehow he attached himself to me when I was injured. Without him I do not believe that I would be alive today. He is worth three men in a fight."

"Owen, eh! You'll be a Welshman then! Good man, we'll find room for you. I see that you have the Lieutenant's baggage there already, so bring it along to the carriage and we'll be off."

Whilst all this was happening, Matthew was practically bouncing with excitement, pulling on his brother's sleeve and asking questions one after the other without waiting for an answer. "Steady on there", said Merriman, laughing, "I'll tell you all in good time, but let's get home first."

Home was a small manor and estate near Burton, in the countryside north-west of Chester, which Captain Joseph Merriman, fortunate in the matter of prize money and a small inheritance, had purchased many years ago. It was a comfortable, late 17th century gentleman's residence with stabling and coach house and the servants quarters properly concealed round the back of the main house. From the raised position of the house there was a fine view over to the wide estuary of the river Dee.

As the carriage turned into the driveway the grey-muzzled old dog lying on the front step of the house slowly climbed to his feet, sniffed the air and gave a tentative wag to his tail. Half blind as he was he knew that there was something new. When Merriman stepped down from the carriage the dog launched himself off the step, took a few confirmatory sniffs at Merriman's leg and then broke into a fit of wild barking, jumped up at him and then whirled round and round in a frenzy of excitement. As his master bent down to scratch his ears his tail wagged so violently that it seemed liable to fly off at any moment.

"Old Jack hasn't forgotten you it seems," said Matthew with a grin.

"No, he's pleased to see me, that's obvious," replied Merriman, kneeling down to make more fuss of the dog, which rolled over on to his back and squirmed in a paroxysm of delight as the man scratched his stomach..

The sound of the carriage wheels on the driveway had brought servants running. The front door opened and Merriman immediately found himself in the midst of chaos. His mother was there with tears in her eyes and her arms open to enfold him, his sister Emily, now some seventeen years old and torn between capering round like an excited girl and showing herself to be a prim and proper young lady. Merriman disentangled himself from his mother, kissed and hugged his sister, made more fuss of old Jack and then tripped over one of several other dogs who, even though they did not understand why, thought it their duty to bark excitedly and get under everyone's feet.

Merriman sat on the bottom step, laughing with pure happiness, the others all smiling and laughing with delight. He caught sight of Annie, his mother's housekeeper and friend, silver haired now but as buxom and round cheeked as ever, standing in the doorway.

"Bless you Master James, I'm so happy to see you again. But you're so thin! We must get some meat on those bones with some of my good cooking inside you."

"I'm sure that if I stay here long I'll get as fat as a pig." He laughed, giving her a hug and a kiss on the cheek and then she bustled off into the depths of the house pushing the servants in front of her.

A growl from Jack diverted his attention and he turned to see his dog sniffing suspiciously at Owen's trouser leg whilst the big sailor stood there hardly daring to move.

"All right Jack, he's a friend, leave him alone," said Merriman. "Owen, do you follow them into the house, and I warrant you'll eat better than you have done for many a day."

"Aye-aye Sir!" said Owen who had viewed all the greetings with amazement. The laughing lieutenant appearing to be another person from the serious disciplinarian who had been his captain in the brig *Conflict*. He disappeared into the depths of the house carrying his own small bundle of possessions.

"Now then, inside with you or we shall all freeze out here" called his father, "James will need to freshen up after the journey and then we can gather by the fire to hear of his adventures. Matthew, control yourself, your questions must wait awhile."

In the house, as Merriman ascended the great staircase with his old dog struggling to keep up, the memories came flooding back of his childhood here, of how once he had been frightened of the serious faces looking down from the portraits on the walls; there his grandfather, old Admiral Elias Merriman, here his grandmother, who so the story went, came from a distinguished and noble family that had rejected her when she insisted on marrying the young Captain Merriman. And there at the turn of the stair, the newest portrait, that was his uncle Major Nathaniel Merriman who had fought and died with his regiment during the withdrawal of the British army from Boston to New York in the spring of 1776. That was sixteen years ago and the war with the colonies over these last nine years.

Some of the portraits showed men in full wigs, laces and ribbons of a past age, some in the sober garb of Cromwell's soldiers, but there was no sailor until his grandfather. Merriman suddenly realized that neither of his parents had as yet sat for a portrait painter and he resolved there and then to persuade them to do so.

Here was his room just as he remembered it from his boyhood. From the window the glimpse of the sea off the estuary of the river Dee. His model boats were still there by the bed, built to fight imaginary sea battles on the local duck pond, that imagination fed by the tales told by his old grandfather, of wild deeds and terrible gales, of fights with pirates and savages under tropical skies, until his mind could foresee no other future than to be a naval officer.

When he returned downstairs he found the family gathered in the largest reception room of the house before a blazing log fire. Candles had been lit and the room was almost as bright as day. His father was pouring claret into some long stemmed glasses and passing them round, even to young Matthew. As they each sat or stood, holding their glasses he said "A toast to our returning hero, may he bring more honour to our name and end up as an admiral."

"But Father, I'm no hero" protested Merriman.

"Not what I hear and read" retorted the elder Merriman, "We hear about it all eventually and I have the gazette posted to me regularly. As far back as the Battle of the Saintes your mettle was quite clearly revealed in Admiral Rodney's despatch when he commended your actions; in a footnote I know, but that you came to his attention did no harm to your career I can tell you, especially as you were still only a midshipman."

"Yes to be sure, but that was years ago and since then there has been little activity to provide opportunity for promotion – the war with the American colonies is over. France is busy with the guillotine and the revolution, and Spain is-------"

"Oh we know all that," his father interrupted, "But we heard about the brilliant action against the privateers off the Malabar coast. Your captain was pleased enough with you to put you in the captured brig as prize-master and you were confirmed in command by the Admiral at the Cape of Good Hope before being sent back to England with despatches. Besides, you have been fortunate to be employed when so many fine officers have been on the beach on half pay since peace was signed."

"That's as maybe, but that's all I've been doing for the last four years, carrying despatches, little more than a messenger really, and since then I have lost my ship *Conflict* and many good men and disobeyed orders into the bargain. If it had not turned out so well I could have been disgraced and sent home, the cripple that I am." And he raised his bandaged left hand in emphasis. "What career will I have now?"

As if in understanding, Jack pressed against his leg and whined softly.

His mother took his hand in hers and said gently, "James, dear James, how bad is your hurt, you still have your hand and the use of your arm, that I can see."

"Yes Mother, but it cannot grasp and hold anything with any strength and my arm has a piece out of it which prevents rapid movement; no, a bird with a broken wing I am and of no more use to the navy" he said bitterly.

His brother, who had been making heroic efforts to control his impatience cried out, "There are many officers with a hand, an arm or even a leg missing, who continue in the navy, James, why not you? And you have not yet told us what happened,-- was it cannon fire, a sword cut or did you ---------"

"All right I'll give you the details, but I see that Annie is signalling that the meal is ready, so let us be about it for I must confess I'm famished."

Over the meal the story of Merriman's progress in the navy was re-lived. From his appointment as midshipman at the age of twelve to a frigate commanded by Captain Edwards, one of his father's friends, his good fortune to be on Admiral Rodney's flagship at the battle of The Saintes and his passing the examination for lieutenant at eighteen. After that his steady progress from fifth officer to third officer, dead men's shoes really and then his appointment, with Rodney's recommendation, as second officer on a frigate sailing for India.

As the servants quietly moved about removing the dishes and lighting fresh candles, young Matthew burst out, "James, I have been patient long enough. Can't we hear how you were wounded and lost your ship?"

"Indeed you have, young man, and now you shall find out, but I think that your mother and sister should retire, as this is a tale of killing and bloodshed, not fit for a lady to hear."

"James is right," said his mother, "Come along Emily, we shall leave the men to it." As the ladies left the room, the men settled themselves more comfortably, their glasses recharged, and Merriman began.

"You know that I was captain of the *Conflict* for nearly four years, employed only to carry despatches and such, as fast as possible between England, Gibraltar, Jamaica or anywhere else the Admiralty directed. An uneventful and boring time it was until last April, when we were returning to Gibraltar from Cape Town. My orders were to make the fastest passage I could as the documents we carried were of extreme urgency. I was to avoid all other ships."

"It was a glorious day and I had every sail set. The ship was fairly flying along, crashing through the waves with the spray bursting over the rail in clouds. I remember standing watching some of the hands helping the sailmaker stretch out a sail for repair; others were splicing, painting or doing some of the endless work needing to be done on a ship of war and we had even organised a shark fishing contest. Life aboard was going well, there had been no punishments for over three weeks and none of us had any idea of what was about to follow, but it happened this way……

Merriman's Court Martial

The scorching sun beat down from an almost cloudless sky and sparkled from the waves and spray as His Majesty's brig *Conflict* crashed through the long Atlantic swell, the legacy of the north-westerly gale which the ship's company had fought for the last three days.

The wind had since veered to the south west and *Conflict* was making good the time lost. The sunlit scene, and the strong wind on the larboard quarter made for conditions which should have delighted the heart of any seaman, but the officer dressed in grubby white trousers and faded, salt stained coat saw none of it.

Lieutenant James Merriman stared gloomily and unseeingly along the length of the main deck. When he took command of the ship he had such high hopes, and since then there had been nothing, absolutely nothing to break the monotony of life at sea. Oh, he knew he did his job efficiently, keeping the ship and crew ready for any eventuality, but all he and the ship had done for four years was to carry despatches. God, he was bored.

He contemplated the earlier years of his career. There had always been plenty of excitement and action to keep a young naval officer's life interesting, indeed the last action of note he had been involved in was the capture of a French brig off the Malabar coast by the frigate *Calcutta*.. The captain of *Calcutta* had sent him with a prize crew to Cape Town where he had been confirmed in command of the brig, renamed *Conflict*.

So lost in thought was he that at first he did not notice his First Lieutenant Alan Jones hovering nearby, obviously not wanting to break into his captain's reverie. Lieutenant Jones was a stocky, red haired young man, the possessor of bright green eyes, the legacy of some Irish ancestor no doubt. The two young men had formed a friendship which although never crossing the line separating the ship's captain from his officers, was nevertheless a close one.

Merriman dragged his mind back to the present, "Yes Alan, what is it?"

"Morning report Sir, as in your standing orders."

"Of course. My apologies, my mind was far away. Anything new?"

"Nothing Sir. The storm damage is all repaired except for the torn tops'l, and that is going back aloft even now. Seaman Smith's broken leg is healing well and he'll be fit to return to duty in a day or two. Oh! and that fool Biggins has been up to his tricks again, making a nuisance of himself round the ship. But apart from that the ship is in all respects ready for action."

The man Biggins that the Lieutenant referred to was simple minded and fond of playing harmless but annoying tricks on his messmates. The crew tolerated the poor fellow and kept him from causing too much bother, indeed he was something of a mascot to them and they helped him with his simple duties to ensure that he did not fall foul of authority. The livid scar on the side of his head received in some long ago fight with the French probably explained his mental disorder.

Lieutenant Jones coughed apologetically. "Sir, there is one more thing."

"Yes?"

"The men have asked if they can fish for shark Sir. The Bos'n has made some very serviceable hooks and there's that tub of rotten meat we found yesterday which would make bait Sir," he continued eagerly.

"An excellent idea. All work and no play……..eh! But we'll make a competition of it; that should make a welcome break in routine and cheer the men up. Have our two midshipmen select teams, of what, six or ten men each, to fish from each side. And of course there must be a prize. Shall we say an extra tot of rum for the men in the team which is first to hook a shark, two tots if they bring it aboard."

"Aye-aye Sir," said Jones with a huge grin on his face.

When the details of the competition were announced, an excited chattering broke out on deck as the men clustered round midshipmen Andrews and Dalkeith, hoping to be picked. Soon all was ready and waiting for Merriman to give the word to start. He was pleased to see that the strongest men had been selected, as it would take brute strength to haul a struggling, fighting shark aboard. Knowing it would please the men he made a show of inspecting them. Looking at the hooks and lines a thought struck him.

"Mr Jones, they'll not catch sharks with this gear. A shark would bite through the lines too easily. There should be a length of chain lashed between the hook and line. I'm surprised nobody thought of that."

With the chain added and the hooks baited with the stinking, rotten meat Merriman gave the word to start. The hooks splashed down almost together and the teams were running the lines out as fast as they could to the encouraging shouts of their shipmates.

Looking astern it was obvious that the weight of the chain was insufficient to take the bait below the water and it could be seen splashing along on the surface.

"Haul them in lads and add some more chain, that should do it."

It did indeed do it and the towed bait disappeared below the surface, trailing the scent of putrid meat behind. It was not long before the sinister fin of a shark appeared, soon joined by others. The seamen on the lines spat on their hands and took a firmer grip. Men were clustered in the rigging and leaning over the bulwarks, eager to watch the sport and see which team would win. Bets were laid and the air rang with raucous and rude comments about each team's ability.

"Don't know why you was picked, Jimmy you skinny bugger. There's more muscle on a belaying pin" yelled a seaman on the mainyard to his mate in one of the teams. For answer Jimmy raised two fingers aloft, concentrating his attention on settling his bare feet into the sand which had been sprinkled on the deck to provide a firmer foothold.

For several minutes nothing happened, then suddenly the larboard side team staggered and nearly fell as a shark took their bait and impaled itself on the hook. Their supporters burst into cheers and shouts of advice, and then the other bait was taken and both teams were struggling to haul in the frantically struggling creatures as they appeared on the surface.

The first team had their fish almost alongside when another huge shark appeared and bit clean through the body leaving only the head on the hook. All eyes turned to the second team who now had their shark hanging alongside with it's tail just out of the water.

"Deck there! Sail dead ahead." The strident hail from the masthead cut through the clamour on deck. In spite of the excitement, naval discipline had kept the lookouts aloft and the ship's wheel manned.

"Up you go Mr. Andrews. Take a glass and tell me what you see."

"Aye-aye Sir." The midshipman scampered aloft, settled himself on the fore tops'l yard and focussed the heavy telescope. "It looks like an Indiaman Sir, she's lost her fore and main topmasts. There are two smaller ships close by. There's gun- smoke Sir, they are fighting."

"Very good Mr. Andrews, stay there and keep your eyes peeled." Merriman looked round for his first lieutenant, "Ah - Mr. Jones, have those fish cut loose. Beat to quarters if you please and clear for action, lively now. And I'll have the last reefs taken off the tops'ls. Mr. Dalkeith, we'll have the colours hoisted."

Merriman, gloom and boredom and fishing forgotten, watched as the small midshipman called his assistants to the flag locker and began to bend on the ensigns to the halliards. With no marine drummer on board, a ship's boy was beating to quarters somewhat erratically and the ship came alive with the noise of running feet, shouted orders and the bangs and crashes from below as partitions and non-essentials were hastily taken down to the hold.

"Sir, Sir," shrilled young Andrews from his perch, "They must be Algerians, they're full of men and one of them is trying to go alongside the Indiaman."

"Thank you Mr. Andrews, come down now and stay by me."

Merriman's thoughts raced. The Indiaman must have lost her spars in the recent gale which had blown her nearer to the African coast than was usual. No action for four years and now his small ship *Conflict* would have to face not one but two of the typical low, open ships with lateen sails, which would be full of bloodthirsty Algerian fighting men, known as corsairs, probably based in some small harbour on the West African coast which could just be seen as a vague shadow on the far horizon to starboard. From there they could dash out and with their greater speed and handiness, catch any slow and lumbering merchantman they could find, although it was unusual for a fast, well handled Indiaman to fall into their hands. Any male passengers and crew who survived the attack had only a life of slavery to look forward to and as for the women *their* fate could only be imagined.

Merriman thanked his stars that he had insisted on daily gun drill, exercises with half the crew pretending to be sick or injured, seamen given unexpected orders in the middle of sail practice or other manoeuvre so that in spite of grumbles from some, the crew were as well trained as he could make them, although shorthanded due to the usual losses caused by sickness and accidents inseparable from a life at sea.

The lack of crew was only one part of his problem. He was under orders to proceed with all despatch to Gibraltar with urgent documents. If he attacked the two corsairs and he won, he would most likely be court-martialed for risking his ship and the papers and disobeying orders and be dismissed from the navy. On the other hand, if his ship was overwhelmed, the papers would not reach their destination and he would be -- -- well, he would be dead. But, there could be women on that merchantman, how could he avoid the action? He was damned if he did and damned if he didn't.

"Ship cleared for action Sir" reported the first lieutenant, "and we cut five seconds off our previous best time."

"Very good Mr. Jones, that was well done. Stand by."

Merriman was surprised to see how close they were to the other ships. Already they were hull up and could just be seen from the deck. Gun smoke was billowing out around the Indiaman but the sound of gunfire was carried away from them by the wind.

"Mr. Jones, I want all guns loaded with grapeshot and run out. Make sure that every man has his weapons to hand."

Merriman waited until they were much nearer to the other ships before turning to the first Lieutenant, I'll have courses and royals off her if you please and brail up the spanker. We'll fight under topsails and headsails this day."

"Aye-aye Sir" he responded, turning to bawl the necessary orders.

Men swarmed aloft hastened by the curses of the boatswain's mates, each trying to ensure that his group of men was faster than the others. The courses and royals disappeared like magic and the ships ahead were clearly seen.

One of the attackers was now alongside the Indiaman and he could see the Indiaman's crew fighting desperately to hold back the flood of boarders.

He wondered what effect his nine-pounder popguns would have, but they were the best he could do. There was no time for further speculation, one of the corsairs had seen them and was trying to turn to meet them.

"Pass the word to the gun crews Mr. Andrews, we will engage the enemy to larboard first as we pass then we will go about and give him the starboard battery. All to fire as their guns bear, aimed low to sweep her deck."

The midshipman ran off and then they were engaging. The little nine – pounders erupted one after the other in flame and smoke and as they passed, Merriman could see the carnage wrought by the grapeshot as it ripped along the packed deck of the corsair.

The gun crews were working like madmen to sponge out and reload as Merriman ordered "Bring her round Mr. Jones." The sails were shaking and flapping as *Conflict* turned across the wind, the seamen hauling madly on the sheets and braces and then she was round and under way again, close hauled on the other tack..

Merriman felt the old excitement gripping him again.

"Ready lads, pound the devils hard. Fire!" The starboard cannon roared out and Merriman saw the screaming mass of humanity heave as the blast of shot hit. Blood was running out of the scuppers of the corsair and much of the rigging seemed to be gone.

The single mast swayed and fell. A few hardy souls still brandished swords and muskets and screamed oaths but they were finished as a threat to *Conflict*.

"By God Sir, two broadsides and nothing in return" shrieked Andrews, capering about with excitement.

"There will be" retorted Merriman, "Now we'll see what we can do against the other ship." He turned to the First Lieutenant, "Round again Mr. Jones, if you please." The ship spun about and the guns delivered a third smashing blow to the corsair as she passed.

The gun crews were again working frantically to reload, the hours of gun drill proving their worth. Now they were passing the stern of the Indiaman and the second attacker came into view.

"As your guns bear" roared Merriman. Again the ship trembled as the cannon thundered, the shot tearing into those men still aboard the corsair. Merriman felt his hat plucked off his head by a musket ball and saw a seaman fall by one of the guns, his eyes wide with shock and his shout of agony cut off by the blood pouring from his mouth and splashing over the other men in the gun crew. In the heat of the action they took no notice and simply dragged him out of their way. Their reaction would come later.

The simpleton Biggins was clinging to the ratlines, shaking his cutlass at the enemy and screaming curses at them. "Bastard French buggers, I'll skewer you all, I'll cut your bleedin' 'eads off, I'll ……..!" He carried on telling them what he was going to do to them until two seamen dragged him down, still cursing, into the dubious shelter of the ship's bulwarks.

"Keep down you silly sod, you'll get yerself killed," shouted one, "they're not French, they're bleedin' pirates."

Merriman observed this with part of his mind while still alive to what was going on about him. "Mr. Jones, have the larboard battery loaded with grape-shot again, then we'll lay her alongside and board," he roared above the noise.

As the ship turned and lost way when the sheets were loosened to spill the wind from the sails, midshipman Andrews was flung backwards onto the deck. He struggled to his feet clutching at his shoulder, blood running down his arm as Merriman steadied him.

"Get below Mr Andrews and have that wound attended to."

"Can't I stay Sir, please. I want to see -----."

"Do as you are told boy" said Merriman, "That's an order." Looking forr-ard Merriman could see the naked sweating backs of his gunners waiting to fire, whilst the rest of the crew gathered in their allotted boarding parties clutching their cutlasses and pistols. Others ready with grapnels to fasten the ships together.

" 'ere Sir, you'll be needing this," said a burly seaman, handing him a cutlass. Merriman realized that his own sword was still hanging, forgotten, in his cabin. As they crashed alongside the guns flamed again, the grapnels were thrown and then the two ships were locked together.

"Now lads, boarders away" yelled Merriman. As he leapt across and down onto the enemy deck he glimpsed Lieutenant Jones, sword in hand, leading his boarding party from the foredeck.

He parried a sword wielded by a turbanned Arab and sliced the man across the neck, a seaman by Merriman screamed as a spear was thrust into his stomach, his assailant immediately falling to a vicious slash from another seaman. Merriman felt splashes of blood and matter across his face as a seaman brained a screaming negro with a boarding axe. There was no time for fancy swordsmanship. All was confusion, it was cut and slash, thrust and parry, stamping forward, slipping on pools of blood, stumbling over bodies and parts of bodies that yet twitched and writhed, with shouts and screams of fear and agony ringing in his ears. Then suddenly they were across the corsair's deck with the Indiaman's side rearing above them.

Up they went, wild with fear and rage, men grappling with each other, stabbing and hacking in a fury, up onto the deck where the Indiaman's passengers and crew, now fewer in number, had retreated to the poop deck and were hemmed in by the enemy.

Merriman hurled himself forward with the rest of his men, something hit his left arm and head a ferocious blow and he found himself lying on the deck, looking up to see two seamen astride him fighting like demons to protect him. One was Biggins, laying about him with a bloody axe in one hand and a bent cutlass in the other, still screaming his hatred of the French, before falling to a pike thrust through his thigh. And then it was over, the corsairs were either dead or leaping overboard to escape the ready swords of the victors. Merriman climbed to his feet with the help of the brawny seaman who had defended him. He stood there swaying, trying to force his dazed mind to comprehend that he was still alive.

"Mr. Jones, how many have we lost," he asked.

"Mr. Jones is dead Sir" said a voice behind him.

A tall gentleman, elegant despite the sweat and blood on his attire and still holding a bloodied sword, stepped in front of him.

"I am Lord Stevenage Sir. I must thank you for your most timely arrival. We had almost despaired when your ship was sighted but that gave us hope to hold on and keep on fighting. May I congratulate you and your men on a most gallant rescue." The voice seemed to come from a long way away.

"Lieutenant Merriman my Lord, I am pleased to be of service to you Sir, I hope that -----". He swayed, everything whirled round and he heard a voice cry "Catch him" before all went black. ....

As he recounted the details of the fight with the two vessels attacking the Indiaman, Merriman could see from the gleam in his father's eye that he was following the narrative with keen attention, and as for Matthew, his wide eyes and open mouth were as Merriman himself must have looked when listening to his grandfather's stories.

"And that was all I remember" said Merriman to his Father. "I came to my senses three days later. I had lost my First Lieutenant and friend Alan Jones, my Second Lieutenant Mr. Hamer, the bo'sn and fifteen seamen. Many more were injured including Mr. Andrews the midshipman. The Indiaman had lost her captain, twelve crew and several male passengers."

Young Matthew was staring at him with awe and his Father's eyes were staring into the distance, no doubt he was remembering sea fights in his own career.

"But how did you lose your ship." persisted Matthew.

"In another gale," he replied. "We stayed alongside the Indiaman whilst the survivors of both ships made repairs to the Indiaman's masts and rigging. It appears that the ship's captain, in the interest of making a fast voyage, had held his canvas on too long and lost his topmasts as a result. If he hadn't, the corsairs wouldn't have caught him."

"We had no further trouble from them. The first one had sunk, the second one was too badly damaged to be worth much, besides, we were too short handed to spare a prize crew, so that one was set afire. None of the remaining Algerians survived. Those who hadn't been killed were swiftly taken by sharks when they jumped overboard."

Merriman paused for a moment or two. "I'm glad I didn't see that, he said reflectively. "Anyway, as soon as we were able we sailed together for Gibraltar. On that night it began to blow and by the following morning it was a full gale. I was unconscious in my bunk, there were no officers left and Mr. Andrews and a master's mate were in command of the depleted crew with the help of Mr. Dalkeith, the youngest midshipman, only fourteen years old. They were desperately short handed and exhausted."

"On the second night the wind veered suddenly and the ship was taken all aback, loosing the foremast and main topmast which trailed alongside. Before they could be cut loose they'd pounded a hole in the ship's side."

"By dawn it was obvious that the ship couldn't be saved, the crew was exhausted and the sea was gaining over the pumps. Mr. Andrews, to his credit, decided to abandon ship before she sank. Fortunately the Indiaman was still nearby and was able to take us all aboard."

"By the Gods, James, that was a wonderful account," exclaimed the elder Merriman, "It reflects great credit on you and your crew. That young Midshipman, what's his name? --- Andrews, he did well."

Merriman nodded, "Yes he did, very well. The more so when you remember that he was wounded and in pain all the time. He kept his wits about him and even remembered to go to my cabin to collect my orders and the documents we were carrying, before abandoning ship. But his activities didn't end there. When we arrived in Gibraltar he took himself off to the port Admiral and made a verbal report, following which the Admiral ordered myself and the rest of my crew brought ashore."

"Had you not recovered your senses by then?" asked Matthew.

"No" replied Merriman, "I developed a fever and can vaguely remember thrashing around in a cot and Owen holding me down whilst the surgeon from the flagship probed, cut and sewed and bandaged me up."

His father nodded, "This man Owen seems to have attached himself to you."

Merriman smiled, "Yes, I don't know how he did it, but when the rest of the men from my crew were sent to other ships, he remained and has acted as my servant ever since. He can't read or write and he isn't an imaginative man but it seems that his honesty and loyalty have been proven. He is a first rate seaman and obviously a tremendous fighter as he is one of the two men who protected me when I received my injury."

"He may not be imaginative as you say, but I think that he had the wit to realize that you are an officer likely to go far and he could do worse than attach himself to you."

"Then what happened?" asked his brother.

"Several days later I was well enough to write a full report for the Admiral, after which I was transferred to the flagship to await the inevitable court-martial."

Matthew groaned, "Oh, it seems so unfair after all you had done."

"Naval regulations," said his father. "Whenever a King's ship is lost from any cause, the captain always faces a court-martial. However I gather that yours went well James."

"Indeed Father, I was very fortunate. My report had been seen by the officers called to form the court and they questioned Mr. Andrews and Master's mate Varley very closely on all the events that had happened. I felt from the demeanour of the court that I might survive, but the biggest surprise was still to come. A note was handed to the chairman of the court, Admiral Stokes, which raised his eyebrows. 'Permit the gentleman to enter and find him a seat,' he ordered.'"

"When the gentleman was seated and the chattering of the spectators had been stilled, the Admiral spoke."

'I believe My Lord, that you have something to say in Lieutenant Merriman's defence. You may address the court Sir.'

'Thank you' said the new arrival, rising to his feet. 'I am William D'Ablay, fourth Lord Stevenage and I was a passenger on the Indiaman. There is no doubt that I and all aboard that unfortunate ship would have perished but for the gallant service performed by Lieutenant Merriman and his ship and crew. I cannot commend him highly enough for his actions and I do not believe that this court would wish to deprive His Majesty's Navy of such a brave and competent officer.' "

Continued Merriman "After that the court retired and when I was brought in again I knew immediately that I was cleared."

Matthew broke in impulsively, "How did you know that James?"

Merriman grinned, "Because my sword was on the table and the hilt of it was towards me. If I'd been found guilty then the point would have been towards me. Then the Admiral announced that all charges were dismissed and he commended me in the warmest possible terms. After the court had adjourned he told me that he was promoting Mr. Andrews immediately to Lieutenant although he had not yet taken his examination, and both Mr. Varley and Mr. Dalkeith would have favourable mention in their records."

"All ended happily then," said his father, "The very fact that Andrews was promoted shows approval of your actions. You made a good friend in Lord Stevenage and that could help you in the future, of that I have no doubt. As they say 'A friend in court makes the process short'. When your wound has fully healed and you are ready for sea service again, he may have some influence on your career. And now I can see that you are both tired, so let us be off to our beds."

As he prepared for bed, Merriman wondered if he would have any kind of future in the Navy. He was asleep as soon as his head touched the pillow.

Magistrates and smugglers

When he had finished one of Annie's huge breakfasts the next morning, Merriman announced his intention of taking a ride to some of his old haunts along the side of the river Dee and up towards Neston and Parkgate on the estuary. It was a beautiful morning, but a cold one and in the clear air the hills and mountains of Wales could easily be seen. Further up the estuary he observed a few brave souls risking the hazardous crossing over the sands from Flint to Shotwick on foot, as people had been doing for centuries.

He had covered several miles when he observed a lady and gentleman walking ahead of him. As he drew level with them he saw that they were his fellow travellers on the journey from London, Doctor Simpson and his daughter Helen.

"Good morning to you," greeted the doctor, "Won't you dismount and walk with us for a while?"

"Gladly, Sir," he replied, "I fear that I have ridden too far already, judging by my aches and pains. It's too long since I sat a horse and naval life gives little opportunity for riding."

He turned to the girl, "Good morning Ma'am, I hope you are recovered from the fatigues of the journey?"

She smiled "Indeed I am Sir, although my father is less so and is feeling somewhat tired."

The Doctor smiled ruefully, "Helen's right, I've been too eager to show the area to her. It is many years since my late wife and I left here and our daughter was born in India. Sadly my wife died some five years ago and I had promised her that I would bring Helen home." He winked at Merriman, "And find her a rich husband."

"I am sorry to hear of your loss Sir," replied Merriman, "But you should have little difficulty in finding your daughter a husband for she is certainly a fine young lady."

The young lady in question spoke immediately, "I will thank you not to talk of me as if I were not here, as if I was a piece of merchandise to be sold!" and she stamped her foot in anger

"I will not be pushed into a marriage which I do not want."

Merriman cursed himself for his tactlessness while the Doctor hastily tried to calm his daughter down. He turned to Merriman, "I apologize for my daughter Sir, life in India and the lack of a mother to provide an example have caused her to be more outspoken than becomes a lady." The Doctor continued, "We live close by, may I invite you in for a glass of something to warm you for the return journey?"

Merriman looked at Helen who was standing with her back to them, "Thank you Sir, for the invitation, but I think that this may not be the right time." He mounted his horse and turned for home. "Good-day to you Sir, Ma'am."

As he rode, Merriman found himself thinking about Helen Simpson. *"There was a young lady of spirit, good looking too. She would make some fortunate man a fine wife. But not me,"* he sneered at himself. *"What could you offer such a girl, a handicapped naval officer on half pay with poor chances of employment or promotion. She could do far better for herself, plenty of young men of the gentry far wealthier than me who would be eager to know her. Forget her you fool, she wouldn't even consider you."* Even as he spoke to himself thus, he could not forget her; anger had made her dark eyes flash and they swam before him in his mind's eye. He did not know it then, but he was to become much better acquainted with her.

When he arrived back home he found his man Owen waiting for him, looking fidgety and unusually nervous. It appeared that his family, at least his mother and younger brother, lived somewhere along the North Wales coast and he was eager to go and see them for a few days.

"But only if you can spare me Sir, and I'll come back Sir, honest I will. I won't run." It was not unusual for seamen in those days, given the chance, to desert or 'run' in naval parlance.

Merriman grunted "I know that, man. I'll give you a letter to show that you are away by my leave, and here's a guinea to see you on your way."

"Diolch yn fawr, thank you Sir, thank you." They went into the house and Merriman wrote a brief note as he had promised "Now be off with you. I look to see you back in three or four days."

Going into the main room of the house he found his father in earnest conversation with a number of distinguished looking gentlemen in front of the fire. He was apologizing for the interruption when his father said, "Never mind that James, I want you to meet these gentlemen and learn of our problems."

"Gentlemen, this is my son James of whom I have been telling you." They immediately rose and came forward to shake his hand.

The elder Merriman made the introductions. It was apparent that they were all men of consequence in the district, landowners, magistrates, wealthy merchants and the like. The senior customs official from Chester was also present and was introduced as Mr.Flitwick.

"Now James," said Captain Merriman when they were all settled again, "We have been discussing the serious situation that has developed here in this part of the County of Chester and in North Wales. Things are beginning to get out of hand with the damned smugglers. Oh, I know what you are going to say James, we have always had smugglers along the coast. But things have changed in the time you have been away."

"In the past, most of us have considered it the duty of the revenue service to catch smugglers and the duty of those of us who are magistrates to punish them if they were caught.

Nobody was unduly concerned, even the merchants, as there was no evidence of a great volume of smuggled goods. If we found the odd bottle of good French brandy on the back doorstep it was accepted as simply a form of tribute, but even that has stopped."

"The smugglers used to go to great lengths to avoid any contact with the Revenue men, but now they are openly aggressive."

"Yes", broke in Mr.Gordon, a small man with a rubicund face who had been introduced as a landowner and magistrate from nearby Neston, "You will not have heard about the latest outrage. The Revenue cutter *Pilote* was anchored just off the Point of Air and snugged down for the night when it was attacked. All aboard were killed except for a boy who got away in a boat Of course a search was started but all that was found were corpses washed up on the shore. The ship has disappeared."

"When was this?" asked Merriman.

"Why, only two weeks ago. The boy was found by fishermen and brought ashore. He had a pistol ball in his shoulder and was suffering from cold and wet, but he recovered sufficiently to be able to tell what had happened. Apparently one of the seamen jumped over the side with him and got him into the boat but was killed before they were clear. The boy is still alive but very ill."

"It's unbelievable," said another man, a merchant from Chester, "To think that these cursed smugglers can get away with murder and piracy so near to authority."

"How do you know it's the same smugglers to blame?" asked Merriman, "I cannot understand why they would change so much after years of trying to be secretive. Couldn't it be another gang of ruffians altogether?"

"There, what did I say" said his father. "James has hit the nail on the head. A good honest smuggler is one thing, but these men are vicious. Besides, why would smugglers steal the Revenue cutter which is so well known in these waters?"

"I don't know, but the Free Trade as they call it is not as profitable as it was since the Consolidation of Duties Act was passed back in "87 and since then the Government has reduced many duties still further," put in Mr. Green, a thin man, possessor of a large paunch, who was another merchant and magistrate from Chester. "Also you mustn't forget that piracy is no new thing in the Irish sea, although there has been none in recent years. Perhaps they intend to sell their prize. I remember that in March of 1780 two packet boats belonging to the post office, the *Hillsborough* and the *Bessborough* were captured by a privateer, the *Black Prince,* I believe, under an Irish captain and flying the American flag."

"Yes, but we were at war with the Americans then and you must admit that it was an audacious move by that captain. It cost the post office well over a thousand pounds to buy their property back.."

"Gentlemen, if I may suggest!" As all eyes turned towards him, Merriman said thoughtfully, "The stolen cutter is actually a small ship of war armed with a few six-pounder cannon and some swivel guns, and with a crew of perhaps thirty or forty men, is that not so?"

Several heads nodded so he continued, "It occurred to me that to capture such a prize would take an exceptionally large, well organized gang, certainly one with a very capable leader."

"Further, they must have been planning their attack for some time and knew in advance where the cutter would be, how many men aboard, maybe even their state of readiness to repel an attack.."

Merriman warmed to his theme. "Do you know if the cutter regularly anchored at that point or were it's movements made at random?"

"At random I believe," said Merriman senior, "I spoke to the unfortunate officer in command only a few weeks ago, and he said that he tried to make his movements erratic so that smugglers might be taken by surprise, but Point of Air was one of his favourite anchorages. Poor man, it was he and his crew that were taken by surprise."

"That argues that someone in the revenue service may be passing information to the gang, or at least someone who has access to that information, maybe even a member of the crew of the cutter. Have there been any other strange or unusual happenings recently that may have some connection?"

"Nothing that I can think of," said the man with the paunch, "Nothing that is except for the usual trouble with the spalpeens."

"Spalpeens, what are they?" asked Merriman.

"Irish labourers," was the reply. "Half naked many of them, barefoot even. They come over to find work on the land, usually most of them in the Autumn for the harvest, but you can find some at almost any time. Many of them actually walk from here down to the south of the country. If they can't find work they are reduced to begging and thieving until they are rounded up to be sent back to Ireland. The law classes them as rogues and vagabonds, even the women and children, and they're kept in a House of Correction at Parkgate or Neston until a ship can be found to take them back."

"Are they a great problem then?"

"Not a great problem, but I confess I feel sorry for them. They are so desperately poor and they hope to earn cash money to pay their rents as cash is in short supply in Ireland. Those that do find work aren't paid much and their unluckier fellows are quite ready to rob them."

"Ireland has been a thorn in England's flesh for centuries," said another voice. "Though I must say that some of the grasping English landlords over there treat their tenants worse than cattle, causing more resentment and storing up worse trouble for the future I'll be bound. And then there's the French."

"The French," repeated Merriman, "What have they got to do with this? We aren't at war now."

"Probably nothing, but we all know that you can't trust the French. I have it on good authority that French agents used to land in Ireland and then slip over to England during the recent war and they are at it again, I'll be bound. I agree that they are very busy cutting off people's heads at present, but there'll be war with France again before long. You mark my words!"

"Well, Sir , You may well be right," replied Merriman, "but to return to the stolen Revenue cutter. Doesn't it seem likely that the people who took it may have a purpose beyond that of handicapping the Revenue men? That they may need to actually use the vessel for some nefarious purpose other than running a few bales of silk and barrels of French brandy. After all, they have managed up until now with simple fishing boats."

"Gentlemen, I believe James has the right of it again," said his father, "A fresh mind brought to our problem is what we needed and now we have it. Well done James."

There were murmurs of agreement from around the room and the Revenue Officer, Mr Flitwick, who had not yet spoken, said "I quite agree with what your son has suggested. There must be something different behind this affair and somebody organizing the criminals who is in a position to know what the Revenue intend to do."

"The difficulty is finding out what we need to know. I've had Riding Officers out along both sides of the estuary but nobody knows anything, or is too frightened to tell what they know. Two weeks since the tragedy happened and we're no nearer to finding out who the damned culprits are than we were then. All the local constables are making enquiries as well, but nothing has come of it. Neither have there been any sightings of the vessel. I'm at my wits end to know what to do next."

"There seems to be little more that we can do at present," remarked Captain Merriman, "except to keep our eyes and ears open and hope that some helpful information comes our way. And now Gentlemen, another glass of this excellent wine before you leave?"

"A bad business," commented the Captain as they watched the visitors depart, "Because I am, or was, a naval man, they seem to imagine that I know the mind of seafaring men and can tell them what these villains will do next. Anyway James, enough of that now. Did you enjoy your ride? Tell me where you went."

"Yes, I enjoyed the ride, although I found the saddle much harder than I remembered it. I found muscles I'd forgotten I had." His father laughed as Merriman continued , "I saw nobody I know except a doctor and his daughter with whom I had travelled from London."

"A doctor eh! That is interesting. You remember old Doctor Jenkins who looked after the family for many years? Well, he passed away two or three months ago and as yet we haven't found a replacement for him. What do you know about this fellow traveller of yours?"

"Very little really, Father. His name is William Simpson and he spent twenty or more years in India in the service of

John Company. His wife died out there and he has returned with his daughter Helen, as he promised his wife, to show her where their original home is. Apparently they live not too far from here."

"Excellent," said his father, "You must arrange for them to visit us James, A new face at table is always welcome, especially someone who may have something new to talk about. I'll have a word with your mother about it. And that reminds me, your mother and I are worried about your hand and arm. It is many months since you were wounded and you are still wearing that bandage. Surely it should have healed by now?"

"Yes, Sir, but it still pains me if it strikes against anything, which is why I keep it covered and I think it is healing, at least as best it can." To change the subject he sniffed the air, saying "I'm hungry and I'm sure Annie will have one of her special pies on the table."

His father shook his head and followed him inside.

For the next few days nothing occurred to disturb the peaceful existence to which Merriman was slowly becoming accustomed, a far cry from the hectic life at sea where there was always some decision for the captain of a King's ship to make . The chief revenue officer had sent a message by one of the riding officers to tell them that a new cutter was to be supplied from the yard of John Gely of Cowes on the Isle of Wight.

"Fine ships he builds," said the officer "but it will be some time before it arrives here, though we are to have one that is almost completed and intended for another station, even then we will have to find a local crew, which won't be easy after what has happened."

Four days after his departure, Owen returned. When Merriman saw him trudging up the carriageway, he looked so downcast and miserable that it was obvious that he was not the cheerful sailor that had so looked forward to seeing his family again. Merriman immediately called him into the front hall of the house.

"What's the matter with you man? You look as if you'd just been flogged."

Owen shuffled his feet, coughed and mumbled, "I'll be alright Sir."

"Damn it man, speak up. You are my responsibility now, so if you have problems I want to know about them and help if I can. Come on, out with it."

Owen looked up with such misery on his face that Merriman was quite taken aback.

"Here, come inside and sit down man. Get this brandy down you and tell me what the trouble is."

In his agitation, the Welsh lilt in Owen's voice became more pronounced.

"Aye, Sir, very grateful Sir, that helps. Well Sir, you'll 'ave 'eard about the Revenue ship taken by pirates or smugglers; my young brother Aled was in her, part of the crew 'e was, all killed, not a man left alive. When I got home Sir, seems that me Mam died only three days ago. The shock, you see. She were old and wore out Sir, and with me being away and Da dead of drowning years gone, she depended on Aled. They tell me she asked for me before she-------before she ----if only I'd been home a few days earlier she might not -----." He couldn't go on, his face twisted with misery.

Merriman put his hand on the man's shoulder. "I'm sorry Owen, really sorry. If there's anything I can do; perhaps you want to go back home for a few days more?"

"No Sir, there's nothing to go back to now. I've seen the grave Sir, they were both put in with my Da. No, I've nothing now. Even the house belonged to somebody else."

The big sailor lurched to his feet, "I'd dearly like to find the scum who did this and set about 'em with a cutlass Sir, straight I would."

"Yes, I know you would," replied Merriman. "Meanwhile, the authorities are doing all they can to discover who is responsible and I'll tell you if there is any news. Remember that you are part of this household now and my responsibility. Be off to the kitchen now and ask Annie for something to eat. We'll talk again later."

Later that day, after giving the matter some serious thought, Merriman called for Owen to come in again. "Owen, when you were over in Wales, did you hear anything, anything at all which may have a bearing on this bad business?"

"No Sir, not that I know Sir, except that they told me the only survivor was a boy. It was my brother what saved him Sir, and the fishermen who found them adrift in a boat, said my brother was still alive then, but all 'e said 'fore he died was something about French and Irish. Dunno if that means anything, I reckon 'e was just rambling. But I did go to see the boy sir."

"Did you, and how is he? Did you learn anything from him?"

"He's recovering Sir, they got the musket ball out and his Mam told me that 'e should be on his feet again in a few days. He couldn't tell me anything except that 'e was wakened by shouts and shooting and then my brother grabbed him and jumped over the side with him. They was both shot when they climbed into a boat tied astern. Another man cut the painter before 'e was killed. That's all Sir."

"Little enough I'm afraid, but I'm sure that there must be more to learn." He paced up and down, hands clasped behind his back..

"If you were to go back, do you think that by spending time in the inns along the coast there, perhaps pretending to be the worse for drink, you might overhear odd snatches of conversation which might give us some clue?"

"Maybe Sir," said Owen doubtfully, "But me bein' a stranger to most folks, there's some as would wonder why I was there."

"You could say that you were on the run. That when you got back here you were shown no sympathy and you determined to be finished with the navy for good. You would need to be careful though, for if you do come across people who know something or who are involved, your life could be in danger."

Owen stood in silence for a few moments, then he straightened up with a determined look on his face. "Be no more dangerous than furling frozen tops'l canvas in a gale Sir, or boarding an enemy ship. I'll do it. I'll feel better knowin' I might be able to do somethin' to help."

"Very good! You're a sensible man Owen, I rely on you to be careful, but if you think, at anytime, that you are in danger, get away immediately and come back here. Remember, discretion is the better part of valour. Now then, you had better have some money with you, in small coins. It would be better if you hid some of the money, otherwise it might be wondered why a "run" seaman had so much about him. I suggest you go in the middle of the night as though you'd left without leave and with stolen money in your pocket."

He thought hard, "As for a weapon, you will have to make do with your knife, You cannot be seen with a pistol. Can you think of anything else?"

"No Sir, and thank you for giving me this chance Sir. I'll not let you down Sir."

"Never thought you would Owen, here is some money, ask in the kitchen for food to take, but tell no-one where you are going. Now good luck to you and, I emphasize, be careful."

A brief "Aye-Aye Sir," and Owen was gone.

A chance meeting in Chester

The next morning, Merriman's parents announced that they would be going into Chester the following day to allow the ladies to look round the shops and possibly to visit friends.

"We'll probably stay at the White Lion in Northgate Street if Mr. Paul has room for us, or The Feathers in Bridge Street. We shall see what entertainment there is at the New Theatre or any of the Assembly rooms in the evening," said Captain Merriman, rubbing his hands together in anticipation. "All after a good dinner, of course."

Merriman recalled the invitation to dinner from his friend Captain Saville and determined to send a message to him immediately by one of the stable boys.

He told his parents about Captain Saville saying, "I'll go with you to town. If my friend cannot meet me for dinner, I'll go to the theatre with you."

"Excellent, good idea, send the boy right away. He can also go to the White Lion to reserve rooms for us."

So, next day they set off. Merriman's mother and sister excitedly chattering about laces, ribbons, silks and dresses, whilst Matthew kept on finding questions to ask about life in the navy.

In the late 18th Century, Chester was a bustling city of some fourteen to fifteen thousand people, well known for the quality of the products produced by its clockmakers, pewterers, cutlers and silversmiths and famous for the 'Rows' which had existed from medieval days, consisting of two rows of shops, one above the other. The upper row was set back with a walkway over the lower row. From that upper walkway people could look down upon the crowds in the street below.

There were delivery boys, street traders ringing bells and shouting to attract custom, servants on errands, apprentices rubbing shoulders with ostlers and stable hands and here and there the inevitable painted whore trying to elicit business, to entice clients into some ramshackle, flea ridden boarding house down one of the innumerable vile and filthy alleys behind the better properties lining the street. There were people window shopping, gossiping in groups or simply strolling about showing off their new fashions. Moving amongst them would be the inevitable pickpockets and street urchins on the lookout for whatever they could steal and beggars, some disfigured or limbless, whining and holding out a cap in the hope of being given a coin or two.

Into this noisy, smelly, heaving bedlam the Merriman family coach slowly forced its way and finally drew into the relative quiet of the stable yard of the White Lion inn, one of the more than one hundred and forty hotels, inns and taverns in the city, from the better class frequented by the gentry and professional people, to those serving the lesser gentry and wealthier business people, to those lower taverns patronized by the working classes and seamen from the port. All in all it was a typical Georgian city.

They were quickly settled into their rooms by the innkeeper Mr. Paul and after an early lunch they separated. Mrs. Merriman and her daughter were to visit some of the proliferation of dressmakers, mercers, milliners and glovers to buy some dresses, silks and ribbons. Women's fashion demanded ever larger bustles and dresses were ornamented with a profusion of bows and ribbons and lace. Hair styles too, were highly complex, wigs being decorated with fruit and flowers and even stuffed birds.

"Let the ladies go their own way James, they'll take half the afternoon to buy what they want and the other half looking in shop windows," said Captain Merriman, "we're better to keep out of the way, otherwise we'll be asked our opinion which they'll take no notice of anyway."

James grinned, "Obviously you speak from experience Father, what shall we do whilst they are occupied?"

"Well, you need some clothes other than your uniform if you are to stay ashore for some time James, and Mr Osgood is an excellent tailor. He'll have you fitted out as a country gentleman in no time, with breeches, shirts, coats and everything else you need, and I suppose you'll want some of these dammed trousers which are becoming fashionable nowadays."

After an exhausting afternoon the family came together again at the inn. The ladies confessed to being quite fatigued and went up to lie down in their rooms, still chattering as women do, about what they could have purchased instead of what they actually did buy, whilst Merriman and his father relaxed over a drink, discussing what they had seen.

Merriman was looking forward to meeting his new friend Captain Saville, who had replied to his message, saying that he would meet them at the White Lion, and so, later that evening Merriman entered the public rooms downstairs to find the soldier waiting there.

I'm delighted to see you again Sir," smiled Merriman, "And I you Sir," replied Saville, "I've asked the landlord to keep us a table, but perhaps you would like to sit here a while with a drink before we dine?"

"An excellent thought Captain, let's do just that."

After the drinks arrived, the soldier said "I'd be happy if you would call me by my given name which is Robert, instead of Captain, which is, I think, a trifle formal."

"Gladly I will, if you'll use my name which is James."

The two young men grinned at each other in complete accord and fell to discussing and comparing naval and military life.

"I can't think how you endure life aboard a ship of war James. No room to move about, rotten food and water and all the while the wretched thing is heaving up and down. I feel positively nauseous at the very thought, sink me if I don't."

Merriman laughed, "It is something that one gets used to and there are compensations for the sailor's lot. To see a tropical sunrise at sea, or a sunset which puts quite spectacular colours in the sky is to confirm in one the majesty of creation. But best of all I love to be aboard a ship thrashing to windward close-hauled, with the spray flying and the ship's rigging taut as fiddle strings, all sail set with just a tweak on a bowline here or a sheet there to have the ship on her best point of sailing." He lapsed into momentary silence, a little embarrassed at his own enthusiasm.

"Besides, there is always the prospect of some action, or at least the interest of visiting strange foreign places and don't forget, the sailor travels with his home around him. I see many places every year whereas you soldiers stay in one place too long, so even if you don't like it you can't change it."

"Well, you're right there, I must agree, but if it is a good place, one can put down some temporary roots and get to know the local folk, the best clubs and so on. There are always dances and social events with mothers looking for prospective husbands for their daughters. An army officer can have plenty of fun without being tied down with a wife."

"I suppose so," said Merriman, "How long have you been in the army?"

"Nearly ten years, my father purchased a commission for me as Cornet when I was sixteen and I went to America to join the regiment just in time to come back home when the war over there ended. The Regiment was so depleted that there were only some one hundred and ninety four other ranks left. Many officers had been killed or died of disease so there were several vacancies. My father was able to purchase my Captaincy two years ago. And you James, how long have you been in the navy?"

"Since I was twelve, when my father persuaded a friend of his, Captain Edwards to take me as a midshipman. I passed the examination for Lieutenant seven years ago, since when I was given command of a small brig carrying dispatches."
He hesitated, "I suppose you might as well know Robert, I lost my ship and received this injury to my arm earlier this year, so my naval career may be at an end."

"I certainly hope not my friend, especially as you so obviously enjoy it."

"Time will tell I suppose, but to change the subject, tell me why are you staying in Chester when you said your regiment is in Ireland?"

"Yes, it was in Cork but is now in Armagh. As for me, I'm recruiting for the regiment James, the good old 22nd, the Cheshire Regiment. We number some four hundred and fifty men now but hope to raise this to a thousand in the next six months. It is hoped that the improved uniform and the bounty paid to each new recruit will bring them to the Colours. Anyway, I'll be moving round the county and beyond for two or three months before leaving for Ireland."

"Surely you are not on your own in this, Robert, and what is the bounty?"

"Three guineas, to be paid to each new man when he signs or makes his mark, although most of it will be taken off him to pay for his equipment. No I'm not alone, the recruiting party is usually made up of seven or eight officers, eighteen sergeants and corporals and perhaps ten other ranks including drummer boys. We separate into smaller parties and eventually we'll take all the new men to Armagh."

"I wish you luck Robert, in the navy we must resort frequently to the Press Gang when we cannot find enough volunteers, though I must say I feel sorry for men dragged from home and family. Sometimes we get volunteers who think service aboard may be a better choice than prison Little do they know that they could only be exchanging one sort of hell for another, but the King's ships must be manned, the country depends on them for her safety. By the by, what do you know of the local Revenue service and the smugglers."

"Very little I'm afraid, although I have heard of the loss of their cutter. I do know that the army is available to help if we are called upon, indeed I remember we were involved in burning boats believed to belong to smugglers back in eighty four down in Kent."

At that moment Merriman's family entered the room and seeing the two men, moved across to them. As they rose to their feet Merriman made the introductions.

"This is my friend Captain Robert Saville of whom I have spoken Robert, meet my father Captain Merriman, my mother, my sister Emily and my brother Matthew."

"Captain Merriman, your servant Sir." The elegantly dressed soldier bowed over Mrs Merriman's hand, "Honoured Ma'am to make your acquaintance." He turned to Emily and took her hand. "Delighted to meet you Miss Merriman. James, why didn't you tell me that your sister was such a beauty. I'm positively dazzled, sink me if I'm not." He again bowed and held onto Emily's hand for longer than was really necessary before releasing it and turning to Matthew. "Your servant Sir. Glad to know you."

They all murmured the usual words. All that is, except Emily who, to her own discomfort, had blushed to the roots of her hair.

"We're about to go into dinner Captain, and would be pleased if you would join our table," suggested Mrs Merriman. "Capital idea my dear," boomed Captain Merriman, "let's all sit together."

"I thank you Ma'am, I should love to. I had a table saved for James and myself but I'm sure the innkeeper will have someone else wanting it."

During the meal, Robert Saville proved himself to be a lively and congenial companion, keeping them entertained with talk of London society and the latest fashions. His anecdotes had them laughing so much that Mrs Merriman, holding her sides, had to ask him to desist or he would be the death of her.

Merriman listened quietly and was amused to see that his sister was stealing glances at Robert beneath her lashes, whilst Robert was trying not to be too obviously looking at Emily. The convivial meal drew to a close as Merriman's father said to his wife, "Well my dear, we shall have to be going if we are to be in time for the concert you wished to see."

"Emily and Matthew are coming with us James, do you and Robert wish to come with us also? We are going to the "Yacht" to see what has been advertised as -----," he pulled a piece of paper from his pocket and read, "-----A Fashionable Entertainment of Music, Recitation and Imitation By Mr.

George Saville-Carey who has appeared for two seasons at the Freemasons' Hall in London and also before Their Majesties at Windsor."

"I actually saw the performance whilst I was in London" said the soldier, "It is really very good. But I hasten to assure you that this Mr. Saville-Carey is of no relation to myself."

After a look at his friend, Merriman replied, "Thank you Father, but no, Robert and I have a lot to talk about so I believe we'll stay here."

As they prepared to leave, Mrs Merriman pressed on the soldier an invitation to visit them in the near future. "You really must come out and see us Captain, as soon as your duties allow."

"Thank you Ma'am. My duties are little enough I assure you. I'll be delighted to call on you."

The family departed, leaving Merriman and his friend to spend the rest of the evening getting to know one another better over the remains of a bottle of brandy. Eventually, they moved into the entrance hall of the inn, the soldier to return to his own quarters and Merriman to climb the stairs to his room.

As they said their goodbyes, the door of a small room suddenly opened and Merriman saw their coaching companion, the lawyer Jeremiah Robinson emerge, deep in conversation with a thin, dark featured man followed by a tall, slim man who kept his face averted, and who seemed vaguely familiar. There was another large man with them who, catching sight of Merriman rushed out of the front door before his companions. The lawyer saw Merriman at the same time and hastily ushered his companions out of the hotel door before turning to say "A pleasure to see you young gentlemen again."

"Indeed Sir, and to meet you. We've just spent a most excellent evening together, the Lieutenant and I," announced the soldier, "I'm about to walk back to my rooms, perhaps you would accompany me."

"As I am sure that your rooms are near the castle Sir, I regret that I cannot, as my way lies in the opposite direction." And with a brief adieu he nipped quickly out of the door and disappeared.

"Strange fellow," mused Merriman later as he prepared for bed, "He didn't seem very pleased to see us, in fact he was positively agitated, and the way in which he pushed his companions out before we had chance to get a good look at them was most strange. I wonder who they were?"

The next day, after he had made another visit to the tailor, the family returned home Three days later, the tailor arrived as he had promised, with all the new clothes for a final fitting. He fussed about as Merriman tried them on, tucking here, easing a seam there until Merriman was ready to explode with irritation. Finally the man expressed himself satisfied and left, promising that all would be delivered the next day without fail.

A Revenue ship is taken

The coast of North Wales and the mountains of Snowdonia stood out clearly. Early rain had cleared the air and Merriman was enjoying the view as his horse ambled along on the Cheshire side of the Dee estuary. His intention had simply been to take a ride because it was such a fine day and he had no particular direction in mind, but his brother had asked to join him and without really thinking about it they had set off on the road to Neston. It was bitterly cold and both of them were bundled up in gloves and scarves and overcoats. They were in no hurry and between his brother's chatter he was deep in thought about his man Owen, wondering if he had discovered anything about the smuggling gang and when he might return.

Merriman suddenly shivered. "Too long in the tropics, that's what it is" he told himself. "Come on Matthew, I'll race you to that far gatepost," so saying he set spurs to his horse and thundered off ahead of his brother who tried valiantly but unavailingly to catch him.

They pulled up, almost together, laughing with excitement.

"It wasn't a fair start James, you were away before I realized what you were doing."

"Ha, you need to keep your wits about you little brother," laughed Merriman.

Approaching the town, they realized that a market fair was in progress with the country folk selling vegetables, eggs and chickens, milk, butter and cheese and the like. People were buying foodstuffs, ribbons and cloth, pots and pans, and all sorts of cheap goods and gewgaws from itinerant traders who had set up their stalls under scraps of canvas. A small group was gathered around a seller of magical potions which he absolutely guaranteed would cure anything. "The recipe for this wonderful elixir was given to me by a dying Holy man in far off India. It will cure impotence and gout and will cause barren women to conceive," he told his wide eyed and gullible listeners.

Leaving their horses tied, Merriman and his brother wandered about, amused by the chatter of the stall holders, occasionally pestered by beggars, when all at once Merriman saw Helen Simpson talking to an old lady who was selling ribbons.

"Good morning Ma'am, you must allow me to buy those for you. No, I positively insist upon it, I hope it will help to make amends for upsetting you the other day."

"Thank you Sir," she replied with a small curtsey, "But really, I had quite forgotten all about it. And who is this handsome young gentleman with you?"

Merriman hastily introduced Matthew who nearly fell over his own feet trying to bow over the lady's hand.

She continued, "From our last meeting, you know that my father and I live close by, so in my turn I must insist that you accompany me there. I know that my father will be pleased to see you again."

"With the greatest of pleasure Ma'am. Matthew, will you collect the horses and follow us. Miss Simpson will show us the way." The cold had brought the colour to her cheeks and with her dark hair and sparkling eyes she was as pretty as a picture. Merriman was entranced and couldn't take his eyes off her.

"You are staring Lieutenant, why don't you look at the countryside Sir? It is much more attractive than I."

"Yes Ma'am, I mean no Ma'am, that is, I mean, well, I think you are – it isn't, what I meant was ---." He stumbled on until he realized that he was making a fool of himself and shut his mouth. Matthew was grinning all over his face at his brother's embarrassment and Merriman growled at him to mind his manners.

After only a short walk they arrived at a small but well appointed house with a modest range of outbuildings, stables and coach house, standing apart from its neighbours, She led the way inside followed by the two brothers, to be greeted by Doctor Simpson who had seen their approach.

"My dear Lieutenant, this is a welcome surprise, and you have a companion?" Merriman introduced his brother to the doctor, who turned to a maid who was hovering in the background and giving her the key to the tea caddy, asked her to bring some tea for the visitors. "Unless you would like something stronger?" he asked.

"Thank you Sir, a dish of tea would be most acceptable."

As they sat and enjoyed their tea, the doctor explained "We really became quite addicted to the drinking of tea whilst we were in India, indeed, we brought a good supply back with us. I find it an ideal beverage to relax one and it is also efficacious in the calming of patients after any painful surgery."

"Indeed Sir, I am sure that you are right. I believe there are many different teas from the various areas of India and China, but although I find it very refreshing, I haven't drunk enough to be able to determine one from the other."

"You mentioned surgery Doctor, may I enquire if you intend to continue in the practice of medicine now you are home?"

"Only in a small way perhaps, for I fear that with my advancing years I am not as active as once I was, although Helen will miss it as she's been my assistant for many years and knows almost as much about medicine as I do."

"My father has mentioned that our doctor for many years has recently died and has not been replaced. I was wondering if you might ------ er, perhaps, well anyway, my parents extend an invitation to you to visit us for a day or two. May I suggest Friday of next week for the weekend?"

"Thank you, we would be honoured. Would you think it impertinent of me to ask if my sister be allowed to accompany us? I should explain that although this house is mine since our parents died, my sister Jane moved back here when her husband was killed in a riding accident two or three years ago. Since then, she has lived quietly here alone and rarely ventures into society. I'm certain it would do her good to visit you. At the moment she is visiting a sick neighbour and so you cannot meet her now."

So it was agreed and details were decided upon, following which Merriman and Matthew left to ride home, to inform their parents what he had arranged. His mother was overjoyed at the prospect of new friends to entertain and immediately began to plan with Annie what should be prepared.

"James, why not invite your friend Captain Saville for the very same evening," she said. He is such an agreeable young man and it would ensure a lively gathering."

Captain Merriman drew his son on one side. "I'm glad you have arranged for your friends to come here James, but there is something else I wish to ask you about. Your man Owen hasn't been seen for over a week now and I fear he may have gone for good."

"No Father, he hasn't. He's trying to find out what he can about the gang who took the revenue boat. I kept it quiet for fear that word may get around, servants tittle-tattle you know." And Merriman told his father all that he and Owen had arranged.

"That seems to be a good idea James, let's hope that he hasn't found himself in trouble."

"He is a good man Father, and I trust him to take care." He shrugged, "But there is nothing to be done except wait for him to come back."

The next few days passed slowly for Merriman. He was unused to having time on his hands and he found the waiting for news from Owen intolerable. His father did his best to interest him in the workings of the estate but it was obvious that his mind was elsewhere. Answering Matthew's endless questions about the navy passed more of the time and to his embarrassment his mother and sister insisted on seeing him in all his new clothes.

Welshman Owen joins the smugglers

Evan Owen sat on a rough bench in the darkest corner of a small and scruffy alehouse in a village near the coast, nursing a pot of ale from which he took infrequent sips. On the table before him was a platter containing the remains of some stale bread and a rind of strong cheese. The usually smartly turned out sailor was unshaven, his clothes dirty and he tried to adopt a furtive air so as to look as though he was hiding from authority.

It was now several days since he left the Merriman household and he had spent the time wandering along the roads and byways near the coast, begging at cottages and farms for food, sleeping rough under hedges and hayricks and showing himself only in the meanest and poorest looking alehouses. By this means he had hoped to attract the notice of anybody who might think him to be willing to do anything to earn some money.

So far his efforts had been in vain and he had been ignored, although in each tavern he visited, the local people, mostly fishermen and farm hands regarded him with suspicious sideways glances. He took another pull at the indifferent ale, staring gloomily in front of him at the beaten earth floor, pondering on what else he could do to find out the information he needed. If nothing happened soon he might as well give up, but the thought of giving up his quest depressed him still further. He finished his drink and decided to have another.

He approached the bar which was no more than rough boards supported on barrels, and was surprised when a man who had been in conversation with the tavern keeper turned and offered to pay. Owen muttered his thanks to the man who followed him back to his seat in the corner.

"Not seen you around here before have I. Where are you from?" asked the man, a dark featured person and obviously a Welshman.

"Originally not far from 'ere, along the coast a bit. My family were all fisherfolk but they're all dead and gone now."

"Sorry to hear that," replied the stranger, but it's obvious you're a seafaring man, what ship are you from?"

Owen looked at him slyly for a moment, then said with a nervous grin, "Been at sea for over twelve years, in 'is Majesty's bloody navy I 'ave. Lately topman in the brig *Conflict* and before that in the old Indy an' before that --------"

"The old Indy, what's that?"

"The Indy, don't you know nothin'? That's the *Indefatigable*, everybody knows that. Why, I remember one time aboard her and the cannon balls flyin' as thick as 'ail when the cap'n says to me ---------"

"Yes, alright, I get the picture. So what are you doing here if you are still in the navy and no family to stay with? Have you run?"

"You're a bit nosey aren't you mate, what is it to you what I'm doing?"

"No offence meant, but I'm looking for a likely lad or two for a little job and I thought you looked as though you needed some money without being too concerned what had to be done to earn it. Am I right?"

Owen decided this could be the lead he had hoped for, so he replied slowly and in a way he hoped the other would think to be reluctance to reveal too much about himself.

"Well, I could use some more money, that's sure and somewhere to sleep, It's bloody cold out in the open."

"I know, you have my sympathies. Anyway, if you want some work be here the same time tomorrow night. I pay well for a man who can keep his mouth shut. What's your name?"

"Owen, what's yours?"

"Mine you don't need to know, just be here tomorrow night. Thomas there will let you sleep in his barn" he said, rising and indicating the fellow behind the bar before disappearing through the door into the night, leaving Owen to mull over what he had learned.

The following evening, Owen was on the same rough bench as before when the man who had approached him previously entered the tavern and brusquely ordered Owen to follow him. Outside, the night was pitch black which the flickering candle in the small lantern carried by the other man did little to dispel. They had walked only a few yards when suddenly Owen was surrounded by a number of men and his arms seized so that he could barely move. A knife pricked his throat and a hoarse voice growled in his ear, "If you speak to anybody about what you see and do tonight I'll see your throat cut for real, not just this pinprick. Do you swear to keep your trap shut?"

Owen nodded, the grip on his arms relaxed and the knife was removed. He touched his throat and felt the slipperiness of blood from the small nick in his skin. He was pushed rather than led in the direction of a cart, which, as his eyes became used to the dark, he could see already carried several men. He climbed onto the back of the cart and sat down on the floor. A foul smelling hood was dragged over his face and the same voice admonished him not to try and remove it.

As far as Owen could tell, the cart was moving inland, but after a journey of well over an hour he could again smell the sea. The cart halted and rough fingers whipped the hood off his head taking some of his hair with it. Rubbing his scalp he looked around him. There was a group of about fifteen men on a sandy beach and the men on the cart joined them, Owen with them. He could see the vague shape of what might be a fishing boat anchored offshore and two small boats being rowed to the beach. The men were pushed into lines, one for each boat and led into the sea as the boats grounded. Each man in turn was fitted with a sort of harness over his shoulders carrying two small kegs and they moved off up the beach to where a number of horse drawn carts waited.

Not a word was spoken as Owen in his turn was loaded with two kegs. He followed the other men and deposited his load onto one of the carts. Each of them must have made at least ten trips back and forth, so that Owen reckoned at least four hundred kegs of brandy had been landed. And that it was brandy there could be no doubt as the smell from a leaking keg was unmistakable.

Following the brandy they carried various boxes and bundles ashore, possibly silks and laces, many of which were loaded onto horses as well as carts and as each cart was loaded it was driven away. The loaded horses were tied one to another and led away into the darkness. The boats had already disappeared out to sea. It was obvious that the complete operation had been done many, many times before as each man knew what to do without the need for orders. When all the goods had been loaded and dispersed, Owen and the last few men climbed onto the cart, the hood was pulled over his head again and they were taken back to the tavern. The hood was removed, some coins were thrust into his hand and he was left alone with a final threat ringing in his ear "Be ready for tomorrow night and you'll keep a shut mouth or else! There'll be a lot more work if you're willing."

In a corner of the barn behind the tavern, Owen lay on his rough bed of filthy straw and considered what he had learned. That the smugglers were exceptionally well organized and efficient in their handling of contraband goods and were prepared to pay well for help in unloading and dispersing the cargo was obvious, but that was all he knew apart from the face of the man who had recruited him. He didn't even know which beach had been used. As for a link between the smuggling and the taking of the coastguard cutter and the death of his brother, perhaps he would be able to discover more about that in the future. At least, now he had made some progress. With a satisfied grunt he settled down to sleep.

The following night saw a repetition of the last. He was hooded and taken with others to another beach, obviously a different one as the carts had to be left further away, but as before he had no chance to talk to other men and so learned nothing. Then for the next two nights there was no activity and he stayed close by the tavern, keeping his ears open for any scrap of information he might hear and eating such coarse fare as the landlord could provide. "No worse than some I've eaten aboard ship" he told himself, thinking longingly of the food provided in the kitchen of the Merriman household.

The fifth night was simply a repetition of the first two, but on the sixth night there was a change. He was collected by the cart and hooded again, but he could tell that they were traveling in different direction than before. Eventually the cart stopped, Owen was helped down, still with the hood on and led into a building. There was a buzz of conversation and then a voice said "You can take the hood off now."

Owen did so and, blinking in the sudden light, looked about him. It was a big old barn, with the roof supported on huge oak beams and illuminated by half a dozen lanterns set in the form of a circle. Crowded round, sitting on straw bales or standing behind were some twenty five or thirty roughly dressed men. To one side, Owen saw the dark featured man he had first met in the tavern sitting on a small cart, with a little round table in front of him on which were two candles in rather tarnished brass candlesticks, a wooden mallet, some papers and a small leather bag.

The man, obviously the leader, stared at Owen for several minutes without speaking, then said in a loud voice "Bring in the prisoner."

Two men appeared from the gloom in a corner, dragging another man between them, pale faced, sweating profusely and with his hands tied behind his back.. He was pushed to his knees in front of the man behind the table as a roar of curses and execration rose from the assembly.

"*By God,*" thought Owen, "*It's a sort of trial.*"

"What's the poor devil done?" he asked the men near him.

"You'll find out, he's a traitor, not to be trusted."

Indeed Owen did not have to wait long to find out. The 'judge' pounded on his table with the mallet and shouted for silence. The noise died down and the 'judge' addressed the prisoner, speaking in slow measured tones obviously intended to convey gravitas to the proceedings.

"You are one Alun Humble are you not?"

"Yes Sir I am but I 'aven't done anyth------."

"Silence, you will have a chance to speak after we have heard the evidence against you."

"You were a member of the crew of the Revenue cutter *Pilote* which we seized a few weeks ago and it was you who sold to us the information about the movements of that vessel. Am I not right?"

"Answer me," he shouted as the frightened man looked round, perhaps for sympathy, of which there was none on the faces around him.

"Yes Sir, that's right."

Owen's heart leaped, at last here was a connection.

The 'judge' continued, "You betrayed your shipmates for money, how can we be sure that you won't betray us for money."

"I wouldn't Sir, if I go to the authorities and tell them what I know and how I know it, they'd hang me. I'll have to keep well away from any damned Revenue men now. I can't, I wouldn't, you can trust me Sir."

The 'judge' banged on the table with his mallet as the wretched man began to babble incoherently. "Silence there. Will the first witness step forward."

A small man, a farm labourer by his dress, stepped into the circle, nervously twisting a ragged hat in his hands.

"Is your name David Williams?" he was asked.

"Aye Sir it is that."

"I want you tell the court what you saw the prisoner doing three days ago."

"Aye Sir, well it were like this, I were walking back to the farm where I work when I sees one of the Revenue men, a Riding Officer talking with this man. They didn't see me 'cos I was be'ind the 'awthorn 'edge."

"Yes alright, and then what did you see?"

"I saw the Revenue man give him like a small bag or purse Sir. It all seemed suspicious. He put the bag in his shirt and went off. The revenue man rode away."

"And then?"

"I followed him at a distance and then met a friend of mine, Jim Evans, 'im over there, and told him what I'd seen. We grabbed 'im and asked what the Revenue man had given 'im. He said 'e 'adn't seen any Revenue man, so we knew 'e was lying. We searched 'im and found a bag with money in it."

"Is this the bag?" asked the 'judge', lifting the small bag off the table and showing it round.

"Yes, it looks like it Sir."

"Thank you, you may sit down. Come forward Jim Evans." Evans stepped forward to be addressed in turn.

"Evans, Can you corroborate what Williams said?"

"Can I what Sir?"

"Was what Williams said correct and the truth?"

"Oh aye Sir, just like 'e said."

"Thank you, sit down now."

The 'judge' upended the small bag and two golden coins fell onto the floor in front of the prisoner, where they lay twinkling in the lantern light.

"Now then fellow, we don't pay you in gold and a man like you wouldn't be paid in gold for whatever work you do, so where did this gold come from.? Have you anything to say for yourself?"

"It's all lies, I didn't do it, these two put the money in my shirt, I wouldn't betray you." But his voice was drowned out by the shouts of the men round him.

The 'judge' pounded on the table again and as silence fell he asked the men what should be done with the prisoner.

"Kill him, cut his damned throat, drown him, break his bloody neck, the suggestions came thick and fast but all really meaning the same, - death.

The leader raised his arms to quell the noise, looked at the miserable sobbing wretch in front of him and said "There it is then, you are sentenced to be executed without delay for your treacherous activities."

"Who among you will carry out the sentence?" There was no rush of volunteers, just a murmuring among the men as they shuffled their feet and looked askance at each other or at the floor.

"Very well then, I shall choose. We have a new man amongst us who has yet to prove himself to be one of us," and he pointed at Owen. "Come forward Owen, you shall be the instrument of this court's justice."

Owen had no choice. If he refused he would probably be killed himself and the man would still die anyway. He hardened his heart, thinking of his brother who had died because of this man's misdeeds. The man deserved to die and in truth Owen had no serious qualms about doing it. He had killed many men in the course of his service in a King's ship, men who were armed and trying to kill him, but to kill a man who had his hands tied behind his back, that was different.

A cutlass was thrust into his hand which he swung round with practiced ease before plunging the blade into the floor where it stood upright, swaying gently.

Surprised at himself, he heard himself say, "I'll not murder a helpless man in cold blood. Cut him loose and give him a sword."

A roar of approval followed his words as the men saw the prospect of entertainment. The difference between the big bronzed seaman and his smaller opponent was so marked that there seemed to be no possibility of an even contest, so the leader nodded and the prisoner's hands were released. He stood for a few moments trying to rub some life back into his fingers before taking the cutlass handed to him.

It was as though he was determined to make a fight of it although he must have known it was hopeless, even if he beat Owen he would never leave the barn alive. The two men faced each other and the condemned man immediately attacked. From the outset it was clear that he had no real ability with a cutlass, Owen parried his furious slashes with ease and quicker than the eye could follow his blade thrust into the man's stomach and up into his heart. He was dead before his body hit the floor, his blood forming a pool round him.

The men crowded round Owen, congratulating him and slapping him on the back, one of them offered him a drink of rum from a small flask which Owen was only too pleased to accept. The leader of the men still in his seat of judgement, called out, "That was well done Owen, though I suspect you have a streak of chivalry which may be unsuited to our business."

The Doctor operates on Merriman

The Friday of the Simpson's visit finally dawned and Mrs. Merriman was all fuss and bother, making sure that Annie and the servants knew exactly what was expected of them, directing Matthew on what to wear and to mind his manners, discussing with Emily which of her new dresses to wear and in general, acting just like any mother when guests are expected.

"Mother," laughed Merriman, "It's not nobility coming. Why all the fuss?"

"I know who it is," retorted his mother, "But the Simpsons are travelled people and Captain Saville has moved in society circles in London. I will not have them think that we are only rough country folk."

The soldier was the first to arrive, riding up on a big bay horse.. A stable lad took charge of the horse and led it away. Shortly afterwards the Simpsons arrived and Merriman was soon busy making the necessary introductions. As he did so he wondered where his sister Emily and young Matthew were, as neither had appeared.

The doctor's sister Jane Prentice proved to be a quiet lady of middle age and she and her niece Helen were very soon engaged in conversation with Mrs. Merriman who quickly whisked them off to see some of the new things she had purchased in Chester.

Meanwhile, Captain Merriman ushered the men into another room., sat them down and provided them with drinks. The conversation soon turned from generalities to the Doctor's experiences in India.

"For most of my years on the sub-continent I was in the employ of the East India Company and situated at their fort in

Calcutta. It's a completely different way of life, as I am sure you know if you have ever been there in the course of your service, strange and colourful. Colourful in respect of the natural surroundings and clothing, but strange in the matter of customs and habits, religion, medicine and much else. I confess that I grew to love the life and people, as did my dear wife. Most of my contemporaries treated the people as nothing more than troublesome children and inferiors, but I found that they responded well to kindness and several of our servants became devoted to us. Because of this I was able, over time, to study their medical ideas, and it came as a bit of a shock to find that in many ways they were ahead of our European knowledge."

The doctor laughed, "I think I was looked on as a bit of a fool for it, but I also think many people are too bigoted to benefit from new ideas. However I certainly learnt a lot from my experiences."

"Have you had occasion to use any of your new-found knowledge Sir," asked Captain Merriman.

"Not here Sir, for I've had no opportunity since we returned, but I *have* used it many times in India with remarkable results. One must not forget that Eastern peoples were civilized far earlier than we were in the past, and have much to teach us if we will only listen."

"I don't doubt it Doctor, I don't doubt it. But tell us about your daughter if you will. I understood my son to say that she was your assistant, which seems to me to be an unusual occupation for a young lady?"

"Indeed it is Sir, but Helen is not one to be satisfied with the empty life so many European ladies lead in tropical places. She has an intelligent enquiring mind and although I know it isn't fashionable, I've always encouraged her to take an interest in everything around her. From a very early age she used to travel round the villages with me and from then on, gradually developed her interest and knowledge. I taught her almost everything I know and she has been of immense help to me as an assistant."

"She certainly seems to know her own mind," commented Merriman ruefully, thinking about their earlier meeting.

"Yes, there is no doubt about that, but for all that she is a daughter to be proud of. Many of the empty headed young men in the Company service would come to the house like bees round a honey pot, including officers from the garrison, but she treated them all with courtesy and sent them on their way."

Robert Saville, who had been sitting in silence the while, stood up and moved over to a cabinet containing a number of swords and daggers.

"This is a fine collection of weapons Captain Merriman. I see that you have some from the far East. That dagger with the wavy blade is from Malaya I believe."

"Yes it is. It's called a Kris. This is my little hobby which I started many years ago when I was a midshipman. I tried to find something different wherever my ship called." He opened the cabinet and took out a big curved sword. The hilt was covered in gold and a ruby glowed in the pommel.

"This is my favourite one. I took it off a pirate in the Arabian Sea. You see the nick in the blade? My sword did that. His swordsmanship consisted of wild slashing, I parried the blow and my point was through his throat before he could recover. It's a fine weapon and must have belonged to some rich eastern prince or the like. There must be an interesting story behind it if we only knew."

The men were soon engrossed in the subject of swords and their preferred weapon. The soldier was expounding on the virtue of the rapier against the curved hanger or the short cutlass and saying that whilst a longer curved blade was alright for a man on a horse he preferred the long straight blade.

"The long blade is fine in it's place," said Captain Merriman, "if you have room to move, but the shorter weapon is more easily managed if you are climbing a ship's side or fighting on a crowded deck."

"That I heartily agree with, although I think it would be to advantage to learn some of the skills needed in the effective use of the long blade," said the younger Merriman.

"There is a fencing master in Chester that I have heard of," observed Saville, "He is a Frenchman and is reportedly very good. I'm going to go to him for some lessons, perhaps you would like to accompany me James?"

The conversation on the merits of the different types of sword continued and the men, except the doctor, were demonstrating various parries and thrusts until interrupted by the arrival of the ladies.

"Joseph my dear, please put those horrible things away," said Mrs. Merriman, "I'm sure that Mrs. Prentice doesn't want to see them."

"Very well my dear," said her husband and the men rather sheepishly returned the weapons to the cabinet.

The conversation then became more general and Merriman took an opportunity to quietly ask his mother where Helen and his sister and Matthew had disappeared to.

"Shh! James. Matthew came in covered in mud. He told me he had been down at the duck pond you used to play in, showing his friends how you fought the corsairs. I told him not to show himself until he was fit to be seen in company."

"And Emily?"

"She is dressing herself up to make a grand entrance, and Helen is helping her. I think your friend the Captain has made quite an impression on her," she whispered.

Matthew presented himself, scrubbed and dressed and looking quite the young gentleman and was duly introduced to the doctor's sister, she being the only one he had not met.

Then, as Annie announced that the table was ready, Emily made her entrance, followed by Helen. The men all rose and Merriman stood there with his mouth open. Was this lovely young lady really his skinny little sister? Then he reminded himself that she was seventeen going on eighteen years old and he had been away for five years.

She was wearing one of the new mantuas recently bought in town, a sort of tawny brown which perfectly complemented her eyes and hair colour. Her hair was done in one of the latest fashions of the day, all ringlets, piled up with an ornament of fruit set at a jaunty angle on top. It was obvious that she had prepared herself for this moment as there was no trace of the blushing girl who had been so taken by surprise by the soldier's speech when they met in Chester.

But when Merriman's eyes fell on Helen his breath was really taken away and he felt his heart give a great throb. She too had changed and was wearing a simple dress of some dark material with little in the way of ornamentation but which perfectly complemented her dark hair and complexion. The decolletage revealed that she was not lacking in those attributes men find most attractive and it was with an effort that Merriman tore his eyes away from her full breasts which swayed and trembled as she walked across the room.

As the introductions were made, Merriman caught sight of his friend's face. Saville couldn't take his eyes off Emily and as the party moved into the dining room, he hastened to offer her his arm. Merriman was amused to see that she pretended not to notice and took Matthew's arm instead.

After an enjoyable meal with the soldier once again entertaining them with his tales of London life, the ladies left the men folk to their brandy and cigars. As they left the table, Merriman saw his mother nod to his father who nodded back He wondered what that was about but he didn't have long to wait to find out.

Once they were settled down again, the doctor asked to be excused. He returned a few moments later with something in a cloth bag. Bowing to Captain Merriman he said, " In return for your hospitality Sir, I would be pleased if you would accept this gift as a small token of our thanks. You will see that it is a bottle of unusual shape. It contains a liqueur of exceptional quality, a few bottles of which I brought back from my travels in India, though I believe it originates from even further East."

"Well thank you Sir, most generous of you I must say, most generous." He beamed at the doctor and passed the bottle round for the others to see, calling for fresh glasses to be brought to the table.

"Small glasses if you have them," said the doctor, "this is best taken in small sips."

At the first taste, Captain Merriman's eyes opened wide. "By God, Sir. This is exceptional, what say you gentlemen?"

They all signified approval except for poor Matthew. His face went red, his eyes watered and he gasped for breath.

"Powerful stuff, Matthew," said his father with a grin. "Sorts the men from the boys eh? Thank you again Doctor. I'll keep the rest of it for special occasions."

"Now Doctor, I hope you won't mind if I mix a little business with pleasure. My wife and I are of a mind that if you are agreeable we would like you to be our doctor. Our previous doctor has recently passed away and we have not yet approached any other. What do you say Sir?"

"I had anticipated that you might ask, Captain, after your son touched on the matter when we last met. As you know, I came home to retire, but I am prepared to take a few patients and would be happy to count your family amongst them."

"Capital, capital, Doctor. And your first patient shall be James here. Be silent James, your Mother and I are most concerned about your wound. It's several months since he was wounded Doctor and it still troubles him. As you see, he still keeps a bandage on it and won't let anyone see it. Now James, no more protests, we insist on it being seen. Doctor?"

"I am more than willing to examine it, perhaps tomorrow morning would be suitable if the Lieutenant -----?"

"Oh, very well then," said Merriman with an ill grace, "if I must, I must."

"It's for your own good James," said his father. "let us say no more about it for now. Captain Saville, I would like your opinion of this excellent brandy, and yours Doctor. I wouldn't be surprised if duty hasn't been paid on it as we found it on the doorstep some six months ago."

The conversation turned to the subject of smuggling and the awful fate of the Revenue cutter's crew. Captain Merriman told the visitors as much as was known of the affair although Merriman noticed that he was careful not to mention anything about his man Owen.

"Now Gentlemen, I think we have kept the ladies waiting long enough. Shall we join them? I know that Emily has been practicing on the harpsichord and hopes to entertain us."

Merriman was surprised to see how fluently his sister's fingers moved over the keys. She played well and he noticed how quickly Robert placed himself to be able to turn the sheets of music for her. He also noticed that his father was keeping an eye on the young soldier. The rest of the evening passed pleasantly enough, Mrs. Merriman sang and the soldier surprised everyone by quoting passages from plays by the Irishman Richard Sheridan.

In the morning, the Doctor suggested that he and Merriman find a quiet room upstairs so that he might examine the wound. As he unwound the bandage, he asked how it had occurred.

"I was told that it was lead shot and nails from some kind of blunderbuss. I didn't see the man that fired it, but I believe I was lucky in that most of the shot missed me and killed one of my men. One piece hit my head a glancing blow, and my arm and hand, which must have been raised at the time, took the force of several other pieces."

"Hmm, I see. Hmm, ah-ha, hmm," said the doctor in the non-committal way that doctors assume the world over . "Raise your arm, if you please, hmm, ah yes, a little further please. Now bend it at the elbow, good, good, now then grasp my hand as tightly as you can. Ah, I see that it pains you and your hand does not have a great deal of strength. Am I not right?"

"Yes Sir, you are, but I am sure that it will improve given time."

"And I Sir, am certain that it will not. In fact I would expect it to become a great deal worse." He pressed his thumb on a point below Merriman's elbow on his forearm. Merriman winced and groaned and sweat broke out on his forehead.

"There is still a piece of something buried in your arm, you see, that will have to come out before the arm will improve."

"But the doctor who cared for me in Gibraltar put me through hell, with his digging and probing and declared himself satisfied that he had found all the pieces."

"Well young Sir, I can tell you very definitely that he was wrong. I'm sure he did his best, but he missed one. I'm surprised that the wound has not festered. If it had you would have been fortunate not to have lost your arm entirely. I strongly recommend that you allow me to deal with it as soon as possible."

Merriman sat down with a bump, clutching his arm, his eyes closed in anguish at the thought of more surgery.

"I know what you are thinking" said the doctor, "You're like most people, you would rather face an enemy broadside than the surgeon's knife. However, I can promise you that you will not feel anything at the time though there will be some discomfort while it heals."

"Very well then, you had better do what you think is best Doctor."

When they returned downstairs they found Mrs. Merriman waiting in the hall.

"Oh Doctor, how is it, how is James' arm?" she asked anxiously.

"Don't fret Ma'am, all will be well. I must open the arm and remove a piece of shot, but I am sure that it will heal satisfactorily. Now if my carriage can be called I'll go home to collect what I need and return as fast as I can. The sooner I do this the better."

"Thank you Doctor, you see James, I was sure that you needed help."

"Yes Mother, you were right as usual." said Merriman resignedly, "I must go and have a large brandy before the good Doctor starts cutting me up."

"No Sir, no spirits of any kind. As your doctor I forbid it. I shall be giving you a draught to make you sleep and it does not mix well with spirits."

The doctor departed and Merriman and his mother joined the rest of the family and guests to tell them what was to happen.

"Pleased to hear it," said Captain Merriman, "we were sure that something could be done for you."

In due time the doctor returned with his bag of necessities and he and Merriman retired upstairs after instructing a maid to bring up some boiling water.

"Please strip to the waist and lie down James. I trust that you do not mind if I call you James." He busied himself with a small phial of some clear liquid. "Now James I want you to drink this. It will send you into a deep sleep and all will be over when you waken."

It was even so. Merriman came to his senses some time later to find his mother sitting beside him holding his good hand. His other arm was bandaged from the elbow to the fingertips but apart from a dull throbbing he could feel nothing.

"The doctor tells us that you will be right as rain in a few days," she said .

"That's right James" said another voice. He turned his head to see the doctor on his other side. "Would you like to keep a souvenir of my efforts?"

The doctor extended his hand. "This is what I removed from your arm whilst you slept." Merriman saw a piece of metal about an inch long together with a small nail.

"Thank you Doctor, I was foolish to doubt you. I suppose I was frightened to admit I needed help."

"Never mind that James. Now If you feel able to sit up, your mother and I will make you presentable. Everybody wants to come and see you."

Merriman sat up on the edge of the bed. The room spun round a few times then settled down. His mother and the doctor helped him on with a fresh shirt and the doctor tied a cloth round his neck supporting his arm. "I want you to keep your arm as still as possible for the next week," he said, "it will help the wound to heal."

They helped him into a chair and his mother fussed around him, sponging his face and combing his hair. "Mother, I'm not a complete invalid," he protested.

"I know dear, but it gives me great pleasure to do it for you. It's been too many years since I could."

The whole family wanted to see him. His father cheerful and hearty, Emily giving him a kiss and a hug and brother Matthew rather subdued, perhaps only now really understanding what the King's service demanded in terms of pain and suffering.

The next to enter was his friend Robert, with a big smile on his face. "How is the wounded hero? Your father has been telling me of how you came to be hurt. A fine action I hear. I must go back to town now but there is someone else who wishes to see you."

He opened the door to reveal the doctor's daughter Helen. She moved towards Merriman, saying "I am pleased to see you looking so well Sir, I hope, no, I'm certain that you will be yourself in a day or two."

"Thank you Ma'am for your concern. I shall be about as soon as I can."

"Now," said the doctor, "That's enough for now. Mrs. Merriman Ma'am, I look to you to ensure that your son has complete rest and does not agitate his arm at all. I'll call again in three day's time but if you need me earlier pray do not hesitate to call for me."

As he was left alone, Merriman was annoyed to realize that he felt as weak as a kitten but his good sense brought him to the realization that it would pass and hopefully he could look forward to using his arm and hand properly again.

As promised, the doctor returned, inspected Merriman's arm and pronounced himself satisfied with its progress. "As you see James, The cut is healing nicely and I'll be able to remove the stitches in another few days."

"Doctor, I'm surprised at the neatness of your stitches. I've seen many a wound sewn up by our navy surgeons but none of them was as good as this."

"Oh, didn't you know. It was Helen who did it, not me. She is far more skilful with a needle than I am."

Merriman was about to make some kind of remark about the unsuitability of such a thing for a young lady to do but he thought better of it.

"The next thing I want you to do James, is to hold this small tightly bound ball of rags and try to squeeze it. You will find it difficult at first, but if you persevere you will find it easier each day. Keep the arm in the sling for a few days longer and practice with it as much as you can. It will strengthen the muscles of your arm and hand."

It was difficult and Merriman often swore in frustration, but as the days passed he found that his grip was becoming stronger as the doctor had told him it would.

Merriman reports to the Admiralty

Eventually, one morning at breakfast, one of the servants whispered in his ear that Owen had returned late the previous night and wanted to speak with him.

Owen looked tired and his clothes were dirty and torn but he had an air of satisfaction about him when Merriman met him. On seeing Merriman his face split into a broad smile, "I've done it Sir, I've done it, I've found out a lot." Then his face fell, "But I 'ad to kill a man Sir, in cold blood it were and I regret that, even though 'e needed killing."

"Right then, wait there until I bring my Father in. Then you can tell us everything."

When they were settled, Merriman indicated to Owen that he should begin his tale.

"Well Sir, I did as you suggested and pretended I'd run, I took to sleepin' under 'edges and stayin' in the shadows in some of the taverns used by the fisherfolk and farm people. Most of 'em looked at me suspicious like, but nobody spoke to me until one night a man approached me and bought me a drink. He was a Welshman, no doubt of that. He said 'e could see I was a seafaring man and started asking questions, like who was I and what ships I'd served on. and such, 'e seemed satisfied and told me to go back the next night as 'e might find work for me, but 'e wouldn't say what."

Owen went on to relate all that had happened.

"An interesting story, these smugglers are well organised I must say," Captain Merriman said with some asperity, "They seem to have no fear of discovery."

"No Sir, and that's not all," continued Owen. "The same thing 'appened for two nights more. I helped with more landings of brandy and such but I don't know where we were taken those times though I kept my eyes open. I must 'ave pleased the man in charge because I wasn't blindfolded again."

Owen finished his account and stood there, nervously waiting to see what effect his tale would have on his audience. Both of his listeners looked at him for a long moment without saying anything, then Captain Merriman rose to his feet and paced up and down, his brow furrowed in concentration. He turned to his son, "James, what do you make of this man's story? I'd like your opinion."

"I believe it Father. Don't forget that he didn't have to go, it was my idea and as for killing that man, Owen had no option and the fellow would have been hanged if the authorities had managed to get hold of him."

"My view exactly. I don't like killing if it can be avoided, but in this case I believe it to be justified." He swung round to face the big sailor. "Do you understand what I am saying? We attach no blame to you for the man's death, but not a word about this affair must go beyond this room.."

"Aye-aye Sir, and thank'ee Sir, I'll not tell a soul," said Owen with a relieved look on his face. "But that's not all Sir. I found out where they take some of the stuff to in Chester."

"Did you by God!" said the Captain, "Maybe we'll be able to catch these rogues before too long. We could go to wherever it is with the Revenue and catch them red-handed, what do you say James?"

"I think we should hear what more Owen has to tell us before we make any precipitate plans Father. As we've said before, there must be somebody with a good brain behind this affair and we don't know if the man that Owen met, the leader of the gang, is the one we want."

"Blast it! You always were the thinker James, and you are right again. I'm too ready to lay alongside and give 'em a broadside. Right then, tell us the rest of it"

"Well Sir, as I said, after I killed that man they seemed to trust me a bit more because one night I was taken in a loaded wagon into Chester. O' course it was dark and I was told to keep under the cover, so I couldn't see the name of the tavern we stopped at but I reckon I could find it again. It *was* a tavern Sir, I know, and the wagon turned into a big yard at the back of it."

"The driver said I was there because I looked strong enough to do the work of two men and we set to to 'elp unload the wagon. There were three other fellows there and we moved the load and split it up between three smaller wagons. We 'ad to be quiet and could only work by the light of a couple of lanterns. As each wagon was loaded, one of the men drove it away."

"Have you any idea where they were going?" asked Merriman.

"No Sir, sorry Sir," replied Owen, shaking his head. On the way back I asked the driver about it, casual like, but he told me to mind my own business. I didn't want to press him Sir, in case he got suspicious."

"No, quite right. You have done well Owen, I'm very pleased."

"Thank'ee Sir. Mebbe I can learn more when I go back.."

"Going back may not be easy. How did you manage to get away to come here?"

"I told 'em I wanted to see my sister who works on a farm near here. O'course I 'aven't got a sister but I think they believed me."

"Well we certainly need to know as much as we can about these fellows, but you must be sure of your safety. I suggest that you do exactly what you are told to do and don't try to come back here unless you have something really important to report, or if you think that you may be in danger."

"Aye-aye Sir, I'll do that." And with that he left Merriman and his father alone.

"You've got a good man there, James. When you return to sea with a command you could do worse than take him with you and make him your Cox'n."

"If I am given a command again, which is unlikely with no war and so many officers on half pay."

"I don't like to see you so bitter James, your arm is healing nicely according to Doctor Simpson and your court martial cleared you. You have everything to look forward to and I should be very surprised if the Admiralty forgot about such a capable young officer."

"I hope you are right Father, but we shall just have to wait and see."

Captain Merriman's optimism appeared to be well founded when a letter arrived a day or two later bearing the Admiralty seal. Merriman opened it with some trepidation, not knowing whether to expect good or bad news. Beneath the usual headings and greetings it appeared that their Lordships of the Admiralty, assuming that he was healed of his wounds, ordered him, "required and requested him" in Admiralty parlance, to report to a Captain Edgar at the Admiralty in London, a week from the date of the letter at two o'clock in the afternoon.

"Good God, that's only three days after today," said Captain Merriman when James showed him the letter. "We'd better send a message to the White Lion to ask if Mr. Paul can reserve a seat for you on the Royal Mail Coach tomorrow evening. It will have you in London about twenty-six hours after leaving Chester. That's a lot quicker than the old rattler you came home on, eh!"

"It certainly is Father, I'll do that right away. Also I believe that I should go and see Doctor Simpson right away as these stitches are due to be removed."

Arriving at the Doctor's house, Merriman was admitted by a maid and ushered in as the Doctor rose to his feet

"Welcome James, come and sit down by the fire. What brings you out on such a cold day?"

Merriman told the Doctor about his summons to the Admiralty and that he would be leaving the very next day. "So you see Doctor, I thought you should examine my arm again before I go. I understand that the stitches should be ready to come out now."

"Quite right, I'll call Helen down to do that, she stitched you up so she can unstitch you. Her fingers are so much more nimble than mine."

The Doctor rang a bell and when the maid appeared he asked her to ask his daughter to join them.

"Helen is reading to my sister at the moment. Jane has a slight indisposition and has taken to her bed for a day or two. No, nothing serious," he said as Merriman began to murmur the usual condolences, "She'll be up and about again tomorrow. I must say that she has hardly stopped talking about our visit to your family. She enjoyed it immensely and hopes to have found a friend in your Mother."

Merriman laughed, "I know that my Mother enjoyed your sister's company, They didn't stop chattering all the time they were together."

Just then Helen entered the room. As she offered her hand, Merriman rose to make a bow and surrender his seat beside the fire.

"The Lieutenant has come to tell us that he has been called to London and he will need to have his wound unstitched before he goes," said the doctor.

"So soon Lieutenant? It seems such a short time since we travelled home. Are you sure that you are quite well?"

"Yes Ma'am, I feel quite well thank you, and my hand is improving daily thanks to your father's ministrations and the hand exercises. Besides, I am a serving officer and when duty calls I must go, well or not."

"Well I don't think it fair that you should have to go away again after so few weeks at home with your family. Can you not ask for more time?"

"Ma'am, I cannot refuse. Although I have no idea why I am wanted in London I would be risking my career not to go. If their Lordships have some appointment for me it would go to some other officer. I would lose the opportunity, and probably not get another."

"Oh, you men, all you think about is duty. I had thought that we could be friends as I know no one else here. I shall miss your company." She coloured slightly as she said it and poor Merriman, not knowing what to say, said nothing, which only provoked her still further.

"I see that I'm as good as talking to the wall Lieutenant. I'll remove those stitches and then you can go back to your precious navy."

She flounced out of the room and Merriman turned helplessly to her father, who simply raised his eyebrows, shrugged his shoulders expressively and held his hands in the air in a gesture which said "I don't understand women any more than you do."

Helen returned with a bowl of hot water and commanded him to remove his coat and roll up his sleeve. She unrolled the bandage and the Doctor inspected the arm.

"Yes, all's well and those stitches must come out now. James, hold your arm over the bowl and Helen will remove them."

The girl's touch was so gentle as she snipped the stitches and carefully pulled them out, that when she suddenly bathed the wound with the hot water, Merriman yelped in pained surprise

"Come Sir, that didn't hurt you a bit, stop making a fuss."

The Doctor intervened, "Keep the wound covered with this clean bandage for the next day or two. You are unlikely to have full mobility in the arm again for some time, but it's certainly better than it was. The muscles of both the hand and arm will continue to strengthen if you continue to squeeze the little ball as I have shown you."

"Thank you Doctor, I'm deeply grateful for all you've done for me. Now I must take my leave of you. I leave for London tomorrow and I have a lot to prepare before then. I don't know where I shall be going or for how long but I do hope we shall meet again soon."

He shook hands with the doctor and turned to Helen and took her hand.

"Good bye Ma'am, thank you for the best stitching I have ever seen."

She smiled sadly, "Good bye Lieutenant, take care of yourself."

Merriman felt a gentle pressure on his fingers and thought he saw a trace of moisture in her eye before she turned away.

"Imagination" he told himself gloomily as he rode home. *"She has no patience with the like of me and my duty, she made that very clear."* The unhappy Lieutenant evidently had a lot to learn about women.

News of French Agents

When the Royal Mail coach arrived in London, Merriman immediately secured a room at an hotel to clean himself up after the journey and to prepare for the forthcoming visit to the Admiralty.

Precisely at five minutes before two o'clock, Merriman presented himself at the entrance to the centre of British sea power, the Admiralty. There an harassed, pink cheeked young lieutenant ushered him into a room where several other officers were waiting. All eyed each other warily, wondering which of them would be leaving with a new appointment and who would not. Many were lieutenants, older men than Merriman himself and doubtless with more seniority. Three of the officers were captains.

Merriman did not have long to consider why he was there. He had hardly settled himself, in anticipation of a long wait, when the lieutenant returned. "Lieutenant Merriman Sir, if you would please follow me." The assembled officers all stared at Merriman, doubtless wondering why such a junior officer was being given preference over themselves.

The lieutenant opened a door and almost pushed Merriman in, saying "Captain Edgar, Sir, Lieutenant Merriman." The Captain proved to be a tall, stooped officer, almost completely bald, who remained at the window for several minutes before turning and staring hard at Merriman for several more minutes. Merriman was beginning to think that he was in trouble when the Captain's face split into a surprisingly warm smile and he crossed the room to a chair on the long side of a beautifully polished mahogany table.

"Sit down here Mr. Merriman." He picked up a wig lying on the table and crammed it on his head. "Damn all wigs, I hate the wretched things, make my head itch most abominably don't you know."

"Yes Sir, I don't care for them much myself," replied Merriman, whose own strong growth was held at the nape of his neck by a fashionable bow.

"Now, Lieutenant", continued the Captain, turning over the pages of a document on the table before him, "I must ask you a few questions. First of all, have you recovered sufficiently from your wound to take up service again and secondly, how do you imagine that your career might suffer if you were out of the mainstream of life in the navy?"

Merriman was taken aback. His first thoughts that he had been summoned to the Admiralty because he was in trouble were dispelled by Captain Edgar's words which seemed to indicate he would be leaving the navy, a prospect that filled him with dismay, although there was the hint of some new appointment.

"Tolerably well Sir, my arm has improved beyond all expectations and inconveniences me not at all. As to your second question, I had not thought of leaving the navy, indeed Sir, I was looking forward to continuing sea service and eventual promotion if I should be so fortunate."

"Good, good, and what do you say to the prospect of fighting His Majesty's enemies in a more discreet and less obvious way?"

"Spying, do you mean Sir?"

"Possibly, Lieutenant, possibly, but only as part of a broader scheme."

"I can only reply Sir, that I am a loyal officer and will do whatever Their Lordships might order me to do."

"Very well then Mr. Merriman, I hoped and expected that would be your reply. Now, I must leave you alone for a few minutes." With that Captain Edgar gathered the documents together and left the room.

Merriman walked to the window and stared unseeingly at the view of the busy street outside, his mind a jumble of thoughts about what had seemed to be said. Unconsciously he clasped his hands behind his back and began to pace up and down in his accustomed 'quarter deck walk', unaware that the door had opened and Captain Edgar and three other people had returned to the room.

A mild voice gently reproved him, "Upon my word Lieutenant Merriman, we shall need to replace the floor if you wear it out like this." Merriman recovered himself with a start, realizing that he was confronted by an Admiral and Lord Stevenage and surprisingly, Mr. Grahame, his acquaintance from the inn at Oxford who acknowledged him with a nod.

"My apologies My Lord, I was deep in thought about what Captain Edgar said."

"I'm sure you were Mr. Merriman, you must be wondering what has brought us together again. Let's be seated and I'll ask Admiral Edwards to enlighten you."

Merriman had immediately recognized the Admiral as that same Captain Edwards, the friend of his father who had taken him into his ship as a twelve year old midshipman at the start of his naval career.

"A good many years ago Lieutenant, your father and I were good friends when we were both young Lieutenants and served together on the old *Terror*. We met on few occasions after he was made post but I've not seen him since he retired, I trust he is well, and also his charming wife?"

"Yes Sir, indeed they are both very well, thank you. My father often speaks of his naval days and your name has often been mentioned. He will be pleased to know you remembered him."

"Couldn't forget him lad, led me into many a scrape I can tell you." The Admiral suddenly realized he had an audience, coughed, cleared his throat, looked at His Lordship in apology and turned back to Merriman.

"Before I begin Lieutenant," said the Admiral, "I must emphasize that what is about to be revealed to you must be held in the strictest confidence and you should be fully aware of the damage which could be caused to the government and certainly to your career if our confidence in you should be misplaced." He held up his hand as Merriman began to speak.

"Say nothing Lieutenant, you would not be here if there was any doubt about your ability and loyalty. Your service record speaks most eloquently on your behalf and it was Lord Stevenage himself who suggested you for this appointment."

Merriman looked at His Lordship in surprise. Although his father had suggested that Lord Stevenage might prove to be a good friend to him, Merriman himself had not dared to hope that it would be so. Evidently his father had been right, but, Merriman reminded himself, he still didn't know what was expected of him.

"You will know Lieutenant, that there has always been trouble in Ireland with nationalists demanding emancipation for the Catholics and parliamentary reform and there were hotheads siding with France in the recent war. Why, only last year a fellow by the name of Wolfe Tone founded a group calling themselves United Irishmen or The United Irish Society or some other damned thing, with the avowed intent of forcing these issues by any means possible."

"Yes Sir, I've heard my Father speak of this, although as you will appreciate, I have been away at sea for many years and I have no real knowledge of these affairs."

Continued the Admiral, "Intelligence we have indicates that these rebellious elements in Ireland are again involved with the French. During the last war French agents landed in Ireland and used the shipping across the Irish Sea to land in England, many of them at Holyhead and Parkgate. Their intent then was to sow discord and dissention and it's common knowledge that they are trying the same again, indeed we are certain of it. These agents are sowing the seeds of revolution in all quarters, from Ireland and the lowest taverns to the Constitutional Clubs in every city. They are a constant threat to the safety of our country."

"We're not at war with France at the present time, but many of us at the Admiralty and some in other circles are sure that we will be again soon, although it's difficult to persuade some of the politicians of this, that man Fox for instance, although I'm pleased to be able to tell you that the fleet is better prepared for war than at any time since the end of the American war, thanks to Mr Pitt the Prime Minister. Only recently were orders given to increase the number of seamen from sixteen to twenty thousand."

Admiral Edwards paused to clear his throat and take a sip of water, which gave Lord Stevenage the opportunity to interrupt.

"If I could continue from here Admiral?"

"Of course my Lord."

"I'm sure Lieutenant, that you know that for the last ten years all Europe has been in a ferment, but since the storming of the Bastille and the start of the French revolution the political situation has deteriorated rapidly. In April last year France declared war on Austria. Not that Austria had provoked them, it was political device to divert public attention away from the social problems in France which have been becoming more serious every day. Prussia on the other hand has been looking to gain territorial advantages from France which is why she entered the war on the side of Austria."

"There was a request from Austria that Britain should enter the war and join an anti-revolutionary alliance but this government is determined to stay neutral as long as possible. Unfortunately, France has defeated the Prussian and Austrian forces and now occupies Belgium and is poised on the border with the Dutch Netherlands. British foreign policy has been founded on the determination that both parts of the Low Countries, both Belgium and the United Dutch Provinces should be kept out of the hands of the French."

He pounded his fist on the table to emphasise his words. "This is critical to our security, not only in the Channel but also on the sea routes to India because of the Dutch possessions at the Cape of Good Hope and Ceylon. As long as Belgium was held by Austria under Habsburg rule it was an ideal situation to prevent French expansion to the north. This country cannot tolerate any further French interference in that area and Mr. Pitt has left the French in no doubt of Britain's resolution to honour treaty obligations to our ally. Do you understand so far Lieutenant?"

"Yes my Lord, I do."

"Good, to continue. Since the revolution started we had considered the turmoil in France to be in our best interests but there has been, and to a degree still is, a part of public opinion in this country which is vocal in its support for the revolution, and as you may be aware there has been a profusion of radical clubs springing up all over the country. This activity has also been increased as a result of the poor harvest this year and the rise in food prices. Many of these clubs send messages of support to the National Assembly in Paris and Paris is the centre where all subversive elements from all countries of Europe, including our own, have gathered."

He paused to gather his thoughts. "However, since the horror of the September massacres in Paris when the mob broke into the prisons and slaughtered the occupants, including innocent tradespeople and aristocrats confined there along with genuine criminals, many of those so called radicals have changed their tune and with the King's proclamation against seditious writings being enforced, we may see some improvement in that direction. Nevertheless, the official French envoy to Britain, the Marquis de Chauvelin, constantly receives deputations from these radical groups, the Norwich Revolution Society, the Manchester Constitutional Society, the London Independent Whigs and the London Corresponding Society to name but a few."

"This last one is expanding rapidly, which shows how great is the attraction of its aims which include universal male suffrage. They have a membership fee of just one shilling and a weekly subscription of only one penny which brings it within the reach of every working man. Our agents keep an eye on their activities which is how we know so much about them. French agents are definitely involved, visiting and addressing meetings and trying to agitate the ordinary people with talk of equality for all and other revolutionary ideas."

"I'd no idea that so many potential revolutionaries were active within this country my Lord", said Merriman. "Can they not be prevented from this traitorous communication with our traditional enemy, France?"

"As the Admiral has said Mr. Merriman, we are not at war with France and the commerce agreements between our countries allows the subjects of both to reside and travel in either without licence or passport. Another thing you should bear in mind, is that the National Assembly declared that all treaties with other countries to be void and called on all European countries to practice self-determination. This means that France has almost, but not quite, declared war on all other governments. So you see, although neutrality would suit us best and allow our trade with the world to expand even faster than it's doing at present, I can see no way that we can avoid another war with France."

"And this is where you and Mr. Grahame come into the matter. The Prime Minister, Mr. Pitt, has asked me, because of my connections with the Treasury, to attempt to co-ordinate the efforts of our own people, the Customs, the Judiciary and especially the Navy in preventing more French activity. Similar measures are being implemented elsewhere but you and Mr. Grahame will be responsible between Ireland and England."

"Mr. Grahame here, with whom you are already acquainted, is my agent in this matter and it's through his efforts that we know as much as we do. We believe that there is some one person at the centre of events who is organizing both the smuggling and the moving of French agents, and who is able to call on extra men for special purposes such as the attack on the Revenue cutter off the coast of North Wales. Further, we believe that person or persons to be brilliant organizers, having knowledge of our political moves almost as soon as they are decided. Also, there must be someone involved who is able to move about between England, Ireland and France without arousing suspicion. Although such persons are but shadows we do know they are there."

"But," and here he wagged a finger at Merriman, "We must proceed cautiously and only move on these people when we're certain of our facts. We cannot speak outright about the French involvement without causing a diplomatic incident which may bring about the war before we are ready."

"So you see Mr. Merriman, we think you are just the man for us, not least because your home is where it is, and surely you know the coast and inland area where these events are happening. We also know that your Father is a magistrate and will be concerned about the smuggling. He must have some knowledge of local rogues who might be bribed to give information."

Here the Admiral broke in, "If you will allow me my Lord, I'll tell the Lieutenant what we propose and require him to do."

"By all means Admiral, pray continue."

"Thank you Sir." He turned to face Merriman. "We are giving you a new sloop of war presently completing at Chatham, the *Aphrodite*. Damn silly name if you ask me but somebody must like it."

"Your duty will be to take station in the Irish Sea with full authority from the Admiralty to stop and search any vessel within our waters which you may perceive to be of a dubious nature. You will have to be diplomatic with foreigners and aware of the consequences should you ruffle the wrong feathers, but we do want you to ruffle a few to see what can be stirred up in the murky pool up there" said he, mixing his metaphors.

"Your ship is, in effect, seconded to the Revenue service so you'll not be entirely a free agent. You'll cruise round, appearing at places apparently at random but in accordance with a general plan conceived by Mr. Grahame here, who will sail with you. You must be prepared to act in concert with him, although of course the ship is your responsibility. The main purpose is to find and dispose of these villains as quickly as possible. Have you any questions?"

"Yes Sir. I'm sure Mr. Grahame will be able to answer any I may have about his plan of action, on our voyage round to the Irish Sea, but do I understand correctly that my new command is ready for sea or is a crew still to be found?"

"All should be ready when you arrive dockside Lieutenant, --- er, that reminds me, you are appointed to the rank of Commander with all pay and benefits thereto from this day. Your commission will be given to you by one of my clerks on your way out and your written orders will arrive at the ship soon after you. You will put to sea as soon as they arrive and start fishing for these damned shadows that his Lordship calls them."

He smiled briefly, "You may be surprised by what you will find aboard when you reach your ship Commander. Oh, and get your uniform sorted out as soon as you can."

As Merriman rose to his feet he knew he was a lucky man. With so many ships still out of commission and many officers on half pay, here he was, promoted and with a brand new ship to command. Post rank was one step nearer. "Thank you Sir, for the confidence you have placed in me, and you My Lord, for your interest."

"Say no more Commander, let us hope that you will be able to deal with the matter expeditiously." Brief handshakes and Merriman was left alone with Mr. Grahame.

As they left the Admiralty, Merriman clutching his papers and his mind in a whirl, the Treasury man spoke for the first time, "I have a carriage waiting, I suggest we lose no time. First we'll call on the naval outfitter to have you measured for a new uniform which will have to be sent to your home; I have some

Treasury business to attend to and some people to see, so I think it will be dawn before we join your ship."

A new Command

In the cold light of dawn the dockside at Chatham was a scene of chaos, or so it would appear to the uninformed eye, but beneath the bustle Merriman could see the organization of one of England's greatest naval ports. Even at that early hour the water was alive with boats of every kind, barges, wherries and flats all loaded with barrels, bales, cordage, timber, canvas, sacks of ships biscuit, barrels of salt beef and salt pork and all the hundreds and thousands of items needed to provision the King's ships. There were buoy boats, hire boats and numerous ship's boats rowed vigorously between the moored and anchored ships and the dockside.

Ashore there was a bewildering array of dockyard buildings, ropewalks, sail lofts, cooperages, smithies, saw pits, carpenters shops and the like. There were dry stores for canvas, rope, tar, oil, rigging blocks and cannon, with a continuous flow of porters, wagons and worried looking clerks carrying papers and files. The Victualling Board had its own stores for ships supplies of food, bread, biscuit and rum and even a brewery from which issued a tantalising aroma of hops which almost but not quite overpowered the stench from the slaughterhouse.

Seeing Merriman and Grahame standing there, a young midshipman seated in a ship's boat, got to his feet and climbed the worn, weed covered stone steps and approached, eyeing Merriman and his companion dubiously.

" I am expecting a Commander Merriman and another gentleman, Lieutenant, do you know if he is here Sir?"

"In spite of the uniform I am Commander Merriman, Mr----?"

"Oakley, Sir, Midshipman Oakley. With your permission Sir." He turned away and called to the boats crew, "Up here four of you and get the officer's baggage into the boat, smartly now."

Seated in the sternsheets beside the young Mr. Oakley, Merriman carefully watched the oarsmen, trying to gain some impression of the crew. Some of them stole guarded glances at him, trying on their part to gain some impression of the man who would have the power of life and death over them. As the boat crossed the choppy waters of the harbour, spray splashed over the bows causing Mr Grahame to utter a smothered oath as he got wet.

"There she is Sir," said Oakley, pointing to where a small ship was just coming into view from behind a huge ninety gun, second rate ship of the line.

Merriman looked at his new command with a keen eye. She was one of the new breed of sloop, with three masts instead of the two as on his last ship *Conflict*, flush decked and of about four hundred and twenty tons. A small version of a frigate really, with a single row of closed gunports hiding what were doubtless nine-pounders. Fore and main masts rigged with square sails and the mizzen rigged fore and aft.

She floated almost level but to Merriman's critical eye it looked as though she would be better down by the stern a little more, but there would be time to change things when he knew how she handled, a new ship with no growth of weed under her to slow her down and her lower hull well protected by new copper sheathing as most warships were by then. *"By God, she'll be a flyer this one,"* he thought to himself.

As the boat approached the *Aphrodite* he saw the bustle of movement on deck as their arrival was noted, the blue and white of the officers and surprisingly, red coats. Red coats surely meant marines which was strange, as a sloop's complement of perhaps one hundred and thirty men did not usually include marines.

"Oars" called Oakley as the boat moved smoothly alongside and the bowman prepared to catch the chains with his boathook.. The oars moved dripping to the vertical and Merriman swiftly climbed aboard his ship. He was a little taken aback to receive the full ceremonial welcome reserved for a captain joining his ship, the boatswain's whistle and the drawn swords of the officers were expected, but the line of marines presenting arms in a cloud of dusty pipeclay was not.

"Welcome aboard Sir" said the officer immediately in front of him. "I am John Jeavons your first Lieutenant. May I present Mr. Laing, your second, Sir, and your third, Lieutenant Andrews?"

"I know this officer well enough, I am surprised to see you here though Mr. Andrews. I trust your shoulder has fully healed?"

Andrews was grinning all over his face, "Yes Sir, completely, it's good to see you again Sir."

"These other gentlemen are Lieutenant St. James in command of the marine detachment Sir, Mr. Cuthbert the sailing master and the surgeon Mr. McBride," continued the first Lieutenant. "Mr. Oakley you have met and this is Mr. Shrigley our other Midshipman."

"Glad to meet you gentlemen, I hope to get to know you all better in due course. This is Mr. Grahame who will be sailing with us. And now ----," he drew from his pocket his commission which every captain joining his ship for the first time had to read aloud to confirm his status. It commenced with the usual flowery verbiage of such Admiralty documents, going on to say 'You are required and commanded to take upon yourself the command of His Majesty's Ship *Aphrodite* and all the ship's company.' There was much more and when he had finished it, Merriman was indisputably the Captain, answerable only to God and the Admiralty. To some of the lowly seamen he probably was God, having the power to flog them or hang them as he felt the need.

Merriman turned to the First Lieutenant, "Mr. Jeavons, is the ship ready for sea in all respects?"

"We are still a few hands short Sir, but in general I'm pleased with what we have and the Warrant Officers, gunner, carpenter, bos'n and their mates are all experienced hands. The last few barrels of water are coming aboard now Sir, but we still need to load powder and shot down the estuary." For obvious reasons of safety, explosives were not brought aboard in the crowded confines of the harbour.

"Very good Mr Jeavons, we shall be leaving as soon as my orders arrive."

"I think they are already here Sir, I signed for a package with the Admiralty seal on it not an hour past and put it in your cabin."

"Show me, immediately" said Merriman and followed the first Lieutenant below. Bending low he managed to avoid crashing his head on the deck beams as Jeavons opened a door and revealed the spartan quarters which were to be his. The dockyard had provided the absolute minimum required, a desk, a table, some uncomfortable looking chairs, a small sideboard and a swinging cot.. The smell of raw, newly sawn timber pervaded the air, together with the usual shipboard smells of tar and paint. There was a small skylight in the deckhead and Merriman found that he could just stand upright beneath it. The Admiralty package was lying on the desk.

"Thank you Mr. Jeavons, prepare to leave for the powder hulks at once. Oh, and I'm sorry but I think you will have to relinquish your cabin to Mr. Grahame."

"Aye-aye Sir", said Jeavons gloomily, knowing that he would have to move everybody else round as a result. "May I ask who Mr. Grahame is, Sir?"

"No, you may not. I'll tell you all that you will need to know in due course." Conscious that he sounded rather pompous he relented a little. "I'm sorry, but all I can say is that Mr. Grahame is very important to the success of the mission we are on."

"Yes Sir, I see Sir."

"You don't see at all Lieutenant, but you will, I assure you."

"Very good Sir. I'll ask Lieutenant St. James to post a marine sentry at your door."

"Belay that for now, we'll sort it out later," said Merriman, wondering again why the marines were aboard.

Merriman sat at the desk to open the package, savouring for a moment to himself the superscription "James Abel Merriman – Master and Commander". A quick scan of the papers showed that the contents merely confirmed his verbal orders received at the Admiralty.

He pondered for a while, gently tugging on his ear lobe which was an unconscious habit he had when thinking. His other hand squeezing the rag ball which had become almost a part of him. The Admiralty had certainly done him proud. A new ship, almost a full crew and even Mr Andrews as third Lieutenant. Lord Stevenage must have had a hand in that too. And why a marine Lieutenant? Marines were unusual on such a small ship and then only with a sergeant in command. That again was something out of the ordinary, and instead of the expected master's mate, the Admiralty had even given him a

Sailing Master, not usual in a ship commanded by less than a post-captain   All rather intriguing. He locked his orders in the desk drawer and went on deck to inspect his new command.

Duties of the ship *Aphrodite*

Three days later the *Aphrodite* was thrashing down the English Channel, close-hauled on the port tack under a grey cloudy sky. As Merriman had thought, she was a flyer, but probably would do better with a few changes he had in mind. Since leaving Chatham he had worked the officers and crew hard to settle them down into a cohesive whole. The watchkeeping bill needed careful drafting to ensure that the few landlubbers and the less experienced men were spread out fairly between the watches, That most of the crew were experienced men helped enormously, and all the Warrant Officers seemed to know their jobs.

Merriman had inspected the ship in every detail from the new figurehead, a well carved, half draped and rather erotic female figure representing the goddess Aphrodite, to the magazine and storerooms, "keel to truck" as the saying went, and he was beginning to remember the names of the officers, warrant officers and some of the crew especially the gunner, Mr. Hodges. That worthy was a small man whose eyes lit with pleasure when talking about his new charges. He had dragged off his woollen cap to speak with his captain, revealing a bald pate surrounded by a bushy fringe of grey hair.

"Almost new nine pounders, Sir, and we've been given two 'Smashers' as well as two bow chasers, twenty-five pounders at that Sir. One of the nine pounders will need some attention, a bush in the touch-hole Sir, but I'll have it right in no time. And I've checked the scantlings Sir, they have all been strengthened to take the strain of firing the bigger guns."

The guns he referred to, colloquially known as 'Smashers', were carronades, short barrelled and light but firing a heavy sixty-eight pound shot. Absolutely devastating at close range they were formidable weapons and were placed one a side amidships. In addition the ship was armed with six small swivel guns for close quarter work.

Aphrodite was well armed which caused Merriman to wonder anew about what his ship would be called upon to do. The 'Smashers' and the twenty-five pounders were unusual in a ship of that size, and those and the marines aboard must be the surprise mentioned by Admiral Edwards.

Merriman paced up and down on the weather side of the quarterdeck. The other officers, and crew whose duties kept them there, were very properly keeping to their own side in the time honoured tradition. Small groups of seamen were working on the standing rigging under the keen supervision of the bos'n and his mates. The new cordage had to be checked regularly for stretching and any slack taken up, but care had to be taken not to over-tighten it.

Forr'ard, Mr Laing was instructing seamen on the use of the heavy sea service flintlock musket with which it was expected that at least three quarters of the crew should be reasonably proficient, although they would rely more on the cutlass, boarding axe and pike if it came to close quarter fighting. The sea service musket was based on the army's Brown Bess but with wooden ramrods and blackened metalwork to prevent corrosion by the sea air. It was a hopelessly inaccurate weapon at anything but short range although some men, with regular practice might hit the target with more frequency than usual.

Undoubtedly speculation was rife throughout the ship about what sort of Captain he would be and the officers would be squeezing every bit of information about him from Lieutenant Andrews. As yet he had been too busy to speak more than briefly to the officers other than concerning the ship. That must change, he had kept them in the dark for long enough. It would be good to entertain them to dinner but due to the haste in coming aboard he had nothing other than ship's fare to offer them. No wine or delicacies of any kind. He resolved to change that as soon as he could.

Evidently Mr. Grahame was not a good sailor. Once the *Aphrodite* left the sheltered waters of the Thames estuary and had begun to pitch and roll, he had turned a peculiar shade of green and bolted below to his cabin. His only response to suggestions of food and drink was a feeble groan and the expressed desire to be left to die in peace.

Grahame had not yet confided his plans to him, so Merriman could not make any plans himself and so perforce must concentrate on working up the ship to the highest peak of efficiency that he could in the short time available. The crew was settling down well although there were one or two misfits and there was a bos'n's mate who was a little too free with the use of a rope's end on the backside of any laggard.

Suddenly making a decision, Merriman turned to the first Lieutenant who was standing not six feet away studiously ignoring his Captain.

"Mr. Jeavons, I would be pleased if you and Mr. St. James, Mr. McBride and Mr. Cuthbert and one of the Midshipmen would join me for dinner this evening. I don't think we can squeeze more into the cabin. Unfortunately, due to the haste with which I came aboard I've no extra stores and can only offer you ship's fare."

"That's kind of you Sir. Thank you, I look forward to it. As the ship was freshly victualled only a few days ago the food is not too bad. If I may presume Sir, the officers have a modest supply of wine and we'd be happy to provide a few bottles and perhaps a chicken." There was a chicken coop in the lee of the bulwarks containing half a dozen noisy hens belonging to the officers.

"Excellent Mr Jeavons, thank you, but you must allow me to replace them at the earliest opportunity. Now, I must take a look at our passenger. My compliments to the Master and I wish to see him in my cabin in ten minutes."

At this period, most naval ships except the smallest, carried a sailing master, an experienced navigator and seaman who was responsible for sailing and navigating the ship. He was under the captain's command for fighting the ship, but it would be a foolish officer who disagreed with him concerning matters of wind and wave.

The Master knocked on the door of his captain's cabin and entered, his hat under his arm. He was a tall man with grey hair and a permanent stoop, his face bearing the lines etched on it by the wind, sun and salt spray of his years at sea. Merriman regarded him gravely for a moment.

"Sit down Mr. Cuthbert, I need to know more about you. I see from the ship's muster book that you have been warranted for ten years and Master's mate for ten before that so I don't doubt your competence. What I do need to know is if you have experience of the Irish sea."

The Master looked at Merriman carefully. He was used to being subordinate to younger men, but this one was younger than most he had served with and was an unknown quantity. True, he had handled the ship well enough up until now, though he carried a bit more canvas at times than the master deemed prudent. So, they were going to the Irish Sea, were they, with winter coming on it would be cold and here he was hoping for the Mediterranean. Ah well, it's a seaman's life.

"I knows the Irish sea like the back of me 'and Sir, born an' raised in Cumberland I was and shipped out of Whitehaven. I haven't been there for what, must be eight or nine years in a King's ship but I knew most of the ports and harbours around there as a lad an' I don't reckon as 'ow they'll 'ave changed much. I've got my personal notes and charts Sir, as up to date as I can make them."

It was usual for ships' masters to pass information between them at all possible opportunities, such as details of newly discovered rocks and reefs, currents, wrecks, winds at various times of the year and anything which was of value to safe navigation. When in foreign parts the master was expected, when time allowed, to use a ship's boat to take soundings and check the readings against the issue charts, sending any revised information back to the Admiralty so that official charts could be amended. In this way a master would build up a large collection of notes even of areas he might not visit for years.

"Very well Mr. Cuthbert, I too sailed those waters as a boy but I shall be relying on you to keep the ship out of trouble. As you now know, we are bound for the Irish sea but under most unusual circumstances which will certainly require us to go close inshore and even to land our people in the dark. More I cannot tell you at the moment."

"Aye-aye Sir, I'll start reading my notes right away."

Soon after the Master left, there was a knock and a pale faced, rather shaky Mr. Grahame put his head round the door. "I think it time we discussed our plans Mr. Merriman."

"Come in Sir, come in and sit yourself down. I am pleased to see you about again. May I offer you some refreshment?" Merriman's servant Peters was hovering round and hastily pushed a chair forward

"Thank you, a little coffee if you would be so kind, and maybe a morsel of dry biscuit. I don't think I could manage anything more at present. I must apologize for my condition over these last few days, but I was never a good sailor."

"Think no more about it Mr. Grahame, now that you are taking nourishment again I warrant you will be your usual self within twenty-four hours."

Whilst they waited for their coffee, Grahame remarked on how well Merriman's servant had looked after him whilst he was ill. "He's been a servant before I should think."

"I don't know about that" replied Merriman. "He was recommended for the job by the First Lieutenant. He's a bit clumsy and I think I'm lucky not to have had my face cut to pieces when he shaves me, his hand trembles so, but I think he'll improve given time. Unfortunately I've not had time to get to know my people as well as I would like. Ah, thank you Peters, that will be all."

As they sipped the steaming coffee, Merriman decided that it was time to tell Grahame his own information about the activities of the smugglers. Therefore he recounted the details of the meeting with his father and other magistrates and the Revenue man from Chester, which revealed nothing more than Admiral Edwards had covered at the Admiralty. Mr Grahame merely nodded and nibbled on a fragment of biscuit, but when Merriman told him that he had a man involved with the smugglers who had already passed on some valuable information he sat up and looked more cheerful.

"Is that the big man who travelled on the coach with you? I saw him at the inn at Oxford."

"Yes, it seems that his brother was one of the crew of the cutter and was killed. He desperately wants to help to avenge his brother's death." Merriman went on to relay to Grahame all that Owen had told him.

"And your man's brother spoke of the French and Irish before he died did he? This could help us tremendously" he said, "One cannot have too much intelligence of the enemy's actions and resources. When do you expect to hear from him again?"

"When I left home I had no idea that I would be coming back to the Irish sea so soon and so he was instructed to go to my father when he has anything of substance to report, and to do everything he could to help the authorities. I will have to go home to find out if there is any news."

"That settles our first move then. We must get ashore and go to your home. I must go with you and hear what your man has to say, if he is there. Then I think you should go to see Mr. Flitwick the Customs Officer in Chester and learn what you can from him, whilst I make a call on someone else who should have more news for me."

"Do you know Mr. Flitwick Sir, is he to be trusted?"

"I've known Jonas Flitwick for many years, in fact he was my superior at the Treasury before he married and settled down.. I would trust him with my life, indeed I have done so on many occasions."

"Going ashore we must be circumspect, and try to avoid making our presence known in the area before we have to. D'you think that the best way might be to stop a small trading ship out at sea which is heading into Parkgate, so that we arrive like a couple of passengers. By the way, have you any clothes with you other than your uniform?"

"Sadly, no, but maybe one of the other officers has a coat I could borrow and I could change my breeches and stockings for a pair of trousers. It shouldn't be difficult to stop another ship, but once the crew get ashore, word of two men transferring from a King's ship will spread rapidly. I believe it would be better to close the shore in the dark and be landed by small boat not too far from the villages of Hoose or Little Meols on the tip of the Wirral peninsula. From there we should be able to hire horses or a carriage."

"An excellent idea Mr Merriman, I can see that we shall work well together. I believe that is as far as we can plan at present. Have you confided anything of this affair to your officers?"

"Only the Master, as I felt it important to know if he had knowledge of the waters of the Irish Sea, so he knows where we are bound and that we are on an unusual mission. I am to entertain some of them to dinner later today so that will be a good opportunity for you to meet them. But I must inform them of what is afoot, especially if I am to leave the ship in the hands of my First Lieutenant."

"Quite so, but make no mention of my connection with the Treasury."

And so it was that Lieutenants Colin Laing and David Andrews kept the deck and Merriman entertained the other officers to a fine meal of roast chicken, salt pork and ship's biscuit, washed down by an excellent claret provided by Edward St James the marine Lieutenant. John Jeavons, the first Lieutenant was a serious, fair haired young man who thought carefully before speaking, whereas the marine officer was a lively conversationalist with an affectedly languid manner. The Surgeon, Alan McBride was slow to join in the chatter at first but after two or three hastily drained glasses, became quite voluble. Mr. Cuthbert spoke only when directly addressed and the little midshipman Alfred Shrigley was so overawed and embarrassed in the presence of his superiors that he could only stammer wretchedly when brought into the conversation although Merriman noticed that the midshipman was not holding his appetite in check and was eating everything in front of him even though the others had finished. Mr. Grahame was also an excellent raconteur and the time passed swiftly and pleasantly.

"Mr. Shrigley, when you have quite finished gnawing on that bone, it is your place to propose a toast I believe."

"Oh Lor', s-s-sorry Sir, I mean y-y-yes Sir." The red-faced youngster groped for his glass, knocked it over, managed to grab it before all the contents were lost and squeaked "The King."

As the time had not yet come when a sailor king would allow his health to be drunk sitting down, the officers stood stooped awkwardly under the low deck-head. After the toast was drunk, Merriman motioned to his servant Peters to clear the table. When that was done and the door closed again, Merriman turned to the serious part of the evening.

"Gentlemen, as you have been kept in the dark so far as regards our purpose on this commission, I imagine the ship is alive with rumours about our destination."

"There are so many different ideas Sir, that the gunner is running a sweepstake on it," laughed the surgeon reaching for the claret again.

"Well then, there may be a winner tonight. I can tell you that we are staying in home waters, the Irish Sea to be precise, so you can all forget thoughts of warm, sunny weather and tropic seas. There is increasing trouble in that area with smuggling gangs, indeed some of you may be aware that a gang went so far as to attack a Revenue cutter a few weeks ago. They murdered all the crew except for a boy who made a lucky escape, and made off with the ship which has not been seen since."

He paused, looking round the table, then continued "Because of this outrage, the Admiralty has decided that a ship of force is to be stationed there. It is to be part of our duty to patrol round the coasts of the Kingdom bordering the Irish Sea to see if we can encounter these ruffians and put them in the hands of the hangman."

There was a murmur of interest and speculation round the table. Merriman's voice rose above it, "I know that you have all been wondering who our mysterious guest Mr. Grahame is and why he is here. Mr. Grahame represents a higher authority than myself and although I am in command of the ship and all activities at sea, we are to be used as he sees fit."

He turned to Grahame, "Perhaps you would like to say a few words Sir?"

"Thank you. I have little to add at this point except to say that there will be secret landings and meetings ashore by both your Captain and myself. These will be for the purpose of gathering, from certain persons in my employ, information which will be of use to us. More obviously, we are empowered to stop and search any vessels which arouse our suspicions. We shall be looking for French agents attempting to cross from Ireland to England so that one way or another there will be ample opportunity for your boats' crews to practice their skills."

He paused for a moment before continuing, "Remember gentlemen, that whilst we are not actively at war with France yet, I know that we most likely will be in the near future. Therefore we are engaged in a quiet war, some may say a bizarre war, but all for the benefit of our country.

"I can see several of you have questions," said Merriman, "Mr. St James, would you care to begin?"

"Thank you Sir. I know we all have been wondering why my marines are aboard, which is unusual on so small a ship. It's made for very crowded accommodation and in the activities you and Mr. Grahame have described there would seem to be little need for us. I hope I can at least post your cabin sentry Sir, It will give the men something to do."

"I don't know myself exactly why you are aboard Mr. St James, but I think that the Admiralty must have had a good reason for your presence here. No doubt those reasons will become apparent in time. Concerning the posting of a sentry, if there were no marines aboard as would be usual on so small a ship, there would be no sentry. Besides, the poor man couldn't stand upright, the deck-head is too low. Next question?"

"How often will you be going ashore Sir, and for how long?" asked Jeavons.

Merriman studied him carefully. Was this an indication that his First Lieutenant did not feel confident in his ability to cope when left alone in command. So far he had proved to be a capable officer but Merriman had no idea how he would act under real stress when he had nobody senior to turn to.

"The first time is likely to be two or three days only. How often after that I cannot say."

"Sir, Sir," squeaked the diminutive Midshipman Shrigley, emboldened by two glasses of good claret, "Will I have a chance of going ashore Sir? It all sounds very exciting and I'd do my best to help."

The others smothered smiles of amusement as Merriman replied with a twinkle in his eye, "I'm impressed by your enthusiasm Mr. Shrigley and I am sure that you would do your best as you say, but as yet I cannot see a part for you to play ashore. You must wait a while for your opportunity."

"Mr. Cuthbert, Mr. McBride, have you no questions?"

"No Sir", said the Master, "After our earlier conversation I checked my notes again and can foresee no problems."

"The surgeon tried to conceal a belch. "My knives are sharp Sir but it seems unlikely they will be required on this voyage so I think that I'll probably manage."

"Very well then Gentlemen, if there is nothing further, I think this pleasant evening must draw to a close." As the officers rose and uttered their thanks for the hospitality, Merriman said "It is I who must thank the wardroom for supplying most of the meal. Goodnight Gentlemen. Oh, Mr. McBride, would you remain behind for a moment."

When the others had gone, the Surgeon remained, slumped in his chair. McBride was red faced and sweating profusely having consumed more than his fair share of the claret. Also he was having great difficulty in keeping his eyes open.

Merriman regarded him silently. It was not unusual for a ship's surgeon at that time to have chosen to serve afloat rather than face a debtor's prison or a cuckolded husband or worse. Perhaps lacking the skills required to make a competent living ashore, the navy was the lowest rung of the professional ladder available.

"Mr. McBride," Merriman's voice cracked like a whip over the Surgeon's head, "You will oblige me by sitting up straight and opening your eyes. I have no knowledge of your professional capabilities but I do know that you are drunk and over fond of the use of alcohol. It has not gone unnoticed that you do not rise for breakfast and when you do appear on deck, it is obvious that you've been drinking. This I will not tolerate. From now on you will come on deck every morning at the change from the morning watch to the forenoon watch in a clean and sober condition and report to the officer of the watch. Should you fail to do so, the officer will have orders to have you brought on deck in whatever state you happen to be in and there you will remain until you are sober. Do you understand me?"

Merriman's words slowly penetrated the man's confused mind. "Oh God, he'd done it again. Why couldn't he keep off the drink?" Every good resolution lasted until the next time a bottle was in front of him. He was filled with self pity and self loathing in equal measure. "Sir you don't understand, I can't ----" his voice trailed off before the anger in the Captain's face.

"I understand only too well" said Merriman, "Bad excuses are worse than none. You must mend your ways. I'll not have a drunkard trying to tend men with shattered bodies, broken limbs or any other injury possible in a ship of war. They deserve better. Now, get back to your cabin, and remember, wine has drowned more men than the sea."

After the man had struggled to his feet and staggered from the cabin, Merriman wondered if he had been too hard. No, he decided, the wretched man must climb out of the pit of misery he had dug for himself and he would need to be helped to help himself. There was probably a sad story behind him but that would have to be ignored. If McBride did not improve, he would have to go.

That decided, Merriman went on deck for a breath of fresh air. Seeing him, Mr. Andrews moved to the leeward side to leave his Captain his own side. Merriman checked the slate by the binnacle. The slate listed alterations of course, sail changes and Captain's orders for the day. Usually made up by the Master, the information thereon was used by both Captain and Master to complete their daily logs. Merriman called the Lieutenant over and showed him what he had just written, his orders concerning McBride.

"Ensure that each officer at the change of watch carries this out until further orders. Goodnight Mr. Andrews."

"Aye-aye Sir, goodnight."

Five days later, delayed by adverse winds, the *Aphrodite* rounded the northern tip of Anglesey, keeping well off to avoid the dreaded Skerries, an isolated group of rocks which had been the death of many a proud ship. It was time to begin her new role.

A visit to the Custom House

In the candlelight, Helen Simpson studied her reflection in the mirror over her dressing table as she brushed her hair vigorously before going to bed. Her long dark hair shone in the candlelight and her complexion was more coloured by the sun in India than society considered right for a lady. "Damn Society", she said to herself, "I don't care what society thinks, I won't be bound by their petty conventions, I won't, I won't".

She sighed, "There I go again, why do I always seem to be at odds with people?" She knew that her father wanted to see her safely married so that her future might be assured, and in truth she had no real objections to the idea, but she had always kept men at arms length. She thought about the men who had tried to win her affections back in India, the company clerks and garrison officers, more boys than men she considered, and the older men, usually married, and often drunk as they tried to assail her virtue. She had grown so accustomed to discouraging them by deliberately not taking them seriously or turning them away with a cutting remark that it had become a habit she was finding hard to break.

Her thoughts moved to Lieutenant Merriman and her expression softened and turned rather wistful. There was no doubt that she was attracted to him, he aroused feelings within herself such as she had not experienced before. But in spite of that she knew that she had upset him with her remarks. "Now he has gone again, back to the sea which he so obviously loves and it could be months or maybe years before I see him again". She sighed again and brushed her hair even more vigorously

She could not know that the object of her thoughts and his companion were even then being rowed ashore at the tip of the

Wirral peninsula. The *Aphrodite* had crept slowly along the Horse Channel guided by the Sea Lights on the coast and the so called Lake Lights and when the Lake Lights were in line dropped anchor near the north east buoy at the corner of the Hoyle bank The night was almost pitch black relieved only by the sea lights and the light from the Schomberg lighthouse on the Point of Air. There were also a few scattered lights to be seen from the small villages of Little Meols and Hoose.

Merriman thought about the orders he had given to the First Lieutenant before leaving the ship. He was harbouring doubts about Mr. Jeavons, especially as he had requested his orders to be put in writing. The orders couldn't be simpler, the ship was to cruise well offshore out of sight of land, ignoring other vessels, and to return to the same place inshore the following night, close to midnight. If they saw Merriman's signal, a lantern flashed three times, a boat was to be sent to pick him up. If no signal was seen then the same orders were to be followed for the next two nights. "Can't worry about Jeavons now" he told himself, "I'll just have to trust him."

Briefly he allowed his thoughts to wander to Alan Jones, his friend and First Lieutenant in the brig *Conflict*, killed in the affair with the corsairs, and what a capable and absolutely reliable officer he had been. "I would have no doubts about him" he thought.

Merriman cursed himself for his inattention to his surroundings as Midshipman Oakley who was at the tiller whispered "Nearly there Sir, good luck." just before the boat scraped on the shore. They were fortunate that it was almost high tide, saving them a weary foot slogging over the muddy foreshore. Two burly seamen dropped over the side and carried Merriman and Mr. Grahame above the tide line to keep their boots dry. Quickly pushing the boat afloat again the two men climbed on board and the boat disappeared into the darkness. No further word had been spoken, all knew what to do.

"Well done Captain" said Grahame, "Horses are our next problem."

After struggling through the soft sand over a stretch of low sand dunes they found a rough track which led towards the village of Hoose. Hoose and the adjacent village of Little Meols overlooked the stretch of sea known as the Hoyle Lake, bounded by the Hoyle Bank and at that time the area containing the two villages was beginning to be known as Hoylake. A brisk walk soon brought them to a small hotel by the name of the Green Lodge. As Mr. Grahame was obviously a gentleman but Merriman looked more like a servant in his seaman's trousers and borrowed coat and carrying a small signalling lantern, they determined to maintain those roles and Grahame was quickly able to secure the hire of two horses from an ingratiating innkeeper. That individual's questions and attempts to strike up a conversation were speedily crushed by a cold stare from Grahame and the injunction to mind his own damned business.

It was only some fifteen miles to Burton where Merriman's parents lived, so it was not long before Merriman was banging on the door for admittance. After a brief wait lights flared in an upstairs window followed by the sounds of movement behind the door. Merriman heard his father's voice bellowing "Who is it waking folk in the middle of the night, speak up now?"

At the reply "James, Father, with a friend," the bolts were withdrawn and the door opened to reveal the Captain wearing a gown over his nightshirt and holding a brace of pistols, one of them cocked. A manservant holding a club hovered in the background, and a maid was at the foot of the stairs.

"Sorry about the pistols James," said his father un-cocking the one and placing it on a side table with its companion. "There are so many villains about that one cannot be too careful. Now then, who is your friend and why are you here when we thought you to be in London?"

"A long story Father, but first may we not go near a fire and have something to warm us? And the horses need to be stabled."

"Of course my boy, forgetting my manners" and turning to Mr. Grahame he said "You are welcome Sir." Giving instructions to the maid to go upstairs and reassure Mrs Merriman that all was well, he led them into the main room of the house where the remains of a fire were still glowing. The manservant quickly re-appeared with some logs and livened up the fire whilst Captain Merriman poured glasses of brandy and handed them round.

After sending the man to rouse a stable boy to see to the horses before going back to bed, he said "Now then James, I'm eaten up with curiosity to know why you have arrived dressed like a servant, and in the middle of the night too?"

Merriman proceeded to introduce his companion and to relate to his father all the events that had happened since leaving home, and Mr. Grahame's part in them. "So you see Father, we came ashore secretly, hoping to avoid spreading the news too soon that a new King's ship was in these waters, before we knew if anything further has developed up here. Mr. Grahame has his own sources of information and will be pursuing those as soon as he can, but have you seen Owen again or have Mr. Flitwick's revenue people found out anything new?"

"No James, I have heard nothing from Mr. Flitwick since you left and there has been no word from your man Owen. I hope he's still alive, it's a dangerous game he is playing."

"It certainly is Father. You know, he hasn't got a sister but he has told the gang that he has, and it might help Owen if it could be arranged for him to have a 'sister' at a farm near here, so that if anybody suspects him and follows him, he could go there to see her rather than come here to the house of a known magistrate. Do you think we can persuade somebody to help in this way?"

"Good idea James, leave it to me. I'm sure that Mr. Green at Burton Farm will help, I'll go and see him tomorrow."

Grahame stood up and moving closer to the fire, spoke quietly, "Captain Merriman, as you will have realized, we are not dealing here with simple smugglers, there is much more at stake than you know. I'm privy to certain information which I am not at liberty to divulge at present but I *will* tell you in confidence that the French are deeply involved. It is also believed that some person or persons of the Quality are mixed up in it and none of it can be to this country's benefit."

"That's true" replied the Captain, "Are we talking about treason, Sir?"

"I believe we are Captain, I believe we are."

"Then damn and blast the lot of them Sir, God's curse on a man who will betray his country. I'll do all I can to help in any way I can, though I don't know what more I can do."

"I'm sure you will Sir, perhaps you could make more enquiries of your neighbours to pick up any gossip or rumour which may have a grain of truth in it, and also follow the Commander's suggestion about the farmer and this man Owen's – er – sister."

"Commander? James, are you then promoted? You did not mention that before. Congratulations, well done, I'll see you an admiral yet."

Continued Grahame, "I would like to be off early in the morning to see one of my informers, and your son is also to go to Chester to see Mr. Flitwick, so if I may be found a little something to eat and somewhere to rest ------- ?"

"Of course Sir, I sent the servants to bed but I'm sure we can find some bread and cold meats in the kitchen. We can go and help ourselves."

As they munched on thick slices of cold beef, pickles and bread spread with fresh yellow butter Merriman's father remarked, "By the by James, a box arrived for you only today from London."

"Ah, that could be my new uniform, I'll look at it later to see that it fits, I can take it back to the ship with me tomorrow evening or the day after."

Next morning, as the sun was beginning to disperse the early morning mists, the two men set off on their respective errands, riding two of Captain Merriman's horses, agreeing to meet back at the house later that day. Merriman was now dressed in his own clothes. His destination was the Customs House where he expected to be able to speak with Mr. Flitwick the Chief Customs Officer. Entering the city, he made enquiries as to the location of the Customs House to find that it was in Watergate Street.

The building was built mostly of brick with stonework round the windows and doors, much weatherworn and set at an awkward angle to the rest of the buildings in the street. Over the main entrance, carved into a stone tablet, a coat of arms appeared to have an Earl's coronet at the top of the achievement. Dismounting, Merriman was surprised to see a small figure he recognized, slipping into one of the other several entrances. It was Mr. Beadle, the lawyer's clerk.

Entering the building which was thronged with porters, merchants, customs men and clerks he saw that the floor was covered with bales of Irish muslin and printed linen, bundles of hides from Ireland mixed with boxes of tea and coffee, small barrels of spirits and other bundles of an indeterminate nature piled to the ceiling. Customs men were busy weighing and measuring to assess the amount of duty payable and the air was filled with a rich variety of aromas and the sounds of fierce argument. Papers and fists were brandished as merchants quibbled with the customs men over the assessments, trying to reduce their costs.

Merriman asked and was told that Mr. Flitwick was on the next floor. Climbing the stairs he could see over most of the ground floor and he glimpsed Mr. Beadle in earnest conversation with one of the clerks in a corner behind a pile of barrels. "Strange, what do those two have in common? Probably friends I suppose, both being clerks" he mused and then dismissed all thoughts of Beadle and his friend when he saw Mr. Flitwick standing behind a row of clerks at desks, watching as they collected money and recorded the details in huge ledgers as merchants lined up to pay.

"Mr. Merriman Sir, a pleasure to see you again. What brings you to this bedlam?" Without waiting for an answer he moved away from the counting desks and continued, "This is what we call the counting room where we collect duties and keep it in strongboxes until it can be sent down to the treasury in London. We also have auction sales of seized goods in this room which is sometimes called the Long Room. Why the Long Room you ask? No good reason really, every Customs

House has one whatever size and shape it is. Named after the one in London I shouldn't wonder."

He carried on this monologue until he had found a clear space near a window where they would not be overheard. "Mr. Merriman, I have some information which may interest you. Three or four days ago one of our small luggers which watches for smuggling round the Isle of Man, encountered a ship which may have been our stolen cutter. It was almost dark but one man who had been crew on the cutter recognized it by the odd shaped patches on the mainsail, rather like an inverted letter 'T' he said. The hull was painted a darker colour than it had been but he was certain that he was right."

"Where exactly was this, and what course was it steering?"

"To the west of the island and heading south, but that doesn't tell us it's final destination does it?"

"No it doesn't, but now we know that it is still in these waters and that gives us hope of finding it."

Merriman went on to tell Mr. Flitwick about his new command and Mr. Grahame's presence aboard. "He asked me to convey his regards and hopes to call on you but it's not certain he will have the time."

"Thank you, Laurence Graham is a very good friend of mine and we have served in the Treasury service together. Perhaps you would give me the pleasure of entertaining you to a meal. I must stay here until mid-day but shortly after I could meet you in the Yacht Inn where I usually eat. It's only a little way up this street."

"That's kind of you Sir, I look forward to it."

Merriman looked around for Mr. Beadle as he left the building but the little man was not to be seen. Mounting his horse, Merriman rode slowly to the Yacht Inn where he stabled the animal. With time to spare he strolled up the street, pausing to look in Mr. Taylor's music shop where apparently one could buy a harpsichord for eighteen guineas, a pianoforte for twenty four guineas, guitars, violins, violincellos and all manner of wind instruments. He moved on to the church in the centre of the town and then down Bridge Street. He gazed into shop windows, many of them the new bow windows developed to show more merchandise and to entice people into the shop.

He was amused by some of the curious items advertised in the pharmacies, "Try Dr. Steer's Apodeldoc for the Cure of Chilblains, Rheumatism and Lumbago" announced one. "Devonshire Tooth Tincture, Relieves Toothache and Prevents Decaying Teeth from Becoming Worse. Restores the Colour and Sweetens the Breath. Two Shillings and Ninepence a Bottle" declared another. More disconcertingly others promised certain cures for venereal disease, among them "Dr. Arnold's Pills" and one with the resounding title of "Abbe Blondell's Grand Chymical Specific." Merriman smiled to himself and moved on.

Later, over a pleasant meal, the conversation between Merriman and Mr. Flitwick was mostly concerning smuggling and the troubles of the Revenue service.

"Do you know Sir, that the source of most of our problems is the Isle of Man?" Merriman had to admit that he did not.

"Used to belong to the Earl of Derby and then to the Duke of Atholl you know. They owned the island and most of their income came from lower duties and customs paid to them on goods prohibited here which were then smuggled into England and Wales, Scotland and Ireland too. That state of affairs continued until the Duke of Atholl was prevailed upon to sell his fiscal rights to the crown and the Revestment Act of 1765 transferred ownership to the Crown. Have some more of this excellent ham Sir, or maybe another portion of the steak and kidney pie, I can recommend it."

Merriman had to admit defeat. "Thank you, but no. I am too full already."

"Very well then, you won't mind if I do" said Mr. Flitwick helping himself to another thick slice of ham and a generous dollop of pickle. "Where was I? Oh yes, the Isle of Man. After 1765 the trade declined a bit until the smugglers re-organised but it is still a significant and profitable trade, although since Mr. Pitt reduced the Duty on many items it must be less so. There are so many boats engaged in smuggling around these coasts that I doubt we catch more than two or three in a hundred, which makes it all the more surprising that the smugglers want to call more attention to themselves with this latest devilment."

Popping another portion of ham into his mouth and speaking with his mouth full, he went on "Now they come from France and Guernsey and unload at sea into smaller boats and wherries to be smuggled ashore. In 1788 Mr. Pitt the prime minister commissioned a report on the trade from a Mr. Frazer who said that he estimated that the amount smuggled into the island at that time was about fifteen thousand gallons of brandy and perhaps five thousand gallons of Genever a year, not to mention tea and other spirits and wines. The loss to the treasury in unpaid duty must be enormous."

"I had no idea that such quantities were involved" said Merriman.

Flitwick carried on, almost unstoppable, "Frazer also reported that many of our own officers were so addicted to drinking that they were incapable of duty and some of them were even connected with the smugglers so that we are uncertain which of them is loyal. There was another more recent report from a Mr. Alexander Cook last year, to the effect that unless more cruisers can be found, together with more Riding Officers supported by more military, then it is doubtful that most of the trade can be prevented. Even so, little has been done to improve matters. There Sir, what do you say to that?"

"I would agree, there seems to be little hope of stopping the trade completely, but if we can catch a few more and especially find out who or what is behind this latest outrage, then we may make some impact upon it."

"Maybe so" said Mr. Flitwick, looking wistfully at the remaining ham. "Maybe so. Anyway, I must settle with the landlord and get back to my duties. This has been a pleasure Mr. Merriman."

"Indeed, and thank you for a fine meal. I look forward to meeting you again Sir."

As he rode homeward in the fading daylight, Merriman pondered on the events of the day. What did the re-appearance of the cutter mean? Was the gang even now killing and looting some other innocent party? Little Mr. Beadle came to mind, what was he doing at the customs house? Was he about his own business or was he on an errand for someone? If an errand, then surely it would be for his employer, the lawyer Jeremiah Robinson. If it was an errand for the lawyer then surely he would have spoken to one of the senior customs officers, even Mr. Flitwick, not to a mere clerk?

Merriman shook his head. Question upon question and an answer to none of them.

French Spies & Irish Allies

On the outskirts of Dublin, an old weather-beaten inn creaked and shook to the onslaught of the wind and rain. A faded sign swung to and fro with eerie screeching from the long un-oiled ironwork from which it hung. On it could just be discerned the words "The Poacher's Rest" but the painted picture which once must have shown the figure of a poacher was so battered by the elements that most of the paint had peeled away long ago.

To the passer-by the place gave the impression of total dereliction, even the gates to the stable yard looked unusable and the roofs of the stables and outbuildings visible over the gates appearing to be in a tumbledown condition. That impression would be wrong. If the passer-by had been able to see them he would have found the hinges on the gates to have been carefully oiled and in the stables several horses feeding contentedly from their nosebags. No light from the single lantern escaped from the stable as window and doors were covered in sack-cloth. At the back of the old inn a feeble light glowed through a crack in an imperfectly covered window.

Two stubby pieces of candle stuck into the neck of wax encrusted wine bottles gave enough feeble light to illuminate the faces of the five men grouped round the rough wooden table in the centre of the room.

Two of the men were dressed in caped overcoats such as a coachman might wear. One of these two was generously proportioned around the waist, whilst his similarly dressed and elegant companion was quite tall and slim. This man wore a small tie wig and carried himself with an air of aristocratic arrogance as though he considered himself to be above his companions. A third man, small in stature, with a furtive air about him stood close beside the fat man. The fourth man, dark featured and dark haired, was roughly dressed, more like a fisherman than a gentleman, and was unmistakably an Irishman. But it was the fifth man who drew the attention of the others. He was plainly but elegantly dressed in dark clothing with a silk lined cloak round his shoulders. He wore no wig but his hair was powdered and tied back with a silk ribbon, a style fast going out of fashion. A deep scar on his left cheek seemed to be emphasized by the candlelight. A simple leather baldrick supported a long rapier at his side which had the appearance of a well used weapon. He stood there with one hand resting casually on the hilt of the sword.

Round the walls of the room five or six other men could be seen, some having the appearance of labourers but others more respectably dressed. Two or three of them held muskets and all of them were armed in some way.

The elegantly dressed man was speaking quietly but he had no difficulty in making himself heard as the others kept a respectful silence as he spoke.

His first words revealed him to be a Frenchman. "I understand that you believe all to be in readiness for our plan to proceed, mes amis, but I need still to be convinced that this is so. Le bateau, I mean the ship, has been disguised and concealed and a crew found from your Irish comrades, this I know, but I am still uncertain how well they can manage the guns or how well they will take orders from my French officers."

"Have no fear on that score Monsieur Moreau" said the dark haired Irishman, "we're all determined that the plan will succeed and the bloody English will find that they are dealing with a harder and better organised group of Irishmen than they can imagine." He scowled briefly and in the candlelight his face took on a malevolent cast. "Your plan cannot fail. The men I sent to help know what is at stake and how important it is to the future of Ireland. They'll control their desire to kill the prisoners, at least until they have served our purpose. And if you need more men I can raise them for you. When we've done what we must, all Ireland will rise in our support and drive the oppressor from the soil of our land." His eyes glowed with fanaticism as the men round the room shouted their approval of his sentiments.

"And then Mister, we will be able to repay France for her help in our struggle. She will be able to use our ports from which to attack England."

"Mon Dieu Monsieur O'Donnell, if your words are true we will succeed ten times over. 'owever there are some items which we must still determine. One, it is essential that we know the actual time that the ship will sail carrying the people we want to capture and the message must be passed to our ships in good time for them to reach the point of attack. How is that to be done?"

The tall, slim and aristocratic man who had not yet spoken replied, "I am to travel to London tomorrow to join the Viceroy's party and I'll send word by courier from there when he and I and the others actually leave London. A courier will travel far quicker than we will so that you will have at least two days in hand. The ship which is named the *Dorset* won't sail the moment the party arrives at Parkgate but will be delayed whilst their baggage is loaded and even then sailing could be further delayed by the state of the tide and weather. So you see, from the moment word arrives from London there will be plenty of time for a boat to sail to where the cutter is concealed and then for it and your ship to meet at the pre-arranged place off Anglesey."

"There will be no escort vessel so that there will be no difficulty in your two ships overpowering the crew of the *Dorset*. Just make certain that your men know who I am. I don't want to be killed by mistake."

The smallest man smirked, "I think Sir William, that we can safely say that our plan is complete in every detail. What can go wrong?"

"Bon, and the second item Messieurs," the Frenchman continued, "The part that is of almost equal importance to France?"

"Ah yes, the graphite or plumbago as we call it. As soon as Sir William's courier reaches Mr. O'Donnell in Chester with confirmation of the time that the party is leaving London, then he'll send a message to the captain of the fishing boat waiting at Parkgate who will then sail up the coast to where the graphite we've already stolen has been stored and hidden. After loading that they'll wait until the cutter joins them after the *Dorset* has been taken".

He laughed, "The mining company has lost so much of the stuff during its journey to London that they have decided to try to send it by sea from Ravenglass. Our friends in Borrowdale have told us that it's being stored in a warehouse on the dockside under guard until they charter a ship. We'll raid the warehouse at night, the guards quietly disposed of, then the casks containing the graphite quickly transferred to the cutter which will then rendezvous with you off the south coast of the Isle of Man. What can go wrong?"

O'Donnell looked slyly at the Frenchman, "You know the value of this graphite don't you Monsieur? What we've already stolen from the mine and from the wagons taking it to

London is worth over forty thousand pounds sterling. We've got more than four hundred casks of it and with the amount in the warehouse there could be over a hundred thousand pounds worth at the price charged for it in London, if not more. We're trusting you to see that France honours our bargain and that we'll all receive our share".

The Frenchman looked at him with contempt. "Have no fear Monsieur O'Donnell, France will pay you very well, but you have still to deliver and complete your side of the bargain".

"Very well then, I repeat, what can go wrong?"

"I think that much can go wrong" growled the fat man who had not yet spoken, "What happens if there is a gale blowing and our boats cannot put to sea? What if our hidden cutter is discovered? Suppose the graphite is shipped before we expect? I think that we have planned for most eventualities but it would not do to be too complacent."

"Certainement Monsieur, you are right, but should there be un tempete, a storm, then no ship will sail and we may "ave une autre chance, n'est ce pas?"

"We're as ready as we can be, said the small man, "All the men on the boats know what they have to do and they're only waiting for the signal to mo---------". He broke off as a shout, a shot and a scream were heard outside. The table and chairs were flung aside as the men around the room all rushed for the door led by the dark featured Irishman O'Donnell. The Frenchman and the other three men waited in silence until the Irishman re-appeared, his face white with shock.

"Somebody has been spying on us. I left a man on guard in the stable and he has been shot to death just outside the window of this room. He must have seen the intruder or spy outside and tried to catch him and been killed for his pains, but he must have made his mark before he died because the knife in his hand has blood on it. He was a good Irishman, we'll miss him."

"But this spy must be found immediately, God knows how much he overheard or if he saw any of our faces!" exclaimed the fat man, mopping his forehead with a large kerchief. "The whole plan may be in jeopardy."

"All my men are searching for him now and he can't be too far ahead of them. The sea is on one side of us and the moss on the other so he must keep to the road and is most likely heading for town. and if he's badly hurt he won't be able to travel fast."

"Can't he cross this moss you spoke of," asked the small man with some asperity.

"No chance of that" replied O'Donnell, "It's nearly all quagmire and quicksand. Many a man has disappeared in there, swallowed up with no trace left of him."

"So gentlemen, nothing can go wrong, isn't that what you said not quarter of an hour ago?" hissed the Frenchman, obviously keeping his temper with an effort. "I am surrounded by imbeciles. Your careless lack of enough guards has allowed an intruder to learn our secrets and if he is not found quickly I may be forced to abandon the entire affair. France cannot yet be publicly involved with your Irish revolution."

"Well, whatever happens we must be on a boat back to England tomorrow morning" said the fat man to his two companions. "I am sure that you Sir William will be travelling the fastest way by packet boat so that you can to be sure of joining the Viceroy's party in time, but my man and I will travel by less conspicuous means."

"Monsieur Moreau, O'Donnell knows where to find us all and he'll let us know if this spy has been captured or not. As we can do no more here now I think we should leave at once and go our separate ways."

The Viceroy of Ireland

Captain Merriman tried to keep a straight face when his son arrived back home but he couldn't prevent a grin spreading across his face. "News James, news at last. I saw the farmer this morning and he agreed to help. He persuaded one of their servant girls to pretend to be Owen's sister and he promised to pass on any messages as soon as possible."

"That's a good start, all we have to do is wait for Owen to come here once more so that we can tell him not to risk coming here again."

"He was here shortly before mid-day, I'd just got back from the farm so I was able to put him right on that. It seems that he's been part of the crew of one of the boats the smugglers use to land contraband and he helped to transfer goods from a larger boat offshore which he is sure was French."

"Good head on his shoulders that man, keeps his mouth shut and his ears open. Seems that he overheard the leader of the gang talking to one of the men on the French boat asking when 'it' was to take place, as the main plan was ready and they would know when the Royal Yacht would be sailing. Unfortunately he didn't hear the answer and we don't know what 'it' is."

"The Royal Yacht? What bearing can that have on the actions of these villains I wonder?" replied Merriman, "Maybe Mr. Grahame can suggest something when he returns."

They fell to discussing the Royal Yacht and speculating what connection the French and the smuggling gang could have with it.

The Royal Yacht at that time was no longer used by Royalty but was reserved exclusively for the use of the Lord Lieutenant of Ireland, the Viceroy, and other notable personages by his permission. The present one was the *Dorset*, built in 1753 specially for the Irish service. Of one hundred and sixty four tons, carved and gilded and with three masts, she was commanded by a naval officer and was usually moored at Parkgate.

At this time, Neston town had given way in importance to Parkgate as most of the passenger trade for Ireland, and most of the imports and exports for the area went through the port of Parkgate. There was no quayside, ships grounded at low water or anchored offshore at Beerhouse Pool. It was what was known as a "legal quay" and as such it had its own customs house with a staff afloat and ashore of some seventeen men. There was a vast trade in goods from Mediterranean ports, the Baltic, Portugal, Spain and other parts of the British Isles.

The Parkgate Packet Boat Company offered very respectable accommodation and ran at least six packet boats with daily sailings to the Isle of Man, Dublin and elsewhere, always subject to the weather conditions, These ferries were nearly all built in Parkgate and so the town had grown to house the supporting trades, shipwrights, carpenters, sailmakers and painters.

Because it was the main departure point for Ireland and in extreme weather conditions passengers having to wait days or even weeks for a passage, there grew up hotels, inns and all their supporting trades of servants, horse and coach hirers, ostlers and blacksmiths. Other services developed including an Assembly Room and as sea bathing had become the vogue there were also bath-houses on the shore. Parkgate in the 1780s and early 1790s was a thriving, bustling small town at the peak of its importance.

"James, do you imagine that the French may be contemplating some venture against the *Dorset*? It is the only idea that comes to mind," said the older man.

"I really can't see why they should, we aren't at war and in any event doesn't she have a naval escort when important people are aboard?" Merriman was perplexed and unconsciously fell into his habit of tugging his ear when thinking.

"Not now. There was an escort when we were at war with America and France, but I suppose it wasn't considered necessary after the peace was signed."

The two men started pacing up and down, hands clasped behind their back, brains furiously at work. Mrs. Merriman, who had entered the room almost unnoticed whilst the men talked, and had been sitting quietly beside the fire, suddenly spoke, "When we were in Chester at the theatre, I remember hearing some gossip to the effect that when the Lord Lieutenant goes to Ireland again in a week or two he will have with him many of the most important people in Ireland. I think they came to London for discussions with Mr. Pitt."

"Mary my dear, you may have hit upon the answer. What about that James?"

"If these people are interested in the *Dorset* which is not a trading vessel carrying anything of value, then their interest must be in the passengers being carried. But why would the French be interested?"

"I don't know James; the only reason I can think of for their interest would perhaps be if they intend to capture them or kill them and as you said, why would the French want to be involved in that kind of thing?"

They continued to pace up and down, brows furrowed in thought, but no solution to the problem presented itself to them.

"When do you expect to see Mr. Grahame again James, perhaps he may have some ideas?"

"We agreed to meet here tonight Father, *Aphrodite* will lie offshore tonight and tomorrow night waiting for our signal, so if he's delayed he could come back here anytime before then."

In the event, Grahame arrived back that night, both lathered horse and rider splashed with mud from head to toe. He asked that the two hired horses be prepared for the road immediately. "I regret having to ride your animal so hard Captain, but it is imperative that your son and I are back aboard the ship as soon as possible. I must be in Ireland tomorrow."

During the fast ride back to Hoylake there was no time for discussing the information that Merriman had, especially as he was encumbered with the signal lantern and the package containing his new uniform and not being a very good rider at best, he found it difficult to keep up with the pace that Grahame set, and he thanked his stars for the practice he'd had when last home. Even when they reached the beach after a breathless scramble over the sand dunes and made the required signal out to sea, Grahame remained uncommunicative other than to wonder where the damned boat was.

The two shivering men stood waiting in the darkness for what seemed like an age but in reality was no more than a quarter of an hour, with Merriman flashing the signal every few minutes. Grahame was irritable and impatient at the delay, but Merriman, with the patience learned in his years at sea stood calmly waiting, knowing that with the offshore breeze the boat's crew would have a hard pull to reach the shore.

"At last, your men will have to do better than this next time Mr.Merriman" complained Grahame as the boat loomed out of the darkness and ran up on the shingle.

Merriman sighed to himself, having learned long ago that it was better to simply accept that all senior officers were short tempered and not to worry about it.

"Back to the ship now, fast as you can" he ordered as soon as they had clambered aboard the boat.

Climbing back on board the *Aphrodite* to the accompaniment of salutes from the officers and marine sentry, he called the first Lieutenant and the Master to him.

"Mr.Jeavons, I'll have the ship under way immediately with all the sail she can carry. Mr.Cuthbert, a course for Ireland if you please." He swung round to Mr.Grahame.

"Will Dublin suit you Sir?"

"That will be ideal Captain. If you can leave the deck, I need to know what you have learned today, and if your man can find me something to eat I would be grateful."

Settled in Merriman's cramped cabin, Grahame demanded to know if Merriman had any news, whereupon Merriman recounted what he had learned from Mr.Flitwick about the cutter probably still being in the Irish sea, and also what Owen had reported about the French ship and the reference to the Royal Yacht *Dorset*.

"Great God! The *Dorset,* is your man certain of that? Could he be mistaken?"

"I suppose it is possible, but knowing him as I do I would wager that he is right."

"This intelligence changes everything."

Grahame stood up suddenly and crashing his head against a deck beam, subsided back into his seat. "Damn it, I always forget how low the ceilings are."

"Deckhead Sir" said Merriman automatically. But Grahame didn't hear. He fell into deep thought, absently rubbing his head where it had hit the beam.

Merriman sat silently, knowing that Grahame would tell him what he had learned when he was ready.

"Mr Merriman, are you aware of the importance of the *Dorset* and her movements?"

"No Sir, I mean I don't know the details of her movements but I do know that she is only used for the passage of important people to and from Ireland."

"Exactly, so why would these villains be interested in the *Dorset* unless they were interested in the passengers?"

"That's what my Father and I agreed on, but we could think of no reason for their interest."

"I can Mr. Merriman, but I hope I'm wrong. The Lord Lieutenant of Ireland, the Earl of Westmorland, is in London at the moment with several of the biggest landowners of that country and has been there for several weeks. Mr. Pitt is discussing with them ways and means of solving the Irish problem and dispensing with the unjust laws preventing free and fair trade between England and Ireland. Unfortunately these very people are the ones who have the most to lose if the law is changed. They stand to lose their lucrative trading monopolies and their powerful positions in Parliament so that Mr.Pitt can make little headway. Westmorland himself has to bribe many of the men of influence to get even the simplest measures adopted. It's certain that they will be returning to Ireland very soon."

"Then there is the reason we are looking for Sir. The Irish rebels would love to get their hands on these people to either kill or hold as hostages to force the government to give Ireland its freedom and Catholic emancipation, and the French would be happy to help them achieve that goal. A free Ireland as their ally would allow them to attack this country from two sides, three, with a foothold in the Dutch Netherlands."

"I believe we have it Mr. Merriman! The reason I'm anxious to be in Dublin is that my agent there sent a message asking me to go over there urgently as he had important news concerning the Lord Lieutenant. It's not impossible that he has some knowledge of this. I'd be obliged if you could land me at a place just south of Dublin as soon as maybe."

"The wind is fair Sir, so you will be there in only a few hours to meet your agent."

They were not to know that Mr. Grahame's agent was even then lying in a ditch with his throat cut.

Patrolling the Irish Sea

"Pick me up here two nights hence Captain, same signal, before midnight. If I'm not there try again the following night. If I fail to appear then you will have to do what you think best about what we discussed" said Grahame. He was obviously worried as he had requested the loan of a brace of heavy pistols and spent almost an hour checking them over and loading them with extreme care. He also drew the charges and reloaded a small double-barreled pocket pistol and asked that his sword be sharpened.

"It is obvious that you are expecting trouble then Sir," remarked Merriman.

"I always do Captain, Ireland is a hotbed of sedition and my people must perforce enter places of doubtful character."

Grahame was put ashore on a deserted beach in Ireland and as soon as the boat was hoisted inboard again Merriman set a course out into Liverpool Bay. He had nearly two days before meeting Grahame and as there was now no reason to try and hide *Aphrodite's* presence he determined to do what Admiral Edwards had instructed him to do, that is to stop and search any vessels he thought to be suspicious.

The Irish sea was full of seaborne traffic, small fishing boats, small coasting traders, large trading ships from the Baltic, France, Ireland, the Americas, the West Indies and faraway places in India and the far east. Not to mention the regular ferry boats plying between the various ports on the surrounding coasts.

The busiest port was Liverpool which was overtaking Chester and Parkgate as the premier trading centre. Much of the traffic from Liverpool and some from Chester, was involved in the infamous Triangle Trade, in which vessels left England with cargoes of cotton goods, cheap metalware and pottery destined for areas of west Africa. Once there, many were loaded with live cargo, captive negroes.

The ships would then head west on the so-called middle passage to the West Indies and America, where the cargo of human misery, those that survived the hellish voyage, would be sold into slavery. The ships then returned to their home port laden with Molasses, rum, sugar and tobacco, making their owners rich men.

It was not long before *Aphrodite* came across a dirty looking, bluff bowed, deeply laden brig heading north towards the Isle of Man.

"Have the gunner send a shot across her bows if you please Mr. Andrews."

"Aye-aye Sir" replied the young lieutenant who was officer of the watch.

The ball splashed down only half a cable ahead of the brig whereupon the ship's master could be seen shaking his fist at the *Aphrodite* but making no effort to heave to or shorten sail in the face of the universally known signal.

"Bring her within hailing distance Mr. Andrews."

Using a speaking trumpet Merriman shouted across "Heave to Captain or my next shot may do some damage." The threat brought instant compliance although the master continued to shake his fist at the King's ship.

"Mr. Andrews, take a small armed party and go aboard. Look at his bill of lading and check it as far as you can against the contents of the hold. And Mr. Andrews, call the captain into his cabin and apologize, tell him some story that there have been one or two cases of piracy and a brig was involved. Tell him he has nothing to fear if he is an honest trader. Take Mr. Shrigley with you."

"Aye-aye Sir, but am I looking for anything in particular Sir?"

"Nothing specific, a shifty expression, a reluctance to allow you to look around, contraband goods, I don't know what. If there are any passengers find out who they are and where they are from."

Andrews returned to report that he found nothing unusual, nothing out of the ordinary and the brig was allowed to proceed. The *Aphrodite* stopped two more ships but nothing was found except the odd few bottles of rum and brandy which could not have been called contraband cargo as there were so few of them.

The fourth ship stopped provided the crew of *Aphrodite* with the first amusement of the day. When the boat returned poor Shrigley climbed aboard to reveal his clothing, hands and face covered in fish scales and smelling to high heaven. Merriman struggled to keep the smile off his face while the officers and crew whose duties kept them on the upper deck stood around grinning and laughing at the boy's discomfiture.

"All right Mr.Andrews, tell me what happened."

Nothing to report about the ship Sir, but when they opened the hold which was full of fish Mr.Shrigley fell in."

"No Sir I didn't. Somebody pushed me when I leaned over the hatchway," complained the little midshipman.

"Well we'd better have you cleaned up Mr.Shrigley. Mr.Laing, have a pump rigged and give him a good sluicing down before he goes below for fresh clothes."

Shrigley gasped and capered under the jet of ice cold seawater applied willingly by two grinning seamen before escaping to the warmth of the gunroom.

Merriman suddenly realized that he was still dressed in the grubby trousers and ill fitting coat he had borrowed for his nocturnal run ashore so he decided that it was about time he appeared on deck properly dressed. In his cabin he changed into his new uniform which was quite a good fit, surprisingly so, considering the haste with which the tailor in London had measured him whilst Grahame had fidgeted and complained about the delay. Peters had managed to remove most of the creases and hovered round trying to do his best to help his Captain get dressed.

"Stop fussing man" said Merriman irritably, "I can manage."

Feeling a little self conscious in the new coat with its pale blue lapels and single gold stripe on each sleeve he picked up his new gold laced cocked hat and went back on deck.

After the fifth ship had been examined, Mr. Andrews climbed wearily back on board to again report that there was nothing to report. "Although I must admit that I've learned a lot Sir. I thought that the crew of a Royal Navy ship knew how to swear but they are amateurs alongside some of the captains aboard these trading ships. This one never stopped or repeated himself all the time I was aboard."

"Well done Mr. Andrews. I think we'll move nearer to the Welsh coast to see what we can find there."

"Yes Sir, and Sir if I may presume, I don't think I've congratulated you on your promotion. It was seeing your uniform that reminded me."

"Thank you, I'd almost forgotten it myself."

Later that day, after dark, Merriman closed as near as he dared to the Welsh coast to the west of the Great Orme. It was a pitch dark night with only stars to be seen and the *Aphrodite* was ghosting along under topsails and jibs only. Merriman had a man in the chains with a leadline and his calls were repeated by a chain of men back to the quarter-deck. Merriman and Mr. Cuthbert had spent some time studying the chart which showed that the coast had many sand banks to trap the unwary mariner.

It was Merriman's hope that they would encounter any vessel unloading a cargo, either ashore or into smaller boats. He had called the ship's company to action stations shortly before although the guns were not run out. "Merely a precaution" he told himself, not being able to rid his mind of what had happened to the Revenue cutter along this stretch of coast. "Anyway, it is all good practice for the men."

"Mr. Jeavons, it's a cold night, have a tot of rum issued to each man and I'll allow half the men to sleep with their weapons handy."

But although the *Aphrodite* cruised along the coast all night, nothing was seen.

The next morning found the ship becalmed only a few miles off the coast As dawn broke all hands were at action stations as was required by naval regulations but there were no other ships in sight apart from a few small coasting vessels also becalmed some distance away.

The First Lieutenant approached him. "Sir, I wonder if we can tell the men something of our purpose here and what we are looking for. There is a lot of talk about smugglers, but nobody really knows anything."

"Right Mr. Jeavons, call the men aft and I'll tell them."

Merriman climbed up onto a pinrail and looked down at the sea of eager faces in front of him. "You're all wondering what we are doing here and why we are stopping harmless traders. First of all we're looking for any sign of smuggling but more importantly we need to find out who it was that seized a Revenue cutter near here whilst it was at anchor. They crept alongside and murdered every man of the crew in the middle of the night."

There were growls, muttering and the shuffling of feet as the men listened and an unknown voice called out "We'll do for them buggers Cap'n, just you lead us to 'em." More growls of approval.

"We believe that the cutter is still in these waters and it's our duty to find her and when we do you can be sure that there will be the chance to avenge those poor seamen."

He jumped down as the same voice called out "Hurrah for the Cap'n lads" and the crew erupted in loud cheers to the dismay of the scandalised petty officers who tried to silence them.

"Sorry about that Sir" said Jeavons "I'll try and find the ringleader and-----".

"Belay that John, it's harmless. We can feel thankful that we are not looking for the ringleader of something worse. Now then, we had no luck yesterday so as soon as the wind returns I want to cruise where we might intercept one or more of the packet boats sailing between Parkgate and Dublin. Have a word with the Master and decide where the best area will be. I shall be below."

Two packet boats were stopped to the indignation of the captains and the consternation of the passengers, but Lieutenant Andrews was by now a past master at smoothing ruffled feelings and neither boat produced passenger names which meant anything to Merriman, except for one, a Sir William Forrester.

"That name rings a bell," mused Merriman, *"I must have met him at some time."* Merriman continued to ponder on it until the answer hit him. His father had introduced them many years ago at the Merriman house and it was the man who had been

with the lawyer in Chester and who had seemed vaguely familiar before being rushed out. Merriman felt a brief moment of disquiet, *"Why would a man like that be meeting his lawyer at that time of night"* Later in the day they sighted another small trading ship, a single masted cutter off the starboard bow and on a course which would take it to the Dee Estuary. The wind had increased and Merriman had changed into his old weathered Lieutenant's coat to save his new coat from flying spray. Idly he picked up a telescope from the box by the binnacle and trained it on the other vessel. It took him a few moments to catch it in the lens but then unconscious habit kept it in view.

As he watched it seemed to him that the vessel was gradually, almost imperceptibly altering course to open the bearing between them. Watching for a few minutes more he was sure of it. "Mr. Jeavons, I'll have the reefs out of the tops'ls, I want to catch that ship and stop her."

"Aye-aye Sir" responded the First Lieutenant, turning away to bawl orders which caused hands to boil up from below and climb like monkeys into the rigging. As the reefs were shaken out the ship heeled to the extra pressure and another dollop of spray hissed over the weather rail. Merriman took another look as they crept close enough for him to see the faces of some of the people aboard. His gaze swept over them, then he drew in his breath sharply as one face seemed to stand out from the rest.

"Mr. Jeavons, I want you to take command on deck. To the people over there it must seem that you are the captain. Mr. Andrews, when you go aboard, take particular note of the people there, their names, reason for travelling, and be ready to give me a description of each of them. I believe that I know a person aboard that ship and I can't think of any good reason why that person should be travelling on a common trading vessel. I shall remain below out of sight."

In his cabin waiting for Andrews to return, Merriman was quite unable to relax. He fidgeted with items on the desk, tried to walk up and down but hampered by the lack of space, flung himself back into the chair his mind in a turmoil. Aboard that other ship was—no, he must be mistaken. What would he be doing on such a craft? One for his creature comforts to look at him, a man unlikely to put up with the primitive conditions found on a small trader.

Desperate to know what was happening, Merriman wanted to rush on deck but he knew that he must maintain his reputation for imperturbability in front of his subordinates.

At last he heard the boat bump alongside and Andrews' feet clattering down the companionway. A knock on the door announced his arrival.

Merriman strove to appear calm and relaxed but was too eager to hear Andrews' report to keep up the pretence. "Well now David, sit down and tell me what you have learned."

"She appears to be an ordinary trading vessel Sir, but there was something about it that didn't feel right. I can't put my finger on it, it's more an impression I had, that the captain and the passengers had a sort of guilty look about them."

"Who are the passengers then?"

"Three of them Sir. A small man, name of Thomas Jones though he doesn't sound like a Welshman. His story was that he had been delivering confidential documents to a lawyer in Dublin. Another was tall and thin with a very dark complexion and black hair, gave his name as John Trevor. He is a Welshman, spoke mostly in Welsh so I couldn't understand what he was saying. The third is a biggish man rather flabby round the middle and has a double chin, his name is John

Richards He said he was a merchant, trading in Irish linen. He had been to Dublin to order more stock. None of them had any papers or anything to prove what they said was true and they said that they hadn't met before boarding the ship. Strange thing is Sir, I caught the fat man glancing at the little man as though for reassurance. That's all Sir, except to say that there was nothing suspicious in the hold or captain's cabin. I hope that is what you wanted to know Sir."

"It is indeed David, I think that this will be most helpful. Oh, one more thing. Can you describe the smallest man again for me?"

"Yes Sir, as I said, a small man, quite inoffensive looking I thought. He wore spectacles to read a small book he carried. Funny little man he was with a face all wrinkled like a walnut. A sort of shifty look he had, wouldn't trust him an inch."

"That's it!" exclaimed Merriman, "You have done well Mr. Andrews. I'm certain I know who those men are. If I'm right it is certain they are up to no good."

"I see Sir", said Andrews, "are we going to take the ship?"

"No not yet, we've no reason to, except suspicion, which as you know is no substitute for evidence. Please be good enough to ask Mr. Jeavons to allow the ship to proceed. We'll follow at a distance until the daylight has gone. My compliments to Mr. Cuthbert and I'd like to see him in here."

When Merriman appeared on deck again the light had almost gone and the small vessel ahead was almost invisible in the gloom. He grinned to himself, "They must be worried men on that ship, wondering why we are following them. Perhaps we have worried them enough for now." He turned to his officers who were standing silently by.

"Mr. Jeavons, Mr. Cuthbert has a course for you to take us back to where we left Mr. Grahame. We must be off that coast not later than nine o'clock tonight."

But although they remained at anchor there for over six hours with lookouts being changed every hour to keep them fresh, no signal was seen. The night was clear so the signal would not have been missed.

Wounded and rescued

The day was fine and cold with a strong, steady wind out of the south-east. *Aphrodite,* with all plain sail set and sailing close to the wind on the larboard tack, sliced through the rising seas occasionally crashing into a larger wave and flinging spray high in the air which blew back over the deck, wetting officers and men alike. Merriman stood high on the weather side revelling in the performance of his ship and thinking of ways in which he could increase her speed. Some weight transferred from forr'ard to aft should help her to rise easier to the seas and giving the rudder more bite as well would allow her to come about a little quicker too,

He called to mind the stowage of stores, water barrels, casks of meat and provisions, powder and shot. Eight or ten tons should make a difference. He motioned to Lieutenant Jeavons and explained what he wanted. It would mean difficult and possibly dangerous work for a Master's mate, the Purser and a working party of seamen but if it increased the ship's speed by another knot or two, that extra speed may prove to be valuable in future. "I'll have the log read every quarter hour Mr. Jeavons. I hope to see a difference over the next hour or two."

Once it had become obvious in the early hours of the morning that Mr. Grahame was not going to appear, Merriman had decided to investigate the north and west coasts of the Isle of Anglesey. The missing Revenue ship had to be hidden somewhere and there was nowhere along the North Wales coast where it could be concealed without being seen by Mr. Flitwick's riding officers and coast watchers. If the plan really was to attack the *Dorset*, then the ship must be concealed near enough for a message to reach it in time to intercept the *Dorset*.

The nearest place was Anglesey, with so many small bays and inlets it offered plenty of places for a small ship to lie hidden from seaward. With miles of grazing and farmland and only scattered villages inland, the chances of discovery would be little enough especially if the local folk had been threatened by the thieves and were too frightened to resist. Besides, the local folk would not want to draw the attention of the authorities because probably they were all reaping some benefit from smuggling.

And so, thrashing south easterly it was Merriman's intention to round Holy Island down to Cymyran Bay keeping well offshore and then to turn back as close inshore as he dared to inspect every possible place where a ship might hide. He reasoned that it would be useless to look into anywhere which dried out between tides as the gang would want to be able to move the ship at short notice.

By the taffrail at the very stern of the ship, the Master was instructing the two midshipmen and a master's mate in the mathematics of navigation but Merriman could see that little Mr. Shrigley was finding it hard to concentrate, his eyes straying repeatedly to where one of the lookouts was precariously perched at the mizzen mast-head.

"Mr. Shrigley, it may be tempting to look elsewhere but if you don't pay attention to what Mr. Cuthbert is telling you, you'll never learn to find your way about at sea. Remember that knowledge is a treasure but practice is the key to it and practice makes perfect. When you have finished with him Mr. Cuthbert, I want to see him aloft with a telescope." The crestfallen Shrigley bent over his slate, his face crimson with embarrassment.

The moving of some weight aft seemed to have had some effect on the speed of the ship but not as much as Merriman had hoped for.

Of course word of what they were doing had spread like wildfire amongst the crew and they were agog with excitement. Merriman had promised an extra tot of rum to the first man to make a sighting of what turned out to be their quarry and once the ship turned North West and closed the shore, extra lookouts were placed on each mast.

"Mr. Cuthbert, I want to be as close inshore as you believe to be safe, just inside the ten fathom line should do, but keep well off round the headlands, I know that several of them have outlying rocks."

"Aye-aye Sir" replied the Master. If he felt irritation at being told his job he was careful not to show it. "I'd like a man in the chains too Sir, with a leadline, it will help to verify the readings on the chart."

"Very well, see to it if you please Mr. Cuthbert".

As the *Aphrodite* moved slowly back along the coast nothing was seen except small fishing boats and lobstermen and the occasional small trader. The normal shipboard noises of the low voices of the working parties, creaking timber and shouted orders were augmented by the flapping of canvas and the squealing of blocks as the ship changed course repeatedly to round the headlands. Over all, the regular shouts of the leadsman "By the mark ten", or seven or thirteen fathoms or some other depth according to the leather marks fastened to the line. Rounding Holy Island again, the strong tidal stream flowing against them slowed the ship but on the whole Merriman was pleased with the way the ship handled.

Past Holy Island the ship turned east then north but still there was no sign of what they were looking for. Rounding

Carmel Head and passing inshore of the West Mouse Rock, which had been the cause of many a wreck, Merriman began to feel a little more hopeful. The north coast of Anglesey had more small bays than the west coast, many of which could hide a small ship. Keeping well clear of the notorious Harry Furlough's Reef, the *Aphrodite* moved slowly eastwards.

"Deck there," the lookout's hail drew everyone's attention. "A ship Sir." The man was pointing to a small headland.

Merriman couldn't wait for anyone else to climb up to report, he had to see for himself. With no time to think about the dignity of his rank, he snatched a telescope from the rack and almost ran up the ratlines to the maintop. Settling himself near the surprised lookout he leveled the glass. "Where is it man? Never mind, I've got it."

It was late afternoon by now and at any other time of day they might not have seen the ship. It was tucked behind a small headland blending well with the land behind it and only visible from a certain angle. Fortunately the sun was setting behind the *Aphrodite* and its low rays reflecting from the window of a small cottage drew the eye and highlighted the mast.

It was indeed a cutter. The single topmast had been sent down but the long jib-boom was clearly visible projecting beyond the headland. Merriman felt a moment of satisfaction that his reasoning had been right and as he slowly climbed down to the deck he pondered on what action to take. Turning to the First Lieutenant and the Master who were trying to look relaxed and unexcited, he said "I believe it to be the ship we are looking for Gentlemen. Some effort has been made to conceal it so a closer look will be needed." He paced up and down for a few minutes.

"We will not alter course for ten minutes so that any watcher there may well think that we have seen nothing to interest us and that we are going away. Then lay a course for Ireland, we must find Mr. Grahame."

Back in the solitude of his cabin, Merriman went over and over in his mind what had happened in the last few days, trying to put events into some kind of order. He ticked the points off on his fingers. First of all the Revenue cutter had been seized. A boy had been saved by Owen's brother who had muttered something about Irish and French before he died. Owen had managed to get himself involved with the smugglers and had killed the man that the smugglers said had betrayed the crew of the cutter. Owen had overheard the smugglers aboard what he thought to be a French ship speak about the Royal yacht and their plans being ready. All these facts together confirmed that the smugglers were indeed part of the gang who took the cutter.

It had been confirmed at the Admiralty that French agents were definitely involved with Irish insurgents and Mr. Grahame had agreed that it was entirely possible that the French and Irish could be combining to make an attack upon the *Dorset*.

And now there was the strange matter of the passengers on the small trader which they had stopped late yesterday afternoon. Merriman had no doubt that one of them was the lawyer Jeremiah Robinson. He had been certain of that when he saw him through the telescope and Lieutenant Andrews' description of the man confirmed it even though he had described himself as a linen merchant by the name of John Richards. And the small man must have been Beadle, his clerk. Merriman suddenly remembered Beadle in earnest conversation with the clerk in the Chester Customs House.

That was the connection with the revenue service and their cutter.

The third man, what was his name? Ah yes, John Trevor, a Welshman, tall with dark complexion and black hair, on the same ship as Robinson and Beadle, could he not be one of the three men that Robinson had been in such a hurry to avoid introducing to Merriman and Captain Saville in the White Lion Inn in Chester? Could that man be the leader of the smugglers that Owen had met? Owen had also reported that a large quantity of contraband was passing through Chester and that the leader of the smuggling gang was a typical Welshman.

There was now no question in Merriman's mind that these men were up to no good, otherwise why would they conceal their real names, and there was also the odd question about Sir William Forrester. That he knew the lawyer was obvious and he was traveling back from Ireland on the same day although separately. Why would a wealthy man like that be involved with smugglers?

Suddenly he remembered the other man with Robinson at the hotel. It was the card cheat from the inn at Oxford, he was certain. How and why were all these people connected?

All the different strands of information were beginning to weave together, Merriman's mind was racing. If the ship lying concealed in the little bay was indeed the stolen cutter, then it was his duty to re-take it. A cutting-out operation just before dawn was the ideal way. He had the force to do it, maybe this was what the Admiralty had in mind when the marines had been put aboard. But there was Mr. Grahame to be picked up tonight, would there be enough time to find him and then retrace their course back to where the ship was hidden?

His restlessness drove him up on deck again to pace backwards and forwards, hands clasped behind him and his head bent down, oblivious to the fact that the frown of concentration on his forehead was so severe that all on deck, assuming him to be angry about something, were at pains to keep well away from him.

None the less, his seaman's instinct subconsciously took note of wind and weather and as the darkness closed in it was the veering of the wind and the sudden bustle of activity as the watch was called to trim the yards, that settled his mind on the best course of action.

"Mr. Jeavons, Mr. Cuthbert, in my cabin if you please, with the chart we are using at the moment." Settled round the table with the chart spread out between them, Merriman told the First Lieutenant and the Master what he had in mind.

"The first thing we must do is find Mr. Grahame. He'll be looking for us before midnight and I intend to be close inshore there long before that." He thought for a few moments, "Mr. Grahame was expecting trouble on this expedition ashore so I think we should have a boat even closer inshore to look for his signal. An armed boat's crew and some marines just in case he's in difficulties. Mr. Laing will command."

"That'll please Mr. St James, he's been fretting that his men were only so much cargo" said the Master. "Something for 'em to do at last."

"Quite so. It is also my intention Gentlemen, to recapture that ship we saw earlier, which I believe to be the Revenue cutter. We'll need to be back there in good time to attack at dawn. Obviously this depends upon how quickly we have Mr. Grahame back aboard but if he's in good time and the wind holds fair, I believe we can do it. What do you think Mr. Cuthbert?"

"Aye Sir, I can have the ship in position in time as long as the wind holds and as you say, as long as we don't have to wait too long for Mr. Grahame. Do you know exactly where you want landfall to be made Sir."

"Yes I do, but I'll hold a council of war later. It is possible that plans might have to be changed if Mr. Grahame has other information, so we must wait until he is back."

Later that night the *Aphrodite* lay hove to close inshore on the Irish coast, approximately at the same point that she had been two nights ago. An occasional adjustment of the sails and rudder kept the ship on station. Lieutenant Laing was ready to take the ship's cutter with a crew of ten armed and eager seamen and five marines with their sergeant. Their orders were to keep their eyes skinned for a signal and to get ashore as fast as they could when they saw it.

"It is imperative that Mr. Grahame is brought off safely Mr. Laing," instructed Merriman. "He should be alone although it *is* possible that he may have another man with him, but if there are any others attempting to prevent him leaving, then you must do all you can to save him. Your men will have their cutlasses and the marines will have their muskets and bayonets."

"You sergeant, will have your men load their muskets as soon as the boat is close inshore so that they'll be able to fire immediately the order is given, though I hope that will not be necessary. I trust that no marine will be so careless as to discharge his musket by accident and that you have five steady men."

"Picked 'em myself Sir, with Mr. St James' approval. They're good steady lads Sir."

"Right then, be off with you now."

As the boat pulled away Merriman strained his eyes to see what he could of the shoreline, but although it was a clear night again all he could see was a faint line of surf and the dark humps of sand dunes.

Laing had the boat holding to a small anchor which kept the larboard side to the beach against a gentle current. All the men were alert and looking for a flash of light which was the agreed signal. The marines had loaded their weapons and now sat silently on the thwarts with the muskets upright between their knees and wrapped in rags to keep the powder dry. An hour passed and another. It was bitterly cold and difficult to remain alert with the eyes constantly confused by the shadows, but the hardness of the thwarts ensured that nobody was comfortable enough to fall asleep.

"Sir, I see something" whispered one of the seamen. Laing recognised him as Larkin, the man who had first spotted the hidden cutter. "What? Where?"

"There Sir, behind us to your left. Looks like three men moving along the beach. Ah, two more Sir, between those two big dunes."

Although he couldn't see the men clearly, they were only vague shadows, it was obvious to Laing that whoever they were they must be looking for Mr. Grahame.

"Right men, easy strokes. You in the bows, bring the anchor in, quietly now. Give way together." Fortunately Laing had kept the oars out and held just clear of the water so there was little noise as the men pulled easily against the current. As far as he could see, the men on the shore had not yet seen the boat but they would as soon as he turned for the shore. Slowly the boat moved along the beach, Laing steering so as to keep as far off as he could whilst still keeping the men in sight. Gradually the boat drew ahead and after perhaps five minutes Larkin hissed "There Sir, the light," pointing along the beach to where

Laing himself could see small flashes of light. The time for caution was over.

"Pull men, pull hard. Sergeant, as soon as we strike the beach I want you and your men out between us and those men advancing along the beach. Shoot if you have to." He swung the tiller over and headed the boat towards where the light had been seen. As the boat grounded the men were over the side, the marines forming a skirmish line and fixing bayonets to the sergeant's order and the seamen looking to their officer for orders. There was no sign of Grahame but as Laing was about to send six of the seamen off towards the dunes there was a shout and two quick pistol shots. A dark figure could be seen making a plunging, stumbling run down from the dunes pursued by three others.

"Grahame, over here," roared Laing leading his men at a run towards them, tugging out his sword as he ran. Even as he did there was the flash and report of another pistol shot and the stumbling figure cried out and fell to the sand. Almost at the same time there was the crash of a volley from behind him and he knew the marines were in action.

"At 'em Lads. Larkin, see to Mr. Graham." A shadowy figure slashed at him with a sword, he parried automatically, disengaged his blade and slashed the man across the face. Another man had fallen to the blades of the seamen and the third was in flight back to the dunes. As the seamen made to follow, Laing shouted "Belay that, back to the boat. Two of you help Mr. Grahame and two of you bring this man along as well." The man Laing had wounded was grovelling on the sand, blood pouring from his face, screaming that he was dying, but the seamen took no notice of his cries and forced him along at the point of a sword.

Back at the boat they found four of the marines standing guard and the sergeant bending over the fifth. "Report sergeant, is your man badly hurt? " asked the Lieutenant. "Sir, there was six of 'em Sir. I waited 'til they was close, then fired a volley. Four of 'em fell Sir and the other two legged it for safety but while we were reloading one came back and threw a knife. Got poor Adamson in the belly Sir, it's bad."

"Right sergeant, get him in the boat." The seamen had already lifted the unconscious form of Grahame into the boat and thrown the whining prisoner in also. They were ready to go and whilst the men pushed off and prepared to row, Laing bent over Grahame, grasping him by the shoulders to move him into a more comfortable position. He then realized that the man was bleeding badly from a wound in his back although he was still breathing.

"Pull hard for the ship men, we've badly wounded men here to get to the surgeon. Show our lantern Larkin, if they see us they'll signal back." The man fiddled with the lantern and then stood up and swung it to and fro until there was an answering signal. Thirty minutes later they were aboard the *Aphrodite* and Laing was making his report to his Captain. The wounded men were in the care of the surgeon whom Merriman had threatened to hang if he was drunk.

Merriman listened in silence as the tired man related all that had happened. "It was fortunate that we had the marines with us Sir, there were too many for the boat's crew to have fought off. Mr Grahame seems to have been badly hit and I don't think the marine will live. Don't really know why I brought a prisoner back Sir, perhaps I was hoping to learn something from him."

"You have done well Mr. Laing and I shall see that you get full credit in my report to the Admiralty," said Merriman formally.

"Thank you Sir" said Laing. "There was one other thing Sir, I'd like to draw your attention to the man Larkin. He must have the best pair of eyes in the ship as he was the first to see what was happening ashore."

"Very good Mr. Laing, it is duly noted. Now go and get some rest."

Merriman had set the ship on a course for Anglesey as soon as the boat had been hoisted aboard; the wind was still in the east although backed a little more northerly and if it held, *Aphrodite* would be able to make the north west corner of Anglesey in good time without the need to tack. The tide was almost at low water and therefore would have turned by the time the ship approached her destination. The strong currents round the west coast of the island would be in their favour and it would be nearly high tide when the attempt was made to recapture the cutter. The only thing which could change his plans would be for Mr. Grahame to have an alternative idea.

Entering the cabin allocated to Grahame he found Peters helping the Surgeon to wrap a bandage round the wounded man. McBride was sweating freely although it was a cold night and his fingers were trembling so much that he could hardly tie a knot in the bandage.

"How is he?" demanded Merriman, "Will he live?"

"Yes Sir, I am sure he will. I managed to extract the ball from his shoulder but the scapula has been broken and he has lost a lot of blood. It may be some time before he regains his senses but he will be very weak and unable to use his arm for a few weeks."

"And the marine, Mr. McBride?"

"I did all I could Sir, but he died. He never had a chance with a wound like that Sir, I did all I could I swear I did Sir." McBride was babbling away and Merriman suddenly realized that the man was terrified and Merriman himself was responsible, having threatened to hang him if he was drunk..

"Calm down McBride, calm down, I'm sure you did the best you could for him. You must now make sure that Mr. Grahame recovers. And what of the prisoner?"

"He has a bad sword cut to the face Sir. I'll stitch him up but he will bear the scar to his dying day. He's had some rough treatment from the marines who know that his friends killed one of their number, but he'll live. They have him under guard."

"Right, when there is any sign of Mr. Grahame coming to his senses pass the word to me at once."

Yes Sir, I will, and thank you Sir." Merriman left the cabin smiling to himself. McBride still had the smell of brandy on his breath but he had managed to appear on deck every morning clean and sober as the orders stated. Perhaps he was managing to pull himself together at last. The man had been drinking but the trembling was from fear not alcohol. Back on deck Merriman called the midshipman of the watch to him. "Mr. Oakley, there will be little sleep for anyone tonight. My compliments to all the officers and I want them in my cabin in ten minutes."

"Aye-aye Sir, in ten minutes" Oakley disappeared below.

When all the officers squeezed into Merriman's tiny cabin there was barely room to breathe. Merriman had the chart spread on the table under the lantern swinging from a deck beam and the men gathered round, some sitting and the rest standing with bent backs beneath the low deckhead.

When they could all see, Merriman said "Gentlemen, we are going to take the ship we saw in the bay yesterday." There was a murmur of approval and pleasure.

The only person who appeared to have doubts was Lieutenant Jeavons, who greatly daring, asked "Are we certain that really is the ship we have been looking for Sir?"

"*We* don't have to be Lieutenant, *I* am sure and if I am wrong *you* will carry no blame" said Merriman sternly, once again wondering about Jeavons' abilities.

"Sorry Sir, I meant no disrespect" he mumbled, ashamed of the implied criticism.

"Very well then, this is how we shall go about it. You will see on the chart that the ship is partially concealed behind this small headland, in a small bay on the east side of Kenmaes Bay. I intend to land the marines in another small bay, Porth Wen, about one and a half miles further east. Mr St James, you will have your own men, now sadly reduced by one, together with a small party of seamen under one officer. You will be in overall command and it will be your task to move quietly along the coast to take up a position overlooking the bay where the ship lies. If any lookouts are found they are to be silenced, but not killed unless absolutely necessary. Mr. Jeavons, have we any men aboard who have been gamekeepers or even poachers, men who might be able to move quietly at night?"

"Two Sir, Salmon a gunner's mate and Jackson, foretopman, both were poachers Sir, who preferred life at sea to prison."

"Good, then they must be in that party and they must deal with any lookouts. Make sure they each have a stout club."

"Your party Mr. St James, must signal to the boats when you are in position. The signal will be three flashes from the headland."

"The main party will be in two boats approaching from the east. The boats will lie well offshore until you see the signal from Mr. St James, when you will pull round the headland which we trust will now be controlled by the marines and round into the bay to take the ship, one on either side. I want all oars to be muffled with rags and the thole pins greased to keep sound to a minimum. Only the marines will have firearms, officers too of course, and the men with their preferred weapon, cutlass, pike or boarding axe."

"The two boats must be round the headland before dawn breaks. so as to achieve maximum surprise. The marines will be able to give supporting fire if needed.. Once you are certain that the ship is ours, Mr. St James, move down to the small village there to stop anyone trying to escape. Remember, I believe these men to be the ones who murdered the revenue men. They must be brought to justice. Mr. Jeavons will command the boat party with Mr. Andrews in the second boat. Mr. Oakley, you will be with Mr. St James. Are there any questions Gentlemen?"

"One thing Sir, are we to apprehend everybody in the village including women and children?" asked the marine officer.

"If some of the women escape with their children it won't matter, it is the men we want. Don't forget that these men are killers who will fight viciously to escape, so see to it that your men are warned what to expect. I expect some of them will be simple Welsh villagers coerced into helping the smugglers to hide, but certainly any man with an Irish accent is to be taken, or killed if he won't surrender. It's possible that there may be some Frenchmen amongst them. If found you must try to capture them alive."

"Finally, once the attacking party has gained the deck, I want a second signal flashed to the ship. I'll then bring *Aphrodite* as close to the mouth of the bay as I can. A cannon shot may convince them that there is no point in further resistance. Now if you are all certain of your duties Gentlemen I suggest that you start your preparations."

The Cutter recaptured

Lieutenant Edward St James crouched uncomfortably in the lee of a small group of rocks with his sergeant just behind him. The rest of the marines were lying in the short tussocks of grass a few yards to the rear. Mr. Oakley and his party of seamen were somewhere ahead. As far as they could tell, the landing in the small bay had been unobserved and apart from one marine falling full length in the water and most of them getting their feet wet the landing had been uneventful. The boat had been hauled well above the water and secured for picking up later.

Oakley had sent the two erstwhile poachers ahead into the darkness and they had returned a few minutes later with the news that a narrow track had been found leading along the coast in the direction they had to go.

Progress had been slow but steady, the only incident being when they had startled a small group of sheep lying in the darkness. The animals had run off making plenty of noise in their haste, occasioning loud whispers from the men about it being time they had a taste of lamb instead of ship's salt pork. They were quickly silenced by the sergeant's snarled threats of dire misfortune to the next man to break the silence.

Now they were close to the headland and waiting for the two advance scouts to return. The smell of tobacco had warned them that there was someone ahead and the men had been sent to investigate. Midshipman Oakley, uneasily conscious of the responsibility which was his, nervously checked for perhaps the tenth time the covered lantern he carried whilst he wondered what was keeping the men.

Jackson suddenly and silently materialised out of the darkness. "All clear Sir. There were two on 'em, supposed to be on lookout. It was easy Sir, they were drunk, but they won't bother us again."

The man's breath smelt of alcohol and Oakley surmised that he had finished off the bottle that the unfortunate lookouts had been using.

"You've not killed them have you Jackson?"

"Lord, no Sir. Just a little tap on the head with me club and they're sleeping like babies. We tied an' gagged 'em to be sure and I left Salmon up there with 'em."

"You're sure that there are no more of them there?"

"Yes Sir, we looked all round but saw no-one. I could see the cutter clearly from up there Sir, but couldn't see anything moving."

"Good man, we can move ahead again then. You, Smith, back to the marines. My compliments to Mr. St James and tell him the sentries have been dealt with and he can come up now."

By the time the marines had caught up with them, Oakley had already taken a look round with Jackson to guide him and could see that they would be in an ideal position. The marine Lieutenant took his own look round with the sergeant and announced himself satisfied. "I'll get the men settled in position Mr. Oakley, while you go and make the signal."

Whilst the midshipman scurried off to signal to the waiting boats, the marine officer placed his small force overlooking the few poor cottages which formed the village of Kenmaes. From there they could also see the ship. "Sergeant, have the men load their muskets, quietly now, I want no man discharging his piece by accident."

The midshipman returned, "I made the signal Sir, and waited until I could see the boats pulling for the shore. They should be here in about ten minutes or so." There was nothing to do now but wait.

Eventually the two boats could be dimly seen gliding round the headland under slow but powerful strokes of the oars. Absolute silence prevailed, not a sound broke the stillness until the boats separated and pulled alongside the ship, one on each side. There was a shout of alarm from a sleeping sentry suddenly woken by the sound of men climbing over the bulwarks and leaping down onto the deck.. His shout trailed off into a scream and then a gurgle as he died without realizing that he was pinned to the rail, transfixed by a boarding pike wielded by a tall seaman.

The dying man's shout had succeeded in waking men below who began to pour up on deck clutching what weapons they had managed to find. The boarders were yelling like fiends, adding to the confusion as the dazed men sought to form some defence, but they were overwhelmed by *Aphrodite's* men, enraged by the thought of the seamen murdered aboard this same ship. Those that chose to make a fight of it were quickly despatched and the rest threw down their arms and cried for quarter.

"Mr. Andrews, take some men and secure the magazine and clear the lower deck of anyone hiding down there" shouted Lieutenant Jeavons.

"Aye-aye Sir." Andrews tumbled below followed by half a dozen seamen eager to find more work for their bloodstained cutlasses to do. All they found was one terrified man cowering behind water casks in the hold. Leaving two of his men to guard the magazine, Andrews returned to the deck, prodding the prisoner in front of him

The other prisoners were sitting in a group on the deck, hands clasped at the back of their neck and looking thoroughly frightened, surrounded as they were by men obviously ready and willing to use their weapons again.

"Ah, Mr. Andrews", said Jeavons, "We are about to have visitors, take a look." He pointed to the village and the beach. The morning was now becoming light enough for them to see where twenty or so men were pushing two boats into the water. Another group of men, armed with muskets, was running along the beach towards the headland with the obvious intention of being able to shoot down on the ship.

On the headland the marines had remained hidden but watchful, but in the face of this threat Lieutenant St James rose to his feet, "Marines will form line" he ordered. As they rose from concealment one of the men on the beach saw them and shouted a warning to his fellows. They hesitated for a moment, but on seeing how few marines there were, came on with a rush, shouting to encourage themselves.

St James would not be hurried. "Marines will prepare to fire, take aim ----". The attackers hesitated at the sight of the uniforms and the threat of the aimed muskets but came on nevertheless. "---- Fire" The muskets belched flame and smoke. Four of the attackers dropped and several more dropped their weapons to clutch at their wounds.

The value of the hours of training by St James and his sergeant showed as the heavy muskets were reloaded in seconds. "Marines will fix bayonets," a pause as the long steel blades were fastened to the muskets, "Marines will advance." As the line of disciplined men moved forwards with their muskets held before them, each musket with its long blade glittering evilly in the growing light, the men on the beach, disheartened by their losses, began to back away. Some of them discharged their muskets at the marines before turning to run and two marines were flung backwards as the heavy balls hit. "Marines will halt, halt. Prepare to fire ---- fire." More men fell, ignored by their comrades as they fled.

Meanwhile the men at the boats were pulling towards the ship. The sudden boom of a cannon caused them to stop rowing and peer over their shoulders to see *Aphrodite* under topsails only, moving slowly across the mouth of the bay. There was heated debate for a few minutes and then the boats turned and made for the beach.

Aboard *Aphrodite* Merriman studied the situation. His mind had been in a turmoil since the boats had left for the shore; he desperately wanted to be with them but he dare not take the chance of being wounded, even killed, whilst the only other man who knew what was at stake lay senseless below. Besides he had to be sure of Lieutenant Jeavons and it was only right that the lieutenant be given his chance to show his abilities.

He was beginning to appreciate the loneliness of command, the need to show utmost confidence in his officers and the orders given to them and to appear calm and unconcerned when men may be dying as a result of those orders. Lieutenant Laing and the Master were on deck and the watch was kept busy making constant sail adjustments as Mr. Cuthbert endeavoured to keep the ship in roughly the same position against the tidal stream.

They had seen the first signal to the boats and Merriman allowed the ship to move closer to the bay as the first pale streaks of dawn appeared in the eastern sky. The sound of musket fire reached them and as the second signal flashed from the headland *Aphrodite* slowly moved across the mouth of the bay. Laing looked expectantly at Merriman.

"Very well Mr. Laing, let them know we are here."

Laing turned and pointed at Hodges the gunner who was waiting for the word of command. Bending down, he jerked the lanyard and the small cannon jerked backwards as it vomited flame and smoke. Watching, Merriman saw the two boats in the bay turn for the shore, the men rowing desperately to reach safety before the advancing marines could stop them.

"Mr. Hodges, take another shot, try and place the ball between those two boats if you can."

"Aye-aye Sir" replied the gunner, adjusting the angle of a second cannon with a handspike. Again the flame and smoke and Merriman saw the splash as the ball fell between the boats, smashing some of the oars to splinters.

"Well done Mr. Hodges," called Merriman, as the two boats drifted together, the men making no further effort to escape. "Mr. Cuthbert, bring the ship to anchor if you please. Mr. Laing, I'll have my gig lowered, I need to see for myself what is happening over there. Have Mr. Hodges keep a cannon trained on those boats in case they have ideas of escape. Don't hesitate to fire if they move. Mr. McBride, you'll come with me."

Climbing aboard the recaptured cutter, Merriman was greeted by his First Lieutenant and a grinning Andrews. "All went well Sir", reported Jeavons. "We lost only two men and a few wounded although none seriously. You were right, it *is* the Revenue cutter, the *Pilote*. The name's been painted over but it can still be made out. My apologies Sir, I was a fool to doubt you."

"Well done Gentlemen, Mr. McBride can see to the wounded, theirs as well as our own. Now, what is the condition of the ship?"

"Almost ready for sea Sir, although the topmast needs to be sent up again. There are plenty of provisions aboard and a dozen casks of water. The guns appear to be in good shape and there is ample powder and shot. She was dragged backwards into this little bay and she is moored by four ropes belayed to rocks ashore. We have sixteen prisoners and there are eleven dead apart from our own. Oh, and one of the prisoners, that one at the back, is an oddity. He won't speak and is better dressed than the others, who by the sound of it are Irish."

"Right Mr. Jeavons, I want the prisoners below under guard, with a pair of swivels trained on the hatchway. Keep your oddity separate but keep a close eye on him, he may be one of the ringleaders. Our own men we'll bury at sea but the other dead can be put ashore for burial. Use some of the prisoners for that. There will be more prisoners to come aboard later and I'll let you have some of the marines. Meanwhile the ship is yours, so determine your prize crew and prepare the ship for sea.."

"Aye-aye Sir, and thank you. Can I keep Mr. Andrews?"

"For the moment, now I'll go ashore."

As the gig passed the two boats in the middle of the bay, Merriman reminded the men in them that a cannon was trained on them with orders to fire if they moved. Ashore, he found a group of prisoners sitting in the sand guarded by two marines and Oakley's party of seamen. A number of women and children were in a huddled group near the prisoners, and others weeping and wailing over the corpses lying where they had fallen to the marines' muskets.

The red coats of marines could be seen dotted around in twos and threes prodding prisoners back towards the village. The thatch of two of the cottages was on fire and Merriman found the marine officer and one of his men standing over two men wearing blue coats. One of them was clearly dead but the other, a younger man, clutched at his arm, his face twisted in agony as blood ran between his fingers.

"Frenchmen Sir", reported St James cheerfully. "Hiding behind some fishing nets. I gave them the chance to surrender but they wouldn't, came at me with their swords so I had no choice but to kill one of them and prick the other. Sorry I couldn't keep both of them for you Sir."

"No matter Mr. St James, we have one of them and a lot of other prisoners. These are the people responsible for the stealing of the revenue cutter and the murder of her crew and so they must be taken back to face trial." He looked at the prisoners that the marines had rounded up and did a quick count, sixteen on the ship, about twenty on the beach and another twenty or more in the boats. They were cowed at the moment but it would not be long before the bolder spirits among them began to look for a way of escape. Merriman reached a decision. He motioned for the Lieutenant to move out of earshot of the Frenchman.

"Mr. St James, we must sort these men into two groups. First of all I want the Welshmen, the villagers in one group and the others whom I suspect to be Irish in another. This Frenchman of yours, have your man there bind up his wound before he bleeds to death and then keep him under guard away from all the others. Search both of them for any documents they may have."

Sorting the prisoners into two groups proved difficult at first, but after Merriman had the idea to let the village women join the men it became easier. They attached themselves to their own men which showed which were villagers and they were moved off to one side with one or two unattached men who, realising what Merriman was trying to do, moved with them. That left thirteen others.

Merriman called one of his seamen to him. "Do you know if any of our men are Welsh and can speak Welsh?"

"None 'ere Sir, that I know, but there's Thomas aboard the cutter Sir."

"Good, take another man and go and fetch him in my gig and as you pass the two boats out there tell them to pull ashore here, do you understand?"

"Yessir, Go an' fetch Thomas an' tell the boats to pull ashore Sir."

"Good, be off with you then. Mr. St James, when those boats come in I want half of your men ready with their muskets to fire if there is any sign that the men are going to resist. They still have their weapons with them. Then have all of them line up and empty their pockets. Take any knives and all money you find."

The two boats approached the beach, slowly because of the smashed oars, but the men had no fight in them and were quickly settled with their fellows who were being lined up and searched by two marines, supervised by the sergeant and St James.

The gig returned and the man Thomas presented himself to Merriman who explained what was required of him. "I want you to talk to those people and try to find out what happened here and why the village people were helping the men on the ship."

"Aye-aye Sir" replied Thomas, "only thing is Sir, I'm from South Wales where we speak different from up 'ere and I've not spoken Welsh for years Sir."

"Never mind Thomas, do your best."

As soon as Thomas began to talk to the villagers they surrounded him all talking at once and pointing to the men sitting on the beach. It was bedlam for a while until Thomas roared at them to be quiet. It was obvious that he was managing to understand and be understood because he fell into earnest conversation with one of the women and the oldest man in the group. After some ten minutes he left them and returned to Merriman.

"Captain Sir, I couldn't understand everything they said but two of them speak English. It seems that the cutter came 'ere one morning at dawn. They rowed ashore and forced everybody out of the cottages onto the beach. One of the menfolk objected so they beat him so badly, he died. Then they took some of the women into the cottages and raped 'em. The man in the blue coat, the one Mr. St James killed, was the worst, he was the one giving the orders Sir. After that they were too frightened to fight back. They are only poor folk and had nothing to fight with anyway Sir, except knives."

"I thought so. You have done well Thomas. Now I want you to go to that other group and see if there are any villagers among those out of the boats."

Thomas returned with four men to join the villagers. "That's all Sir, they told me that there are none of 'em on the ship Sir an' two of 'em were killed by the marines."

That meant that the village menfolk numbered eleven with two dead and the remaining group of men numbered twenty nine still alive plus those still on the ship and the two useless lookouts that Mr. Oakley and two seamen were leading down to the beach.

Merriman stood, head down, hands clasped behind his back, pondering his next move, when the marine lieutenant quietly spoke. "Boats coming Sir, full of bodies it seems."

"For burial Lieutenant. Have your men see if they can find shovels in the village and then a party of prisoners can start digging. Where's Thomas? Ah, Thomas, ask the village people where to bury the bodies."

"I have one of my men dead too Sir, shall we bury him here?"

"No, we'll bury him at sea with the seamen we have lost. I won't have him lying alongside those murderers."

St James looked at him with gratitude "Thank you sir, that was a kindly thought. My men will be pleased."

Merriman continued, "It occurs to me Lieutenant, that as we have two Frenchmen here, and I think another on the cutter, there may be others mixed in with these Irishmen. If so they will need to be separated."

"Very good Sir, I'll have that done immediately." The result was the discovery of four more Frenchmen.

"Right Mr. St James, we have twenty three or four Irish here. I want them transferred to the cutter and secured in the hold with the others. Send half of them at a time. Go with the first lot and bring the Frenchman back here. My compliments to Mr. Jeavons and will he show you which one, and will he send Mr. Andrews and Mr. Mcbride to me here. See if you can find any more French aboard and bring them back as well."

As the Lieutenant busied himself with organizing the movement of the prisoners and the marine guards, Merriman called Midshipman Oakley to him.

"Mr. Oakley, take your party and go back to fetch the boat you left at Porth Wen."

"Aye-aye Sir."

The midshipman dashed off and Merriman beckoned to the seaman. "Thomas, I wish to talk to these people and I may need you to translate for me."

As he approached the villagers, they rose to their feet and the women bobbed in a sort of curtsey and hid behind the men who knuckled their forehead obsequiously. Before he could speak the oldest villager stepped forward and said, in English with a strong Welsh accent and with a simple dignity, "God will bless you Sir for our rescue from these wicked men."

"I regret that two of your people have been killed by my men, but they were amongst the attackers so the marines had little choice in the circumstances" replied Merriman.

"We cannot blame you for that Captain, they were forced to join in, or be killed if they did not, they had no choice either. We count ourselves fortunate that only three of our number have been killed. I think that we might all have been killed before these men left here. What will happen to your prisoners now Sir? They deserve to hang."

"We shall take them away with us for trial and they will be lucky if they don't hang for piracy and murder. Before we leave is there anything more we can do for you?"

"Thank you. Apart from the bad treatment and shaming of our women, they took our food, slaughtered most of our sheep and have left us almost nothing. We Welsh are a hardy people and we can begin again, but it would help if we could have some foodstuffs to help us through. Our boats were burned and if you could spare one we could fish again. Do you think we could have some of the weapons too?"

"Certainly, we will leave some muskets, powder and shot and a few cutlasses and knives for you, and you can have a boat from the cutter." He pulled a pouch from his coat pocket. "This is the money taken from the prisoners. It amounts to no more than five or six guineas but that is more than I would have expected from such a mangy crew. I want you to take it. With care it should allow you to replace what you have lost and help you through the winter."

The old man took the pouch in a trembling hand and turned to the villagers, speaking to them rapidly in their native tongue. They crowded round Merriman, all talking at once, the women with tears in their eyes, some of them even trying to kiss his hand and all the men looking at him with amazement and gratitude.

Merriman was quite taken aback by this display of emotion and found himself unable to move. He looked at the old man for help. "Don't worry Captain, they mean you no harm. We see few English here in Mona, and those we do see are the rent collectors who offer little other than curses and blows. Your kindness is so unusual that they can hardly believe it. You and your men will be remembered in our prayers for years to come."

Finally Merriman managed to extricate himself and found that Lieutenants Andrews and St James were on the beach sending the last of the prisoners off to the *Pilote*. The dead had all been buried and the only people left ashore were the Frenchmen and some marines and seamen.

"Mr. Andrews, go with this boat if you please. My compliments to Mr. Jeavons and I would like a quantity of provisions sent ashore for these people."

"Aye-aye Sir. There was only one Frenchman aboard Sir, he's here with the others. There were more but they were all killed."

At last it was done, the larger of the revenue cutter's two boats was left behind together with the provisions and a few weapons. Back aboard the *Pilote*, Merriman found that in his absence the topmast had been sent up and the decks cleaned of all signs of the fighting. Jeavons reported that the prisoners were all secured below under a marine guard and he was ready to begin the final task which was to tow the ship out of the small bay and put to sea.

"Very well Lieutenant, I'll leave that in your hands. When you are at sea you will take station astern of *Aphrodite*. Mr.

Oakley should be here shortly with the other boat and he can stay with you. Mr. Andrews and Mr. St James will go back to *Aphrodite* with me. Mr. St James, the six Frenchmen will go with us. I want them in irons and a guard posted at all times, so arrange to split your men between the two ships as you see fit. Mr. McBride, if you have finished your ministrations here you will come as well."

"Yes Sir, there is only one wounded marine I'm concerned about and I should like to take him over with me Sir, if you agree."

Merriman had no qualms over leaving Jeavons to move the *Pilote*. It was simple seamanship and he was an excellent seaman with an adequate prize crew to handle any problems that might arise. Climbing wearily aboard his ship, Merriman realized with surprise that it was past midday and he also realized that he was ravenously hungry, not having eaten since the previous night. The Master, Mr. Cuthbert and Lieutenant Laing welcomed him aboard and Laing seemed rather agitated.

"It's Mr. Grahame Sir. He has been conscious for the past hour and has been asking for you, but he is very weak and feverish."

"Below with you Mr. McBride, I'll follow directly."

A traitor to be hanged

Jeremiah Robinson was a worried man. He paced up and down his office, his mind in turmoil. Ever since the meeting at the old "Poacher's Rest" had been interrupted he had been worried that his part in the nefarious schemes of the French would come to light. Then he and Beadle had been seen by the boarding party on the trading vessel. True, the officer seemed to be satisfied with their story, but he was conscious that he must have looked out of place aboard such a filthy ship. In hindsight that had been a stupid thing to do when they could have used the more comfortable packet boat. Yet why did that warship continue to follow them for so long if the Lieutenant had been satisfied and saw nothing wrong?

And in the first place, why was there a King's ship stopping and boarding ostensibly innocent trading ships in the Irish Sea? He knew that the Revenue people would be trying to trace their stolen cutter, but surely the navy wouldn't have been involved. It was a new ship too, never seen in these waters before or so the captain of the trader said.

The room seemed almost unbearably hot and he mopped his brow with a kerchief already soaked in perspiration. What a fool he'd been to get mixed up in the affairs of the Irish trouble makers and the French revolutionaries. It had all seemed so harmless. All he had been asked to do was deliver a letter to an address in Paris and bring back a reply. His regular visits to France and Ireland in connection with his legitimate business had been seen by someone as the perfect cover for subversive activities.

Of course he didn't know that at first. He had been told that it was simply a matter of trade secrets, a way of preventing rivals from learning what a company was doing. How gullible he had been. In truth, he had thought there was something strange about it, but he was so well paid to carry the letters that he had stifled his conscience and carried on. Not until his visit to Paris three months ago, when that damned Frenchman Moreau had been waiting at the address to which he usually delivered the letters, had he fully realized what he was doing.

Moreau had pointed out that he, Robinson, was a traitor to his King and Country, a courier for spies and informers, who would be hanged if he were ever found out. Naturally he had tried to bluster his way out but as Moreau mildly remarked, it was too late to change his mind. He had received too much money, not to mention the favours of women procured for him in Paris. "Boys too I believe," Moreau had said, looking at him in disgust.

"There are witnesses to all of this Monsieur Robinson, who are prepared to testify to the truth of it. Enfin, you will continue to work for me or you will be denounced, or most likely killed as I find most convenient at the time. You will continue to be paid and you will still be required to travel to Ireland as well as to France".

He paused, then continued, "There is more at stake here than you know, but if you continue to do as you are ordered then you will be well rewarded".

Robinson sweated anew as he recalled how Moreau had suddenly drawn that damnably long sword of his and placed the tip to his throat. "You will be watched and you will receive your instructions in a variety of ways." He had gently thrust with the sword until he drew blood.

"Is your situation now clear to you Monsieur?"

Robinson had fled, sweating with terror at the realization that it was a matter of complete indifference to Moreau whether he lived or died. Since that night he had travelled to both France and Ireland several times and become aware of the extent of the plot between Moreau and the Irish rebels.

He flung himself into a chair, desperate to know what to do for the best. His whole life was in ruins. He didn't have the coldness of temperament for this business and he knew that the other conspirators thought him a weakling. If the plans failed they would be unlikely to spare his life.

Why oh why had he got himself involved? If it was anyone's fault it was his wife's, curse the woman. For years he had regretted the marriage. What a fool he had been even then, she had lured him with her womanly wiles, all sweetness and modesty because to her an up and coming young lawyer was a good catch.

Almost from the day of the marriage she had changed into a completely different person, a strident loud mouthed baggage making incessant demands on him for money to spend on dresses and entertaining her idle friends. He had wanted a family but soon after they were married she had told him that she disliked children and very soon had denied him her bed and her body. Since then they led almost separate lives.

Yes, it was all her fault, a better wife would have been content with the comfortable life he could provide, would have wanted children, would not have driven him to seek solace for his bodily needs with other women. Damn the woman, damn, damn, damn, she had driven him to it. Because of her he was a traitor to his country and if he was exposed, he would be hanged.

He put his face in his hands and wept with despair. After a little while he brightened and sat up as a rare thought struck him.

There might be a chance if he could get away. He had some money put by that he had kept from his wife and he knew she kept some in the house together with her jewellery. He could take that and make his way to Liverpool where he might find passage to America, he could make a living as a lawyer there. That was it, no time to lose, if his wife interfered he would give her the thrashing she deserved. If he killed her he would be no worse off, if caught, he could only be hanged once. God, how he hated her.

And Beadle his clerk was another. He hated the obsequious little toad with his sneaky ways. Good at his work but he knew too much of other people's affairs. But then he would need a good clerk in another country, somebody to discuss cases of law with. Could he be trusted? Probably not, but they could help each other to escape.

He was totally unaware that he had been muttering aloud and most of his thoughts had been heard by his clerk who had been listening at the door. Beadle stared at the lawyer with a faint smile on his lips and shut the door as quietly as he had opened it. As he thought, his master would be useless in the crisis about to engulf them and it would be up to himself to organize their means of escape. He would go along with Robinson for the time being but he wouldn't hesitate to abandon him if necessary.

A warning to the Captain of the *Dorset*

Merriman entered the cabin to find McBride trying to hold Grahame down.. The wounded man was struggling to get out of the cot he was lying on, but at the sight of Merriman he fell back with a groan.

"How is he Mr. McBride?"

"Very feverish Sir and weak from loss of blood which has weakened him to the extent that I fear for his life if he won't rest."

"Commander, I must speak with you, privately," gasped the wounded man, clutching at Merriman's sleeve with feeble desperation.

"Carry on Mr. Grahame, I'm listening, and I have some good news for you."

"Water Captain, I need water." Mcbride hastily filled a cup and whilst Merriman lifted the man, he held the cup to his lips. Grahame drank greedily and seemed to recover some of his strength. Merriman gestured to the surgeon, who reluctantly left the cabin with a final request that Merriman didn't tire his patient too much.

"Captain, you know that I went to meet one of my agents who said he had information concerning the Lord Lieutenant. Since sending that message to me, he and another of my men have been following a man whom we have long suspected of being involved in activities against the Crown. Two nights ago they followed him to an old, deserted inn where he met with other men, mostly Irish but some of them English."

Grahame continued slowly, "My agent was discovered but not before he had heard confirmation of what we had suspected, the plot to attack the *Dorset* using the pirated revenue ship with a crew of Irish under French officers. And there is a French man o'war somewhere. Another plan these damned French are up to is something to do with stealing a shipment of plumbago or graphite, which the French are desperately short of."

His voice faded, and Merriman thought he had lost consciousness again, but he opened his eyes again.

"Water, more water. Ah that's better. My man was badly wounded when he was discovered but managed to reach his companion and tell him what he knew and ordered him to meet me. Then he turned to meet his pursuers and try to hold them off whilst his companion escaped. I fear he must be dead."

"I met the man, who told me what had transpired but we were attacked and I barely escaped with my life. These plots must be prevented at all costs Mr. Merriman, at all costs." He closed his eyes for a moment. The increased pallor of his face and his laboured breathing showed what an effort it was to speak.

"Rest easy Sir. Part of this plot has already been foiled. This morning we recaptured the Revenue ship and took the people aboard prisoner, those who were not killed that is. We also took six Frenchmen, two of them officers, but the leader of them was killed by my marine officer. The French are aboard this ship and we have another Irishman captured when you were brought off the beach."

"Thank God," gasped Grahame, impulsively grasping Merriman's hand, "I knew Lord Stevenage was right to propose you for this command. You have done more than I thought possible, but there is more to do, we must find out more about the graphite, why do the French want it? They-------" His voice trailed off and his head fell to one side.

"Mr. McBride, here, immediately" bellowed Merriman. As the man almost fell through the door in his haste Merriman added, "I'll hold you responsible for keeping him alive, d'you hear McBride? No more drinking or it'll be the worse for you."

Returning to the deck he saw that Mr. Jeavons and his crew had safely brought the *Pilote* from her moorings and under foresail only she was moving out to join *Aphrodite*.

"Mr. Andrews, signal to the First Lieutenant if you please, to anchor near me. Then the men who are not part of his prize crew can bring our boats back."

Two hours later, the boats had been hoisted inboard, the dead had been buried at sea and the two ships were heading north-east, gaining sea room. Merriman leaned back in his chair after a filling meal of salt pork and biscuit fried in pork fat and considered the morning's work with satisfaction. Grahame had been rescued, the pirated cutter successfully re-taken with little loss, prisoners captured and the French involvement proven. Most pleasingly the crew were in high spirits after their adventures ashore and had even produced a man who played tunes on a fife as the anchor was hauled in.

Another thought struck him. The crew was probably expecting a share of prize money. If the cutter was simply returned to the Revenue there may not be any prize money. Well, that would be up to the Admiralty and the Revenue to argue over and could take months to settle. In the meantime he had to decide what to do next. There was still the mysterious French ship somewhere, ready to attack the *Dorset*. If the French captain was determined he may try, even without the support of the second ship, because the *Dorset* was not escorted and would be an easy target.

And what was the reference to plumbago or graphite all about? Merriman had an idea it was used for some purpose in the casting of iron but why were the French interested? They had half Europe under their thumb, surely they could find enough there.

Another worry was Mr. Grahame. Was McBride professionally competent enough to save him? And with Grahame unable to help, who could he rely on to investigate the activities of Robinson and Beadle, the lawyer and his clerk whom Merriman was sure had been the passengers seen only yesterday on the boarded trading vessel.

Obviously the first and most imperative action must be to secure the safety of the *Dorset* and her important passengers. To that end he must find out when she would sail and *Aphrodite* must be the escort. There was no other way, he must go to Parkgate to see the captain of the Royal Yacht, the *Dorset*. His mind made up, Merriman's mind raced with plans and ideas and he returned to the deck to give himself room to move and think.

"Gentlemen, your attention. Mr. Cuthbert, a course please, for the Chester Bar. Mr. Andrews, heave to if you please and signal to Mr. Jeavons to come aboard."

When the officers were assembled in his cabin, Merriman proceeded to enlighten them as to what had been learned about the Irish plan to seize the *Dorset* and passengers and the reason why the French were involved. "Damned Frogs" muttered The Master, "Always up to some devilment. We'll be at war again soon enough, see if we're not."

"I'm sure you are right Mr. Cuthbert", replied Merriman, "so it is up to us to do whatever we can to frustrate them now."

"May we know what you intend Sir" asked the First Lieutenant

"Yes. I must go ashore at Parkgate where the *Dorset* is stationed, to meet her captain to see if he knows when the Lord

Lieutenant and his party are expected. We'll take *Aphrodite* as close as we can and anchor off the Point of Air, which is where the unfortunate crew of the Revenue cutter anchored that fateful night. This ship draws too much water to go any further into the estuary. Then I'll take the ship's longboat and sail upstream to Parkgate."

He continued, "*Aphrodite* will remain at anchor until I return. Mr. Jeavons, you will return to this ship. Mr. Laing, you will take command of the *Pilote*. You'll take her to Dublin and hand over the Irish prisoners to the military authorities there. You can take the fellow you captured ashore in Ireland as well. Present my compliments to the senior officer, explain the circumstances of the capture of the prisoners and request that they be held on charges of piracy and murder. As soon as possible I'll submit a complete report to him in person. Confine your report to the loss of the cutter and her fortunate recapture. If possible don't reveal to him the French involvement in this affair, but if he wishes to know where I am, you may say that I'm sailing urgently to England on a matter involving the Viceroy. Is that clear Lieutenant?"

"Yes Sir, and after handing over the prisoners?"

"You'll make all haste to join the *Aphrodite* somewhere off the Dee estuary. I don't intend to return the cutter to the Revenue until I'm certain that we'll not need her. Both ships will keep extra vigilant watch with the men armed and ready. It is unlikely to happen, but I want no repeat of the piratical attack on the Revenue ship."

"Mr. Andrews, you and Mr. Shrigley will go to Parkgate with me. Have the bos'n pick a crew for the longboat and he can go with us. You will wear your best uniforms. Are there any questions Gentlemen?"

"No? Good. Mr. Cuthbert, as soon as Mr. Laing has departed set course for our destination, there is need of haste."

But haste there was not to be. South easterly squalls and rising seas prevented any headway eastwards. Merriman tried to heave to, but before darkness fell a full gale was driving the two ships off to the North West. For two days *Aphrodite* made so much leeway that he began to worry about the proximity of the coast of Ireland. For all that time he remained on deck, lashed to the rail, as the ship was battered by the elements. The wind howled and screeched in the rigging, enormous seas washed over the deck and the air was so full of spray that even in daylight there was little visibility.

It seemed to Merriman, soaked to the skin and half frozen as he was, that the storm had concentrated its full malevolence on his small ship especially to prevent him reaching the *Dorset* with his warning. But, he reminded himself, the *Dorset* couldn't sail until the gale abated. Maybe they would be in time.

He thought about the fine but cold weather of the last few days and of how right the old proverb was. "A fair day in winter is the mother of a storm the next." He repeated it to himself over and over again.

Life for the crew below decks must be well nigh intolerable he thought. Seawater would have found its way below every time a hatch was opened and everything would be streaming with moisture. The close quarters in which the men lived and slept would keep them reasonably warm but the air would be almost un-breathable and there was no chance for the ship's cook to provide anything hot for the men. The constant pitching and rolling of the ship would prevent any but the most hardened seamen sleeping or even resting and what torments the injured Grahame was experiencing did not bear thinking about.

It was not until the third day that the gale began to moderate and when at last Merriman felt able to leave the deck he fell fully clothed into his cot. He was not even aware of Lieutenant Andrews and Peters his servant stripping the wet clothing off him, chafing his limbs to bring some warmth back and then covering him with blankets.

The next thing he knew was Peters shaking his shoulder. "Captain Sir, Captain --- it's Mr. Graham Sir, Mr. McBride is worried about him Sir."

Merriman forced the fog of sleep from his brain and swung his feet out of the warmth of his cot. "What time is it, how is the ship, where ------"

"All secure Sir" came the cheerful voice of Lieutenant Andrews. "It's midnight, and we're making good time on a course for the Dee estuary, Mr. Cuthbert is sanguine that we shall be there at dawn. If Mr. McBride hadn't been so worried about our mysterious Mr. Grahame we would have let you sleep on. Oh, and there has been no sign of the cutter Sir, it's nearly three days now since we saw her."

"I've slept for what, must be over eight hours ? Peters, Find me something to eat and a hot drink and tell Mr. McBride I'll be with him directly I have some clothes on."

A few minutes later Merriman stumbled bleary eyed into the cabin to find a distraught McBride. "I'm losing him Sir, he's dying and I don't know what more I can do." The wretched man was almost in tears as Merriman glowered at him and stepped past him to look. Grahame had been lashed into the cot to prevent him being thrown out and McBride was struggling to stop the cot swinging too violently. The sick man was sweating and thrashing about, his cheekbones prominent above the sunken cheeks, the skin white and waxy looking. Merriman thought McBride was right, the man looked like death but every effort must be made to save him.

"Are you sure you took all the scraps of his clothing out of his wound when you extracted the ball?" asked Merriman, remembering his own wound.

"I, I think so Sir" replied the miserable man.

"Think so, think so, that's not good enough man. Get those lashings off him and turn him over, let's have a look at the wound."

Clumsily because of the movement of the ship, but as gently as possible they managed to get the injured man turned over and his bandages removed. Merriman drew in his breath sharply at the sight of the swollen inflamed flesh round the hole the pistol ball had made. McBride had probably done his best and a couple of stitches attested to his efforts, but it was obvious that the wound was badly infected.

"There, I'm sure you left something in there, you must probe again."

"I c-can't Sir, look at my hands." The man's hands were shaking so badly that there was every possibility that he would make things worse.

"Is there nothing you can do, nothing to reduce the fever?" demanded Merriman,

"I could bleed him Sir, let some of the evil humours out."

"Good God, that's no good, he's lost too much blood already. What kind of a doctor are you? Tie a compress over the wound and then cover him up again. I don't think the lashings will be needed again."

Indeed, Grahame had subsided into a coma and was lying quite still. Merriman watched whilst the doctor bandaged his patient again.

"My cabin McBride, follow me."

In his cabin a furious Merriman turned on the surgeon feeling like strangling the man but controlled himself. "I asked you what kind of doctor you are, from what I see you are useless" he roared.

McBride fell back before the fury in Merriman's face, then attempting to salvage some of his lost pride he drew himself up, as much as the low deckhead allowed. "Not a very good one I know. I never had chance to complete my studies at medical school you see Sir. My father lost his money to rogues and was thrown in a debtor's prison and died there and my mother died soon after. Even my fiancee would have no more to do with me. My life is in ruins Sir. The only post open to me was on this ship, do you wonder I took to drink?" He collapsed into a chair and peered up at Merriman through bloodshot eyes.

It was not an unusual story and Merriman felt some compassion for the man but the fact remained that Grahame was certain to die unless more capable help could be found for him. He realized that the nearest doctor he knew who might be able to save Grahame, was Doctor Simpson at Neston, near Parkgate, where they were heading. There was only one course of action, Grahame must be taken to the good doctor without further delay.

"Get back to your patient Mr. McBride and do your best to prepare him to travel. I'm taking him ashore with me as soon as we reach Parkgate. You'll go too if you can leave the other wounded."

"Yes Sir, they're all recovering well, even the marine I was worried about is on his feet again."

Successful operation

Dawn was breaking as *Aphrodite* under topsails and jibs crept slowly up through the North Deep, past Chester bar and up to her anchorage near the Point of Air, Mr. Cuthbert anxiously checking his chart against the soundings called by the leadsman in the fore-chains. "Here Sir, this is as far as I dare take her. It is slack water now and the tide is turning, so the flood will help you upstream in the longboat."

"Thank you Mr. Cuthbert." Merriman nodded to the expectant Jeavons, the orders were passed, and the anchor dropped down as the sails disappeared like magic. *Aphrodite* rode gently to her anchor, her bowsprit pointing upstream as though the ship herself was trying to make further progress.

Since making his decision to take Grahame ashore, Merriman had driven the ship so hard, carrying more canvas than was wise, that the Master had shaken his head in a mixture of exasperation and admiration for the Captain's ship handling. All preparations had been made and as the ship came to rest the longboat splashed into the water and the bos'n and his crew tumbled aboard and set about stepping the mast. Carefully the comatose Grahame, swathed in blankets and covered with canvas, was swung down on a stretcher and laid across the thwarts, with McBride fussing about him the while.

"In with you Mr. Shrigley" said Lieutenant Andrews, following him down into the boat. Merriman came last as was right and proper. The boat's crew pulled lustily on the oars until the boat was well clear of the ship. The sail was raised and with Andrews at the tiller the boat heeled to the wind and set off up the estuary. Merriman had sailed these waters many times as a boy with fishermen he had befriended, and so he knew where the various sandbanks were, although with the low water many of them were revealed and it was easy to steer clear of them.

As the estuary narrowed, the tidal flood was squeezed between the shores of the Wirral peninsula on the one side and the Welsh coast on the other, which caused it to increase speed, carrying the longboat along with it, so it was not long before Merriman could pick out the houses of Kirby on the larboard side and soon afterwards, vessels could be seen lying aground off Dalpool, the old anchorage. Following the line of the low coastal cliffs they soon reached Parkgate.

The shore was lined with trading vessels lying aground. The ones closest inshore were surrounded by high wheeled carts, and others further off by lighters and small boats as the crews and trades people hurried to unload their cargoes before the tide rose further. The Royal Yacht *Dorset* was easily the smartest ship visible, three masted and embellished with carving and gilding round the stern and at the beakhead. She was not aground but afloat further out with three anchors out to counteract the strength of the tidal stream

"Drop the sail and pull for that ship" ordered Merriman. As the longboat drew closer Merriman saw a petty officer speak to a seaman who disappeared below. By the time they were alongside an officer was on deck.

Merriman stood up and removed his boat cloak. "Permission to come aboard Sir, I need to speak with your captain most urgently." The sight of Merriman's uniform caused a flurry of interest aboard.

"He is not here Sir, I don't expect him back before nightfall," replied the officer.

Merriman climbed nimbly aboard the ship. "Are you in command in his absence then." he asked.

"Aye Sir I am, Lieutenant Chadderton Sir."

"Lieutenant, have you received word when the Lord Lieutenant will arrive?"

"Not exactly Sir, but we have been told that he will require passage to Dublin within the next four or five days. We're prepared to sail as soon as he's aboard."

"Good, that gives us some time. Can we speak privately?"

"Below Sir, in the captain's cabin."

Merriman gave the officer a brief account of the plot which had been discovered.

Chadderton looked shocked, "It's hard to believe Sir, we're not at war with France, are you sure that is what is intended?"

"There is no doubt, Lieutenant, men of my crew have died because of it and I have the Revenue cutter under a prize crew offshore at this moment. This ship must not sail until I have spoken to your captain and formulated some plan for the safety of your passengers. If you know where he is you could send word to him to return to his ship, I'll return as soon as I can. Meanwhile I have a desperately wounded man in my boat and I must get him to a doctor immediately."

Climbing down into the longboat, with a parting admonition to Chadderton to try to bring his captain back, Merriman directed the crew to pull for the wooden jetty projecting from the street in front of the town buildings. Several urchins were dangling lines in the water in the hope of catching a fish and they and a few loungers stared at the smart boat with interest, obviously impressed by the sight.

It would not be easy to get the stretcher bearing Graham up the rickety ladder to the top of the jetty, but no doubt naval expertise and improvisation would do it.

"Mr. Andrews, whilst we get Mr. Grahame ashore, I want you go and find the largest carriage you can hire, with a driver if possible."

Andrews returned with a scruffy looking open carriage, drawn by two sorry looking horses, driven by a morose looking individual wearing a disreputable hat which drooped below his ears. "Best I could find Sir without going too far away" apologised the Lieutenant. Two seamen hoisted the stretcher into the carriage and settled it on the floor between the seats. "Won't fit any other way Sir, it's too long, and one of the doors will have to stay open," reported the bos'n.

"No matter, we're not going far. Now then, Mr. Andrews I want you to stay with the boat. If you see the captain of the *Dorset* return, go out and speak with him. In the meanwhile here's some money. These men will need feeding so send the bos'n to find something. No drinking mind, beyond a glass of small beer."

"Aye-aye Sir, no problem about that" replied the lieutenant.

McBride and Shrigley were already inside the carriage and Merriman climbed up alongside the coachman.

"Neston, as quick as you can. Do you know where Doctor Simpson lives?"

"No, and I aint goin' nowhere until I see some money" the fellow replied.

"Damn your impertinence, d'you think I'm going to cheat you."

"Mebbe, mebbe not. I've been cheated before by the gentry an' likely to be again" said the man gloomily.

Merriman fumbled in his pockets, "Here's some silver, now get on and see if your beasts can trot. I'll show you which way to go."

With silver in his pocket the driver became a changed person. "Yes Sir Your 'onour." He grinned at Merriman revealing a mouthful of rotting teeth, the man's breath almost knocking Merriman off his seat. "These nags 'o mine can trot, never fear." He flicked his whip and cracked it between the two horses heads without so much as touching them. The horses immediately broke into a lively trot and didn't slow down until Merriman had pointed out which was the doctor's house.

"You'll wait for us, I have further to go yet." Without waiting for a reply, Merriman jumped down and walked to the front door which opened before he reached it, to reveal the Doctor himself.

"My dear James, what a pleasure to see you again, what brings you here?" He peered past Merriman to where McBride and Shrigley were struggling to draw the stretcher out of the carriage.

"I'm sorry to trouble you Sir, but I have a man here who I think to be close to death, if you could look to him right away I'll explain all later."

Immediately the doctor was all efficiency. Bring him in, bring him in, I'll call my daughter." Merriman and McBride carried the stretcher inside the house and placed it on a table as the doctor directed.

"What happened to him", he asked, feeling the patient's forehead.

"Pistol ball in the back four nights ago. Mr. McBride here got the ball out and has done all he can but I'm afraid it is not enough."

"Right, help me to turn him on his side." The doctor swiftly removed the bandages to reveal the wound which was even more swollen and angry looking. Grahame moaned and started to thrash about.

"Hold him down" ordered the doctor, "you boy, up on the table and sit on his legs."

Shrigley scrambled up just as Helen Simpson came into the room carrying the doctor's bag. "Why Lieutenant Merriman, had not expected to see you again so soon."

"No time for all that Helen" said the doctor opening his bag and selecting some instruments. "I need hot water and bandages and a glass of brandy. I must open this wound at once."

"Brandy, Doctor?" said Merriman.

"Oh, not for drinking if that's what you are thinking. No it's to wash my instruments before I use them. In India I found that fewer of my patients died of complications after surgery than those of other doctors. I always kept my instruments clean whereas others never bothered. I don't know why that should be, but it certainly was so."

Helen returned with bandages and the brandy, with a maidservant carrying a steaming kettle of hot water and a metal bowl. The maid left the room and Helen poured water into the bowl together with the brandy. The doctor plunged his instruments into the hot liquid and then, selecting a scalpel, he turned back to the patient.

"Hold him tight Gentlemen, unconscious though he is he will feel this." The doctor drew the bright blade across the wound, severing the stitches and opening the flesh. There was an immediate gush of blood and foul smelling liquid pus. Helen was there with rags to mop it away, not in the least upset at the sight. Selecting a pair of long forceps the doctor probed into the hole in Grahame's back.

"Aha, got you" he exclaimed, withdrawing the forceps with a small piece of lead clasped in the jaws. He plunged in again, gently moving the instrument round and extracting it again with what was evidently a piece of Grahame's coat.

"Right Helen, I think the usual medication will suffice." He held a pad of material over the wound while Helen poured a little water into another bowl and added a few drops of liquid from a small green bottle. "Hold him again, if you please Gentlemen." They did as requested and he slowly poured some of the liquid into the hole. Grahame moaned and tried to move but Merriman and McBride held on grimly and Shrigley did his best with the man's legs.

The doctor bent and sniffed at the wound, "No smell of corruption there, Helen, show the gentlemen your needlework." The girl deftly stitched the sides of the cut together with no hesitation even though her hands became smeared with blood. The men watched with amazement, especially McBride who looked absolutely thunderstruck.

"You know that his shoulder blade is cracked I presume" said the doctor. "I want you to hold him upright whilst I bandage him. This pad over the wound will retain any further seepage and the bandage round his body and upper arm will hold the bone together. That's it, now to get a little restorative down him." He held Grahame's head back, opened his mouth and poured in a draught which Helen had prepared. "You can lower him down slowly, on to his side if you please."

"It's a miracle" gasped McBride. Indeed it appeared so. Some colour had returned to Grahame's face and although it was still pale, the waxy appearance had gone.

"I believe he'll recover now, but I would prefer you to leave him here if you can so that we can watch his progress" said the Doctor.

"If you think that would be best, although I had expected to take him to my parent's house" replied Merriman.

"No, James, I'll keep him here, but if you could manage to carry him up to our spare room, strip him and get him into one of my nightshirts I would be obliged."

That done they returned downstairs and the doctor produced the brandy bottle and glasses. "James? Mr. McBride?". McBride shook his head. "Thank you Doctor, but no. I have had my difficulties with alcohol recently and would prefer not."

Dr Simpson poured a measure of brandy for Merriman and himself. "And what about you, young man?" he said to Shrigley.

"J-Just a little Sir, if I may." The midshipman made the mistake of draining the glass at a gulp and was instantly reduced to a coughing, wheezing, eye watering heap of embarrassment.

"Now James, who is the man upstairs and what has happened to bring you back here so soon?"

"It's a long story Sir, but I'll make it as brief as possible. This is Mr. McBride my ship's surgeon, whose training has been all too short and the boy is Midshipman Shrigley." Merriman launched into an abridged version of the events of the past few weeks, from his appointment to the *Aphrodite* to the re-capture of the Revenue cutter, but making no mention of the Royal Yacht or Grahame's position. "He is a Mr Laurence Grahame, who has been sent here by the government to report on the activities surrounding the piracy of the cutter. Unfortunately he got himself too close to the action with the result you have seen."

Merriman stared hard at McBride and Shrigley as if to dare them to disagree with his version of events. "He's well thought of in London and it would not help my career if he were to die when in my care."

"We will take the greatest care of your Mr. Grahame" said Helen, who had not taken her large dark eyes off Merriman's face during his recital.

"I'm certain of it Ma'am, my thanks to you both. And now I regret that I must rush away again. I have not told you all Doctor; there are weighty matters afoot and with Mr. Grahame insensible it falls to me to take his part. I must go to my father's house and maybe to Chester city. If I could impose further, may I leave Mr. McBride here until my return later today? I am sure that he will have a thousand questions to ask you."

"Of course he may stay, will you be able to stay a little longer when you return?"

"I think not Sir, but my ship could be in these waters for some time to come, which I hope will give me the opportunity of calling on you again. Miss Simpson, pray forgive my abrupt departure Ma'am, but it is the King's business and cannot be delayed."

"It appears that we are fated to meet but briefly Sir, but I do hope that we shall see you again soon and for longer". Merriman took her extended hand and bowed.

"It is my earnest hope too Ma'am." Did he imagine it or had she gently squeezed his fingers again. Straightening up he looked into her eyes for a moment before she blushed and averted her gaze.

Little Shrigley was watching everything with his mouth agape and when Helen turned to him, smiled and said "Be sure to look after our dear friend, your Captain, for us Mr. Shrigley, and bring him safely back to us," he blushed and stammered "I will, I will Ma'am, depend on it," he was already her devoted slave.

Welshman Owen returns

Waking the coachman from his slumbers, Merriman directed him to his father's house near the village of Burton. As the battered conveyance made it's way along the country road, Merriman fell into a deep reverie. Shrigley, seeing his captain's serious face, kept himself quiet in a corner assuming him to be considering weighty matters of command. In this he was quite wrong as Merriman was day-dreaming about Helen Simpson.

He was smitten, he admitted to himself. Not that he had had much to do with the fair sex, a sea going life saw to that, but he knew that she affected him deeply. Surely the signals he had received or thought he had received, the slight hand clasp and the blushes could not mean that she herself was not also so affected. But what of it, he was most probably wrong.

He put thoughts of the lady from his mind as the wheels of the carriage crunched on the gravel driveway to his father's house.

"Down you get Mr. Shrigley" said Merriman jumping down himself. He turned to the coachman and gave him another few coins. "Off you go now."

The man grinned and touched his tattered hat with his whip in mock salute. "Aye-aye Cap'n" were his parting words as he whipped his team into motion.

The sound of the carriage wheels brought servants and Captain Merriman to the door.

"James, back so soon, this is marvelous, I have news for you, come inside, both of you," called Merriman senior from the top step.

"Your mother and sister have gone to the town again, and Matthew is with his tutor at school, so I am alone apart from the servants and your man Owen who came back yesterday. They were standing in the hall and Shrigley was looking up in awe at the portraits lining the stairs. "If your young midshipman can close his mouth you may introduce him."

"Of course Father, may I present Mr. Alfred Shrigley, Sir Mr. Shrigley, this is my father Captain Merriman."

Poor Shrigley was already quite overwhelmed with the morning's happenings and now he was face to face with a Captain no less. Merriman was pleased to see the first confusion on the boy's face change to determination as he bowed and said "Your servant Sir" with all the aplomb of a courtier.

"You are welcome Mr. Shrigley" said the Captain "Are you hungry, boy?"

"Yes Sir, I am."

"Thought so, never met a midshipman yet who wasn't. You too James?"

"Me too Father. We haven't eaten since the early hour before we left the ship."

"Annie" bellowed his father, "Annie, hungry mouths to feed."

Annie bustled in, wiping her hands on her apron, "I'm coming, I'm coming. Oh Mr. James, this is a surprise, are you staying?"

"No Annie, we must leave as soon as we have fed, we have to be off again as soon as maybe, so something cold and quick must suffice, thank you." He led the way into the dining room to wait for the food. They sat, and Merriman told his father everything about the re-capture of the Revenue cutter, the French involvement with the Irish and the threat to the Lord Lieutenant's party.

"Good God, you and Grahame have done well to find out all this so quickly. Mind you, it's no surprise to find the French mixed up in this, can't trust 'em, never could," said the older man.

"And if that were not enough, Father, there is another plot to do with a cargo of plumbago or graphite, which the French intend to steal. Mr. Grahame may know more but he has been severely wounded and is now unconscious at Doctor Simpson's house. The French must be stopped but I have no other information to go on."

There was a break in the conversation as Annie and a serving girl came in with plates of sliced meat, chicken legs, bread thickly spread with golden butter, and small bowls of pickles and large bowls of fruit. Shrigley looked at the food longingly, licking his lips in anticipation. He reached out towards the chicken legs then realized what he was doing and looked guiltily at the others.

"Better than ship's fare, eh, boy, go on help yourself," said Merriman. Shrigley heaped his plate and devoted himself to filling his stomach while he had the kind of opportunity which rarely befell a mere midshipman.

"I've been thinking about this plumbago James. Only last week I was talking with a fellow magistrate at a function in Chester. Bankes, that was the man's name, from Saughton Hall at Northop over the other side of the river; seems his family in London owns extensive holdings in Borrowdale, somewhere in Cumberland, with mining at Seathwaite where they extract plumbago, and he was telling me about the stuff. Apparently it has several names. Where it is mined they call it Wad, but it's also known as plumbago, or graphite or even black lead, the poorest quality of the stuff is used for writing materials. He also said something to do with the theft of the stuff. Now what was it?"

His brow furrowed in concentration. "I have it. He told me that they have always been troubled by theft because the stuff is so valuable. Even small amounts are worth stealing and it would be smuggled out of the country in exchange for contraband goods which would be smuggled back in Apparently Cumberland graphite is the finest quality in the world and that found elsewhere is poor stuff by comparison Seems that the miners are often laid off so that production is reduced and the price kept high."

"I know that it is used in foundries to help in the casting of cannon and iron shot and I have heard that it even has a use in making gunpowder", interrupted Merriman, "If the French want to risk stealing it, then they must be short of it. We must stop it falling into their hands."

"I remember something else" said his father, "Bankes told me that normally the graphite all goes overland to London apparently, to the company's sole agents, but it was often stolen before it reached there. They are planning to keep it in a strong warehouse under guard at a port, until they have sufficient to make up a full cargo which would be shipped in a specially chartered ship."

"That must be what the French are after. If their agents among the smugglers have realized what is being arranged then they must be going to try and take that ship. That is another reason they wanted the Revenue cutter. With two ships against them, one certainly armed with cannon, the trading ship would have little chance, even with guards aboard. It all fits together, don't you agree?"

"Sir, Sir," said Shrigley with his mouth full of roast beef, "They haven't got the cutter now Sir, so they might not attack the trader. They might find it easier to attack the warehouse where nobody would be expecting an atta ----- Sir." His voice trailed away as he realized his own temerity in expressing his opinion to a Captain and a Commander.

Merriman and his father looked at the diminutive midshipman in silence for a long moment, then at each other whilst Shrigley tried to make himself as small as he could, not however, ceasing to eat.

"D'you know James, the boy has a good head on his shoulders. That might be just what they will do. Well done Mr. Shrigley, you could go far. It must be considered James."

"Another strange thing Father, when we were in Chester last, I saw Sir William Forrester, and I remembered that you introduced me to him many years ago. He was in the hotel with a lawyer by the name of Robinson who has a clerk called Beadle. I'm certain Robinson and Beadle were on a dirty little trading ship we stopped when coming back from Ireland. If I am right, they gave false names to my boarding officer and I was hoping to take young Shrigley here, who was in the boarding party, to Chester to see if he could confirm that Robinson was the man on the boat, but we won't have time for that now."

"Sir William Forrester eh! I've not seen him for years."

"What do you know of him Father?"

"Not a great deal James, beyond the fact that he is quite wealthy and has vast estates in Ireland. There was talk some time ago concerning him dipping his fingers into government money when he held a government post, but nothing came of it. Why, do you think he is involved in this affair?"

"I don't know, but I am convinced that Robinson and Beadle are up to no good and he certainly knows them. I call to mind what Mr. Grahame told us about treason involving someone near to the Viceroy, maybe this is the man?"

"You could be right James, he will bear watching. Yes, come in." This as a knock came on the door, which opened and Owen stepped into the room.

"Annie said you was 'ere Sir, I thought you'd want to know what I've done."

"Quite right Owen, what news have you."

"Well Sir, I can't go back to the smugglers now. I don't know what I did to make 'em suspect I was a spy Sir, maybe I asked too many questions, but three days gone two of 'em faced me and accused me of working for the Revenue. I brained one with a bucket and ran for it before they could call for help. Took me two days to find my way back 'ere Sir, had to go a long way round."

"No matter Owen, you're safe and you have done well. With what you found out and with intelligence from elsewhere we've managed to re-take the Revenue ship and uncover some other plans. Tell me, have you heard any of the smugglers speak about plumbago or Cumberland?"

"Plumbago, Sir? No, I never heard of that place before."

"Not a place Owen, it's something dug out of the ground which is used in the making of cannon balls in a foundry. And Cumberland?"

"Yes Sir, one time I remember, one of the men said we would be going up to Cumberland, a big run that would make us all rich."

"Did he mention a place name?"

"I think so Sir", the big man scratched his head, "Sounded like a bird if that's any 'elp Sir."

"Ravenglass!" shouted Merriman senior triumphantly "Bankes mentioned Ravenglass."

"Aye, that's it Sir, I remember it now."

"Right Owen, Get your gear together, you can come back to the ship with me. Now then Father, I must leave something else in your hands. He paused for breath, "I must get back to Parkgate to speak with the captain of the *Dorset* and then back to my ship. If you could arrange to have a discreet watch kept on Robinson and his clerk something might be learned. Mr. Flitwick of the Customs House in Chester might help with that but he should be informed that I saw one of the clerks in his employ in close conversation with Beadle. That could explain how the smugglers knew where the Revenue ship would anchor on that night."

"Don't worry about that side of it my boy, I'll deal with it. I'll ride into Chester immediately after you have gone. You'll need the small carriage to take you to Parkgate, I'll send Hoskins with you to bring it back.."

"There is one other thing you might do Father, perhaps tomorrow, is to visit Doctor Simpson to find out how Mr. Grahame is faring. If he has recovered consciousness he'll be desperate to know what is happening so you can tell him everything."

He turned to young Shrigley who was still eating, "My God boy, I don't know where you put it all. Leave it now, we must go."

It was not long before the smart carriage belonging to Captain Merriman drove up to the doctor's house to collect McBride and to allow Merriman to enquire after Mr. Grahame. The doctor announced that Grahame was resting comfortably but was still unconscious.

"I'll have to leave him with you then" said Merriman. "I don't know how soon I may be back but I've asked my father to look in on him and tell him all that has happened since he was wounded, if that will not be inconvenient to you. Perhaps father will take him off your hands when he is able to be moved."

"Your father will be welcome James, but I'll not allow my patient to be moved until I'm certain he's fit enough to travel" replied the doctor.

And so the small carriage, now rather overloaded with the passengers and Hoskins the coachman, set off for the jetty where Lieutenant Andrews and the longboat's crew waited. Merriman was displeased to find quite a large number of idlers had gathered, staring down at the boat and speculating amongst themselves on the reason for the presence of the naval party. Several of the idlers were trying to stir up the boat's crew with abusive remarks and jeers, but under Lieutenant Andrews' stern eye the men remained quiet, although muttering darkly about what they would do if the Lieutenant were not there.

Merriman beckoned to Lieutenant Andrews and they moved away from the crowd.

"Have you news of the *Dorset's* captain yet David?"

"Yes Sir, he is aboard. He is a Captain Knox, a Scotsman. have spoken with him and confirmed what you told the lieutenant, but he wishes to speak with you Sir."

"Good, we'll go over there at once. Mr. McBride, Mr Shrigley, Owen, into the boat with you. You'll remember Owen I'm sure, Lieutenant, he has been of great service to us in this matter. He managed to join the smugglers and has provided us with valuable information but they now suspect him and he cannot go back to them. So, from now on he'll be my cox'n in *Aphrodite*."

"Of course I remember him Sir, a good man to have at your side in a fight, saved your life on the *Conflict* as I recall."

"Indeed, and now let us be off." Both officers swiftly climbed down into the boat, Merriman last as custom demanded. A few strong oar strokes brought them alongside the *Dorset* where the Captain welcomed Merriman aboard and ushered him down to the cabin.

The captain of the *Dorset* was a stout, weather beaten individual with one arm missing. A Post Captain of the Royal Navy he would have been fortunate to be given this command, which, although a responsibility, was also a fairly safe and easy appointment.

"'Pon my soul Commander Merriman, I find this tale of villainy hard to credit. To think that these, these scum, would dare to attack my ship ----," he broke off, spluttering with fury and going red in the face "Is it really true?"

"I regret to say that it is Sir. As you now know, we have re-captured the Revenue ship and I have six French prisoners and perhaps twenty three Irish as a result. From what I have learned from various sources, the Irish rebels were to hold the Lord Lieutenant and his party hostage to force the Government to accede to their terms for Irish freedom. In return for French assistance the Irish would welcome French troops to Ireland, from where they would be poised to attack England. That is the heart of the matter Sir, I'll vouch for it, but I'm not at liberty to reveal the source of all my information."

"An incredible story Commander, incredible." He shook his head in amazement, then suddenly remembering his manners, "May I offer you a glass of something Commander?, I have a new claret here, received from London only last week. I'm told it is rather good."

"Thank you Sir, that I would relish."

Captain Knox poured two glasses of the deep red wine, and handing one to Merriman said "A toast Commander, confusion and damnation to the Frogs, what."

"Confusion and damnation to the Frogs," repeated Merriman. "An excellent sentiment and if I may say so Sir, this is an excellent claret too. Now Sir, have you heard when the Lord Lieutenant's party will arrive?"

"I was told two days ago that I could expect them here in four or five days, which means that they might be here tomorrow or the day after. The *Dorset* is ready to sail immediately they are aboard. Incidentally Commander, he prefers to be known as the Viceroy, rather than the Lord Lieutenant, sounds more important you know. Might be important to you to know that, should you have occasion to meet his party and staff."

"Thank you Sir, I'll remember it. And now, with your permission, I should like to propose what we should do to safeguard your ship when you sail for Dublin."

"Safeguard my ship? I thought the threat was over with the re-capture of that ship."

"No Sir, there is also a French ship somewhere about and I believe they were to meet to attack you together. There is no reason to suppose they'll abandon their plan simply because the weaker of the two ships is lost to them."

"You're right, the Frogs don't lack for enterprise and courage, I've fought them often enough to know," he touched his empty sleeve for a moment, lost in memories. "Do you have any suggestions Commander?"

"When they laid their plans Sir, they would have expected to be able to take your ship by surprise and overwhelm you by sheer weight of numbers before you were able to resist. I know that they have formed an alliance with the smugglers along this coast who must be acting as their eyes and ears, so it is certain that they are aware of the presence of my ship *Aphrodite* anchored off the Point of Air. However, they may not realize that we know of their intention to attack the *Dorset,* and may believe that it was only a co-incidence that we found the Revenue cutter."

"Surely they'll suspect that we have extracted details of their plans from the prisoners and know that they can no longer surprise us," interrupted Captain Knox.

"Yes Sir, that is very possible, but I believe that you should still expect to encounter the French ship somewhere between here and Dublin, probably off the north west of Anglesey, and be prepared for it."

"You say I should expect to encounter the French, will you not be escorting us? This ship has little armament and though my crew will fight, this is not a ship of war."

"I shall escort you Sir, but at a distance. This is what I intend if you are agreeable. Whatever the Lord Lieu ----- the Viceroy says, you must make every excuse not to sail until the morning of the day after tomorrow when the tide will be right. Tomorrow I'll take *Aphrodite* away to the north so that watchers may assume that we are leaving the area. I'll stay well out of sight of land until the day after tomorrow. When you sail, take a course two or three miles further to the north than you might normally do and fly St George's flag at the main. You'll be able to see my tops'ls and I'll be watching you. The moment you see any ship appear which looks suspicious in any way, haul down that flag. It will be the signal to me to close with you. At the same time you should alter course towards me."

"A good plan Commander, it could work but I don't know if the Viceroy will allow it. I doubt not he would prefer you to be in close escort, not over the horizon."

"He may do Captain, if you tell him. You outrank me Sir and this is your ship, but I should tell you that I have been given orders from the very highest level of government to do whatever is needful to apprehend these people. It is important that this French ship is captured and I hope my plan will tempt him to try to seize your ship and then I can bring him to action."

Knox turned and stared out of the stern windows at the view up river. It was a major decision for him to make, to balance the safety of the Viceroy against the need to stop the French. He turned back to Merriman. "What is this highest level you refer to Commander?"

"The Prime Minister himself has charged Lord Stevenage to co-ordinate all the efforts of government agents, the Judiciary the Revenue and the Navy to prevent all French activity between this country and Ireland. I myself met with Lord Stevenage at the Admiralty not many weeks ago and he stressed to me the urgency of this. I need hardly add Captain that what I've just told you is highly confidential and should not be discussed with any others."

"Have no fear Mr. Merriman, I can be a veritable oyster when I choose. Very well then, let us do as you suggest. I'll not sail until dawn the day after tomorrow." A thought struck him, "It may be a day later if the Viceroy's party is delayed."

"No matter Captain, I shall be on station. Now Sir, if there is nothing further, I should be getting back to my ship."

"Of course, another glass before you go?"

"Thank you Sir, but no more."

Knox accompanied Merriman to the ship's side and after a brief handclasp, Merriman descended into the longboat.

"Back to the ship if you please Mr. Andrews. The tide is with us so we should make good time. Yes, what is it boy?"

Little Shrigley was desperately trying to attract Merriman's attention, having to restrain himself from tugging at his captain's sleeve.

"Sir, it's a man in a fishing smack that passed us when you were aboard the *Dorset* Sir. I saw him on the trading ship we boarded, you know, the one with the three passengers, a fat man, a small man and him, Sir."

"Are you sure Mr. Shrigley?"

"Yessir" squeaked Shrigley in his excitement, "I'm sure Sir."

"I saw 'im too Sir" put in Owen, "He's the leader of the smuggling gang. I don't think 'e saw us Sir, an' you remember the fat man you caught cheating at cards back in Oxford? Well e was there too."

"That settles it", mused Merriman. "If you are right, that ties Robinson in with the smugglers, probably with the Irish rebels as well, and by extension, with the French also." Merriman's mind went back to the occasion of the meeting with Robinson and the three men in the Hotel in Chester. The third man had looked vaguely familiar, it must have been the fat card cheat.

Darkness had fallen by the time the longboat drew near to the *Aphrodite.* As they approached a challenge rang out. "Boat there, what boat are you? Keep off or I will sink you."

The bos'n yelled back "*Aphrodite,*" the single word telling the officer of the watch that the Captain was coming aboard.

As soon as he climbed onto the deck Merriman called all the officers to his cabin and explained to them what had been arranged with the captain of the *Dorset,* and what had been learned about the French plot to take the plumbago. "We still do not know exactly when or how they propose to do that, so one or more of our French prisoners must be made to talk," said Merriman grimly. "Yes, Mr. Oakley, what is it?"

"Sir, I know I must seem ignorant, but what exactly i[s] plumbago and why would the French want it so badly?"

"A good question Mr. Oakley. Plumbago is found in vein[s] and pockets in the ground. Shafts and tunnels have to be du[g] and when it has been mined it must be washed and sorted. [I] believe the plumbago, which is also called graphite [or] blacklead, is used in foundries to improve the quality [of] castings of such as cannon and shot, and is also used in th[e] manufacture of gunpowder but how that is done I cannot say. [I] imagine that the French must be desperately short of it to eve[n] consider such a plan, but if they intend to go to war with u[s] again they will need all they can get, as will we. Now M[r.] Cuthbert, Mr. Jeavons, I want the ship on station by dawn, se[e] to it if you please."

French Agent Moreau

Monsieur Charles Henri Moreau, once titled Charles, Count de Treville et Beaupreau, stared with distaste at the miserable French seaman before him, whilst his mind raced to find a way of recovering from the blow to his plans.

Only that morning he had landed at Holyhead, having been rowed ashore from the French corvette *La Sirene*, the *Mermaid*, in high hopes of his plans reaching success.

Not often did he stay ashore and this was only the third time he had come to the miserable little inn on the edge of the town and he hated it. The food was execrable and as for the wine, the wine was only fit for peasants and pigs. He tolerated the place only because there had to be somewhere his agents could contact him or leave messages. The landlord was well paid to keep his mouth shut although Moreau knew that the offer of more money or the threat of violence would rapidly open it .

"So, you tell me that you are the only man to escape when the English ship attacked, how was that possible? Tell me that".

"I wasn't there Sir, I was inland, keeping a watch on the road as ordered. When I heard the shooting I went back to the village but by the time I got there I could see that the cutter had been taken. I saw Lieutenant de Boyard killed by an English soldier in a red coat and Lieutenant Benedict wounded and our men taken prisoner. There was nothing I could do so I hid in the bushes until the English left and then I crept away".

"Boyard dead? But he was an excellent swordsman".

"Well, the Englishman was better. The two Lieutenants attacked him together and he killed one and wounded the other".

"Mon Dieu! There is one man I should like to face with my friend here." For emphasis his hand pulled his long sword partly out of its scabbard and slammed it back in again.

He began to pace up and down the room. So the damned English had found the cutter, well, the plan could still work without the second ship. His own ship was well armed and could easily overcome the resistance of the unsuspecting crew of the *Dorset* And there was no reason to suppose that the English were aware of the plan to capture the Viceroy and his party. His own men wouldn't talk, and the Irishmen hated the English so much that they wouldn't say anything either. Once the *Dorset* and the passengers were taken, the Irish were supposed to kill the crew and sink or burn the ship to ensure that there was no-one left alive to tell tales. He despised the Irish and had expected to be far away when they did their evil work, but now his own men would have to do it although he would take the important prisoners back to France.

Then the second part of the plan could be carried out. The English could know nothing of his intention to seize the shipment of plumbago, so there should be no difficulty about that. The plumbago would have to be transferred to the hold of his ship *La Sirene* instead of the revenue cutter and he would have lost the money that ship would have brought him, but still, if all went well he would have struck a great blow for France.

He had no illusions about his own situation. As one of the hated *aristos* his own head could fall into the basket beneath Madame Guillotine as easily had those of his parents, brother and sister. He was the younger son, and after a monumental row with his father, he had left home, taking only his father's sword and a horse. He had been fortunate to have spent most of his adult life away from the family estates, moving round the world, selling his sword and services where he could.

He had been with the French volunteers under the Marquis de Lafeyette in the American War of Independence, simply taking the name Moreau which was his family name. Whilst he was known to be a gentleman he was not known to be an aristocrat. He hated the revolution for what it had done to his family, but he loved France, and was pragmatist enough to realize that there could be ample opportunity to make a new fortune under the new regime, especially as war with England was almost certain.

With this in mind he had approached members of the National Assembly in Paris to whom he was known and been introduced to a Monsieur Gaillard. It seemed that this gentleman had at his fingertips the strings to all kinds of mysterious affairs carried on in secret on behalf of the Assembly. He had welcomed Moreau as someone he could use and between them they had devised the plot involving the Irish rebels who were, of course, known to French agents in that country. Moreau had been given *La Sirene*, a corvette, the French equivalent of a sloop of war and until now the plan had been successful.

Speaking to the seaman who had stood in silence whilst Moreau had been thinking, he said "I must return to the ship. They will not be sending a boat for me until tonight so we shall have to find a fisherman to take us out there. You will come with me."

Prisoners interrogated

Dawn found *Aphrodite* just out of sight of land, tacking back and forth in a moderate breeze to hold station in a position to be able to see the topsails of the *Dorset* when she emerged from the sandbanks which would keep her close inshore for the first part of her passage along the coast.

As usual the ship had cleared for action ready for dawn, an activity which was carried out in every King's ship. Doubtless some thought it a waste of time as the country was not at war, but Merriman had always insisted on his officers and crew trying to better their previous time, every time. Now, with his knowledge that war with France could not be long delayed, it was more important than ever to keep the men on their toes.

Merriman had retired to his cabin. Peters, who had improved with practice, was shaving him with deft strokes of the razor as Merriman's mind worked over his plans. He was as certain as he could be that his plan for the safety of the Lord Lieutenant and the *Dorset* was a good one, but what about the other business, the French interest in plumbago? What was to be done about that?

His mind was so occupied that he scarcely noticed Peters leaving the cabin and returning with his meagre breakfast. And where was Lieutenant Laing and the cutter? Without the other ship nothing could be done about sending a force up to Cumberland. *Aphrodite* couldn't be in two places at once and he must stay with the *Dorset*.

Merriman went on deck to find room to pace up and down and was surprised to see a few flakes of snow falling, although visibility was still good.

"My God, it's as cold as charity Mr. Cuthbert. Keep your eyes on the weather and move us nearer to the coast if necessary. I don't expect the *Dorset* to sail until tomorrow morning but if the Viceroy is impatient it may be earlier. We musn't miss sight of her when she comes out."

"Aye-aye Sir, I'm watching it. I think we'll have more snow before the day is out. Don't like the snow Sir, cold wet nasty stuff it is, though to be expected at the time of year I suppose."

With surprise Merriman realized that it was already late in December and would soon be Christmastide. For a few moments he indulged himself with memories of Christmas at home before he entered the Navy. The roaring fires and the huge feast on Christmas day when Annie would excel herself in the production of puddings and pies, preserves and confections, and the centrepiece, an enormous joint of meat or more likely several joints. There would be a goose filled with Annie's own recipe seasoning and heaped dishes of steaming vegetables to accompany them. Followed by jelly or syllabub or even ices if the icehouse still contained ice from the previous winter. Merriman realized his mouth was watering as he remembered the huge ale and fruit cake Annie used to bake months before Christmas to allow it time to mature. His parents always invited their friends and his father would ensure that everyone ate and drank their fill. "Nobody should leave our house hungry or thirsty," he would say with a great roar of laughter. Even the elderly vicar, who was always invited after they had been to the morning service, succumbed to the warmth, the food and wine, and his rubicund face would smile benignly on the gathering before he fell asleep.

Merriman did not realize that he had been standing there for several minutes with a smile on his face and came out of his thoughts to see the officers and men on the quarterdeck were all looking at him and whispering amongst themselves "What's this? Has nobody got work to do? I'll soon find you some." he said harshly.

As soon as he spoke the hands hastily returned to the task they were doing and the officers looked elsewhere, all avoiding eye contact except Lieutenant Andrews who ventured to say "You were smiling Sir, happy memories I think."

"Indeed, David, they were, but I -------------" He was interrupted by a hail from the foremast head, "Deck there, sail on the port bow, I think it's the cutter Sir."

"Aloft with you Mr. Andrews, see what you make of her."

It was indeed the *Pilote* and as she approached Merriman ordered the *Aphrodite* hove to, to wait. The cutter rounded to in the lee of the warship and in moments a boat was in the water and Laing was climbing aboard the *Aphrodite* to make his report.

"Now then Colin, did you manage to send the prisoners ashore?"

"Yes Sir, all delivered to the military as ordered. The senior officer is a Colonel Sir Henry White. He had heard of the loss of the cutter and when I told him that the prisoners were to be charged with piracy and murder he was delighted to have them under lock and key. They were moved ashore during the night and he's arranged for them to be confined in the barracks under military guard so that no word might be spread about the capture. The Colonel sends his compliments and congratulations on your success in re-capturing the revenue cutter, and he hopes he may have the pleasure of meeting you and hearing the full story."

"You didn't mention the French I hope," interrupted Merriman.

"No Sir, but strangely enough he said that he would be very much surprised if the French weren't involved somewhere, but didn't pass comment. That's all Sir, we would have returned earlier but for the gale which prevented us from leaving Dublin Bay."

"Thank you Colin, well done." Merriman went on to tell Laing what had been planned concerning the *Dorset* and what Grahame had learned concerning a French plot involving seizing a cargo of plumbago. "I intend to question these French prisoners to see if I can learn anything further about their plan. In the meanwhile, you return to the *Pilote* and stay close. Please pass the word to the First Lieutenant and Mr. St James to come to my cabin."

Merriman pondered on the best way to interrogate the prisoners. He had one wounded French officer, one petty officer and four seamen, all in chains. The seamen may know what the French plan was but probably spoke little English and Merriman himself had almost no French. Certainly the officer spoke some English so he had to be the one to concentrate on.

"Ah, Gentlemen," said Merriman as the two officers knocked and entered the cabin, "Sit down. We have to try and make one of the Frenchmen tell us their plans and I have an idea how we can do it. Do either of you speak French? No, I thought not" he said in response to their shaken heads, "We shall have to resort to trickery."

He went on to explain his idea to them and before he had finished they were both smiling and nodding.

"Right Mr. St James, will you fetch the French officers here with a marine guard whilst you, Mr. Jeavons, make the necessary preparations on deck."

A few minutes later the marine officer knocked on the door, "Prisoners Sir, in chains as ordered."

The Frenchmen, handicapped by the chains and flanked by the Marine sergeant and another marine, shuffled into the cabin to see Merriman sitting at his desk with his back to the door. The senior man immediately tried to move towards him "Monsieur Le Capitaine, I must protest Sir, I am ------," His words were cut off by the marine sergeant who bawled in his ear, "The prisoner will not speak unless spoken to. Stand where you are."

Merriman ignored the man for a few moments more and then closed the book he had been pretending to study and placed it in a drawer. He then turned to the Frenchman and slowly looked him up and down before speaking in a quiet voice. "Yes Monsieur, what are you protesting about?"

"These chains Sir, and the conditions in which I and my fellow prisoners are being kept. I am a French officer and demand that I be shown the courtesies suitable to my rank."

Merriman regarded him with a baleful eye and said nothing. The Frenchman nervously licked his lips and tried again. "It is against the rules of war for an officer to be treated in this manner."

Merriman raised an eyebrow, "Rules of war? But we are not at war Monsieur, and you are not a prisoner of war. If you were you would be treated accordingly. You were captured in possession of a British vessel which you and your compatriots together with Irish rebels had seized, murdering the entire crew. You are nothing more than common pirates and murderers and will be treated as such. The facts are as I have stated and there can be no defence. You know that as Captain of a King's ship I have the power to have you hanged or shot as I see fit. I have decided that your men will be shot and you will be hanged. However, I will give you the mercy of a quick death by shooting if you will tell me all you know about the plot to steal the plumbago. We know most of it anyway."

"That I cannot do, it would not become the honour of a Frenchman. Armand Benedict will not betray his country."

"You talk of honour M'sieur Benedict, a common pirate? Very well, it is all the same to me." He looked at the other Frenchman who had been listening with horror to what had been said. "What about you M'sieur, will you tell me what I want to know?"

"I order you to say nothing, You must not betray M'sieur Moreau. They will not kill us," shouted Benedict to his companion who shook his head and looked at the deck.

"Mr St James , I believe you have the four seamen up on deck, take their irons off and give them time to make their peace with God before they face your firing squad. You can put these fellows back below for the moment."

"Aye-aye Sir," said the Lieutenant, as his men pushed the shouting, protesting prisoners out of the cabin. They were dragged back to the hold, Benedict shouting all the way. "You cannot do this, we are not pirates, you are committing murder yourselves if this is done." But the faces of the marines were set impassively and they took no notice of his cries which redoubled as he saw the four bewildered French seamen standing in front of a line of marines who were busy loading their muskets.

As they were fastened up again, the two of them started arguing and shouting in their own language until the sound of a volley of musketry silenced them. Benedict raged uselessly at the marine guard, then realizing it was hopeless sat down next to his white faced and trembling companion

Ten minutes later the marine Lieutenant called for them to be unshackled and brought up on deck. The first thing that

238

they saw was a pile of four corpses covered with bloodstains lying in the scuppers, and looking up they saw two noosed ropes hanging from the mainyard and two lines of seamen waiting to haul them aloft. The captain and his officers were lined up on the quarter-deck.

"Mon Dieu, he meant what he said," whispered the French officer to himself, resolving to show no fear. His companion began to scream and struggle and fell to his knees as the marines pushed them beneath the hanging ropes and adjusted the nooses round their necks.

"Mr. St James, belay that for a moment, I'll have a word with that snivelling wretch. Bring him to my cabin," called Merriman from the quarter-deck.

Merriman stared at the terrified man who had to be supported by two marines as he was in a state of collapse. "Now fellow, what is your name?"

"Anton O'Flynn Sir."

"You are Irish then?"

"Born and raised in France Sir, My grandfather left Ireland many years ago."

"So, you are an Irish rebel as well as a pirate and murderer that makes three reasons to hang you."

"No Sir, " said O"Flynn, tearing away from the grip of the marines and flinging himself to his knees in front of Merriman "Have pity Sir, I'm French and I never killed anyone Sir, I'm only here because I can speak English."

"Well fellow, tell me about the plumbago plot and I will see to it that your life will be spared."

"Yes your Honour, heaven bless you Sir for the good man you are. May the saints look after---------"

"Stop babbling man and start talking or back to the noose you go."

"Yes Sir, well the plan is to attack the ship taking the Viceroy and the important gentlemen with him to Ireland, keep them as prisoners and kill the crew and sink the ship to leave no witnesses. The cutter we took is --- was, to be used to help in the attack and then it was to go further north and lie offshore to wait for a fishing boat. If they received the correct signal the fishing boat was to lead the cutter into the harbour at a place called Ravenglass and alongside the jetty."

Having started, the man became positively garrulous as the story unfolded. The combined force of the French and Irish would then make a raid on the warehouse and take it before the surprised guards could do anything to stop them. The plumbago would be loaded aboard and the ship would sail for France stopping only off the coast of Ireland to send the Irish and their prisoners ashore.

"The cutter would be sold and we would all share in the money Sir, I swear I didn't know there was to be killing until the cutter was attacked and ----- "

Merriman cut him short. "Do you know where you are to meet the fishing boat and what the signal is?"

"Yes your Honour, one mile to sea due west of Ravenglass between nine of the clock and midnight. It was expected that the attack on the Viceroy's ship would be before mid-day and we could be in position that same night."

"And the signal?" asked Merriman anxiously.

"A blue light over a white light, flashed three times every ten minutes. The answer is a white light over a red."

"What about the French ship, what is she? And who is the M'sieur Moreau that your officer spoke off?"

"A corvette Sir, sixteen guns and the usual crew with more Irishmen aboard. Moreau isn't the captain. He came to the ship with orders to the captain to place himself under Moreau's command. I think he is some sort of secret agent Sir, I hear him say something to the captain about reporting to a person the National Assembly in Paris."

Merriman leaned back in his chair with a sense of relief flooding over him. Now he had it all. It remained to protect the *Dorset* and fight or chase off the French ship and intercept the raid on the warehouse at Ravenglass. But no longer was he mixed up with agents and spies, it was now a matter of straight forward naval action with which he was familiar.

"Take him away, Mr. St James, fasten them all up again but keep this man separate from the rest."

Meanwhile, Benedict was still standing with the noose round his neck, close to fainting with the tension. He saw the marine Lieutenant return to the deck and call to his sergeant that all was over. He was amazed to see the four bloodstained "corpses" scramble to their feet unharmed, grinning all over their faces. He realized that they were not his own men but English seamen wearing his own men's clothing. His face betrayed his feelings as the noose was lifted from around his neck and he realized how they had been deceived.

"Yes, M'sieur, you have been tricked ," said Lieutenant St James, "Your men are alive, we stained their clothing with chicken's blood. Captain Merriman is not a man to execute prisoners out of hand however much they deserve it. Now you'll all face trial for your crimes and I doubt if the judge will be as lenient as Captain Merriman."

Sirene attacks the *Dorset*

Merriman regarded his lieutenants carefully. Jeavons, Laing, Andrews and St James together with the Master were all eyeing him eagerly. "So you see Gentlemen, we now know the whole plot. We must ensure that neither the attack on the *Dorset*, nor the theft of the graphite can succeed. This is what I propose."

"Mr. Jeavons, you will take command of the cutter with sufficient men to handle her. You will take Mr Andrews with you and some of the marines under their sergeant and rendezvous with the fishing boat off Ravenglass, probably tonight or maybe tomorrow night I suspect that it will be the smack we saw leaving Parkgate yesterday with the man aboard whom we believe to be the leader of the smugglers. You know the signals, so if they reply correctly you'll know it is the right boat. They are unlikely to suspect that anything is amiss and you should be able to close and take them by surprise. They are unlikely to fight but a sample of cannon shot over their heads and through the rigging should make them see sense. Remember, I want as many prisoners as possible."

"*Aphrodite* will stay with the *Dorset*. I hope to intercept the French ship and be able to bring her to action, although I have my doubts that she will fight once it is realized that we are ready for her. Do you have any questions Gentlemen?"

"Only one Sir" said Lieutenant Jeavons, "What do you want done with the fishing boat and the prisoners when we have them?"

"I suggest you make your way towards Dublin. Once the Frenchman has been dealt with and the Viceroy is safely delivered, *Aphrodite* will sail to meet you. I'll look for you to the south of the Isle of Man".

An hour later Merriman stood on deck and watched the cutter sail off to the north and the Cumberland coast. It was straightforward mission but he wondered how Jeavons would cope with it. Merriman shrugged his shoulders, it was Jeavons right to be given the chance and at least he had young Andrew with him.

The day passed with no sign of the Royal Yacht. Visibility worsened and a worried Mr. Cuthbert complained to Merriman that they could be aground before seeing anything. It was not until the next morning that the weather cleared sufficiently for *Aphrodite* to take her position out of sight of the coast but from where they would see the *Dorset* emerge from the estuary. About mid morning she was seen from the masthead, flying St George's flag, and moving well offshore as arranged.

"Keep her in sight Mr. Cuthbert, but not too close. We have the weather gauge so we can run down on her very quickly if she signals".

However, it was not until the two ships were well past Anglesey that the lookout shouted "Deck there, signal flag down Sir and *Dorset's* changing course".

Merriman rubbed his hands together, his plan seemed to be working. "Very well, Mr. Cuthbert, set a course to meet her and I'll have all the sail she can carry. Mr. Laing, beat to quarters if you please.

He stood behind the men on the big ship's wheel, watching as the drum roll brought the men racing up on deck. To the shouted orders of the petty officers the topmen were up the ratlines like monkeys, out on the yards and loosing tops'ls and t'gallants which filled with a bang as the braces were hauled taut and the ship heeled over to the extra press of canvas and the spray came over the rail like bullets. Merriman grinned to himself; this was real sailing and no mistake. "Mr. Laing, I'll have that last reef out of the mains'l and another pull on the lee braces if you will."

He caught the look of alarm on the Master's face. "Don't worry Mr. Cuthbert, she'll carry it and more." At the speed they were going it was not long before the tops'ls of the *Dorset* could be seen from the deck. Merriman looked round, "You, Larkin, I'm told you have the sharpest eyes aboard, aloft with you and tell me what you see."

Merriman waited in a fever of impatience while the man climbed to the main topmast crosstrees. "Deck there, *Dorset's* bearin' up towards us and there's another ship beyond her, looks like a sloop of war Sir. Could be a Frenchie by the cut of her sails."

"Stay there and tell me if there is any change" shouted Merriman, beginning to pace up and down in the limited space left to him. He juggled in his mind with the problem of the different positions and speeds of the three ships. With any luck the French would have their attention fixed on the *Dorset* and would not yet have seen *Aphrodite* screened as she was by the *Dorset*. Maybe they could get even nearer. The hull of the Viceroy's ship was now visible from the deck, rapidly looming closer as the two ships converged.

The boom of a cannon and the splash of a shot just ahead of the *Dorset* showed only too clearly the intentions of the French. Now Merriman knew for certain that the third ship was the enemy. He made his decision.

"We'll pass close astern of *Dorset* then round up to put ourselves between the two of them. Be ready with your gun crews Mr. Laing, we may get the chance to give the French a broadside."

There was a hail from Larkin at the masthead. "Deck, Th[e] Frenchie's turning away Sir, she must 'ave seen us."

"Damn and blast them, we may not be able to bring o[ur] broadside to bear now. Mr. Laing, have the gunner stand b[y] his toys forr-ard."

Nearer and nearer they came to the *Dorset* until it seemed a[s] though they would collide with her quarterdeck. There wa[s] Captain Knox frantically waving his one arm and the alarm o[n] the faces of the passengers was clearly visible.

"Ease a point – hold it, hold it" growled Merriman to th[e] seamen at the wheel; mentally juggling the various factors a[t] work, the courses the ships were steering, the force of wind an[d] its effect on each ship. Out of the corner of his eye he could se[e] his officers and seamen waiting for his order. He waited [a] moment or two longer, then "Now" he roared, "Helm down."

Aphrodite seemed to spin on the spot as she turned under th[e] stern of the *Dorset,* close enough to toss a coin across it seeme[d] and then she was round and as the seamen hauled madly o[n] the braces and sheets she steadied, close hauled, on a cours[e] heading directly for the French ship.

Merriman was aware of cheers from the *Dorset* as they swep[t] past and he raised his hat in acknowledgement. The Frenc[h] ship was now heading away with all sail set and even withou[t] his glass Merriman could read the name on her stern --- *L[a] Sirene.*

"Mr. Hodges, fire as you bear." The gunner, crouche[d] behind and between the two twenty five pounders raised h[is] arm in response, waited until *Aphrodite* rose to a wave the[n] tugged the lanyards. Both guns belched fire and smoke. On[e] shot splashed into the water close alongside the Frenchman bu[t] the other smashed through the stern window in a cloud [of] splinters, but without visibly impairing the ship's sailing abilities.

"Well done Mr. Hodges, keep at it" called Merriman. The gun crews reloaded the guns as fast as they could. Hodges bent over, briefly sighted and fired both of them again. Both balls splashed into the sea just astern of *La Sirene* and the next salvo was no better. Hodges turned to the quarterdeck, "Sorry Sir, he's out of range of these guns Sir."

It was true, the other ship was gaining ground quickly whilst *Aphrodite* was still building up her speed after being slowed by the turn. Merriman looked up at the straining canvas, every sail that could be set was set. He pounded his fist on the rail in frustration.

"Damn it! How do the French shipwrights manage to build faster ships than our English shipyards?"

He raised his telescope as he saw a man on the stern of the French ship waving his hat. The glass clearly revealed a tall man dressed in black with a deep scar on his left cheek. He wore a cloak and carried a long sword at his side. "I wonder if that's the Moreau the French officer mentioned" mused Merriman. As though the man had heard, he made an elaborate bow and waved his hand in farewell.

Merriman became aware of Midshipman Oakley trying to attract his attention. "Yes, what?"

"Signal from *Dorset* Sir, reads – break off chase and stay by me to Dublin. Then it spells out Viceroy Sir."

"Very well Mr. Oakley, acknowledge that." Merriman again pounded his hand on the rail, accepting that the other ship would make it's escape. A touch faster and his ship would have caught *La Sirene* he was sure; but he dare not disobey a direct order from the Viceroy. "Mr. Laing, reduce sail and take up station astern and upwind of the *Dorset*." He watched unhappily as *La Sirene,* now well ahead, turned and headed the south.

Moreau cursed his luck. Just when he thought the capture the *Dorset* was certain, a lookout had sighted the Englis warship hidden by the sails of the *Dorset.* It was no part of h plan to risk an open engagement with a warship at this tim even a small one so closely matched to the power of *La Siren* Because of the other part of his plan, he was forced to turn ta and run like a coward. The damned English must have know about the plan to capture the *Dorset* or else someone had talke when the cutter was re-taken. But then again it may just l coincidence, because the warship must have been despatche by the Admiralty weeks ago to be here at this moment. S maybe nobody had betrayed him.

Although he had successfully planted a chain of agents Ireland and England, the plan hatched between himself ar Gaillard in Paris was finished. There was no chance surprising and capturing Lord Westmorland now. If he ha not been betrayed then his plan to take the graphite would n have been compromised. And it was his own plan of whic Paris knew nothing. He had hoped to return to France report a successful outcome to Monsieur Gaillard and to add c the delivery of a cargo of graphite which France desperate needed. The value of the captured ship and such a carg would, at a stroke make him wealthy and establish him wi the Revolutionary Committee as a daring and resourcef agent.

Well, forget the cutter and its Irish crew, he would have th graphite anyway. All he had to do was meet the smugglers the fishing boat off the Cumberland coast and together the could attack the warehouse. The graphite would have to l loaded aboard *La Sirene.* Moreau paced angrily up and dow the deck thinking furiously. He stopped suddenly. The spy at the Poacher's Rest! He must have heard all and managed to pass on the information to a colleague before he was killed. That would explain it . Therefore he could expect the English to know all about the scheme to take the graphite. The warship had gone to Ireland, maybe they had sent the cutter to forestall the raid on the warehouse. Perhaps he could evade the warship and still find a way to seize the graphite and so save part of the plan.

He turned to the ship's captain. "Capitaine, turn the ship about . We must make for the rendezvous immediatement."

The Viceroy delivered to Dublin

The two ships anchored close to each other in the harbour a Dublin and in answer to a signal from the *Dorset*, Merrima had himself rowed across to the Viceroy's ship. Captain Kno met him as he boarded and shook his hand vigorously.

"Damn fine ship handling Commander, thought at first yo were going to ram me for sure, but no, your turn was judged t a hair, never seen a finer piece of seamanship in all my years a sea Sir, never. Now come below, the Viceroy and h companions are waiting to see you. Must warn you thougl he's in a bad temper."

The Viceroy, Lord Westmorland, proved to be an elderl man of medium height, rather portly and of irascibl disposition, who opened his attack before Merriman wa halfway through the cabin door.

"What do you think you are doing Sir, risking the lives c my friends and myself with your hare-brained scheme to catc a pirate who might, just might be involved in some mad plot t seize our persons. Knox here tells me you believe the Frenc are involved. Now then Sir, explain yourself before I send report to the Admiralty about irresponsible young officer acting above their authority." He paused to draw breath an Merriman took the opportunity to reply.

"My Lord I shall be pleased to tell you more of this affai my authority and the reasons behind my actions, but only t you." He looked pointedly round the cabin at the othe passengers who were staring at him as if he was some peculia specimen.

"By God Commander, this passes belief. Do you know wh these people are? Members of Parliament, prominent men c affairs in Ireland and all of us have been meeting with Mr. Pitt himself. Out with it man, tell us what this is all about."

"No my Lord . I cannot until we are alone."

"This is affrontery of the worst kind. Your story had better be good enough to explain your behavior or I'll see to it that you never command a King's ship again. Captain Knox, what do you know of this man?"

"My Lord, I can only say that I believe you should hear him out and in private as he requests."

The Viceroy glared at Knox and then at Merriman before turning to the other passengers. "I'm sorry Gentlemen, but if you would be kind enough to leave us."

Once they were alone Lord Westmorland seemed to relax a little. He leaned back his chair and said "Now Commander, what have you to say that cannot be said before my friends?"

Merriman launched into the account of all that had happened since the pirating of the Revenue cutter, his summons to the Admiralty, his authority derived from no less a person than the Prime Minister and the Admiralty, the information that had come to his ears concerning the plot to capture the Viceroy himself and the other passengers, the recapture of the cutter and the certainty that the ship which had tried to stop the *Dorset* was French. He made no mention of Lord Stevenage or Mr Grahame, merely referring to government agents with whom he was in contact and their understanding of the plotting between the French and the Irish rebels.

During this recital of events the Viceroy's attitude changed from anger to understanding of the situation. "But tell me Commander, why could you not tell me all this in the presence of my friends?"

"Because my Lord there must be a spy close to, or a member of your party. Consider Sir, for the French ship to be in a position to intercept this ship they must have known of your movements. A messenger must have left London even before you did, to make contact with the French ship to warn them of your departure time. They know how long it would take for you to reach Parkgate and set sail for Ireland and could then make a very good estimate of where you would be at any given time."

"My God, what a plan. But for you and your actions we could even now be prisoners of the rebels with little hope of life as Mr. Pitt could not possibly accede to their demands. Commander, I apologize for my earlier attitude, it's clear to me that you are an officer of great ability and my report will say as much. Have you anything more to add?"

"Yes Sir, two things. First, I have no real idea who in your company may be a traitor but it is thought in London that somebody of the Quality is involved. May I ask what you know of Sir William Forrester's movements over the past week?"

"Sir William? Do you suspect him? Well, he only came back to join my party a few days ago. He tells me that he has been up in the north of England for the past week or two so I think you are barking up the wrong tree there."

"It's possible My Lord, but it is certain that he was travelling back from Ireland only a week ago and I know that he consorting with people who are definitely involved with Irish rebels and the French. May I suggest that you give that thought some consideration Sir?"

"Indeed you may," said Westmorland thoughtfully, "I'll keep an eye on him. And the other?"

"The French prisoners Sir. The Irish I captured are in Colonel White's custody here in Dublin, to be tried for murder and piracy and doubtless they will hang. They are rebels anyway and should hang for that alone. I have a French officer and several seamen in irons aboard my ship. I would not like them to share the same fate because they dared not disobey orders. As war with France now seems imminent could they not be considered early prisoners of war?" Merriman made no mention of the man Anton O'Flynn whom he determined to press into his own ship's company.

"Very well Commander, you are very persuasive, Send them ashore and I'll see to it that they are treated as such.. However, you must return to give evidence at the trial of the rebels."

"Thank you my Lord, and now with your permission I would like to get back to sea and find Lieutenant Jeavons and his crew."

"Certainly Commander and may I say it is a pleasure to know a man of action instead of the sycophants and self seekers with whom I am usually surrounded." His eyes twinkled as he gripped Merriman's hand. "When we all thought our two ships would collide before you turned under our stern to intercept the Frenchman I'd not felt such excitement for years. Poor Knox was beside himself with anxiety, oh yes you were Captain, you can't deny it."

Knox grinned at Merriman, "I admit I was worried at the time, but as I said before, it was a fine piece of seamanship."

Back aboard his own ship Merriman was in a fever of impatience to find Lieutenant Jeavons and hear what had happened to that part of his plan. Nevertheless he found time to send Lieutenant Benedict and his men ashore under guard after telling them that they would not be executed but would be held as prisoners of war.

As *Aphrodite* left the lights of Dublin behind and encountered the first swells of the Irish sea, Merriman looked up at the sky. Occasional glimpses of the moon could be see above but heavier cloud could also be seen coming from th north-east. He paced up and down for a few moments befor addressing his officers, Lieutenant Laing and the Master.

Gentlemen, we must find the *Pilote*. If Mr. Jeavons h succeeded in taking the fishing boat, he will set a course to pa south of the Isle of Man to meet us. You will oblige me l taking *Aphrodite* on a course to where we may expect encounter them. The weather will be against us and visibili may be so bad we may not even see her, therefore Mr. Lain you will have extra lookouts placed.

"One other point Gentlemen, the French ship *La Sirene* w heading south when we last saw her. They may not realize th we know of their plan to seize the graphite, so I wouldn't surprised to find that she has changed course to try to meet th fishing boat off Ravenglass. If so, *Pilote* will be in danger. It w be near dawn when we approach that area so I'll have the sh prepared for action earlier than usual, guns will be loaded b not run out. Oh, and have the cook give the men an ear breakfast at their posts. Meanwhile I'll be asleep in my cabi call me immediately there is anything to report."

In his cabin, Merriman called for his servant Peters to brin him something hot to eat and seated himself at the tabl cursing the last order he had given to Mr. Laing. In his wish appear to be the unmoved and iron nerved captain he had on succeeded in tying himself to his cabin. Gloomily he picked the fat pork fried in breadcrumbs which was placed before hir until he realized he was hungry whereupon he ate the lot, wi a toddy to follow which Peters brought from the gall wrapped in cloth to keep it hot.

Later, as he lay in his cot fully dressed except for his co and shoes, and not expecting to sleep, his mind wandered ov the events of the last few days and the orders he had given. Had he thought of everything? Would they find *La Sirene*? Had Jeavons managed to capture the smugglers? How was Mr. Grahame recovering? Was Helen nursing the man? That thought set his mind racing in another direction. Helen, was she really attracted to him or was he imagining it from a blush and a faint hand squeeze?

He pondered the problem, perhaps when this affair was resolved he would have the opportunity to see her again, perhaps they might ------ maybe she would ----- ?

The next thing he knew he was being shaken awake. It was Peters, "Captain Sir, Mr. Laing's compliments and it's almost dawn and they have sighted a ship and would you come on deck Sir."

Terrible weather and the search for *Sirene*

It was a bitterly cold, gloomy morning with wet snow almost rain, falling almost horizontally due to the high wind but John Jeavons was feeling mightily pleased with himself as he walked up and down the area known as the quarterdeck although it was but a small section of the maindeck of the *Pilote*. The entire expedition to capture the raiding party of smugglers had worked like a charm. The fishing boat had appeared shortly before midnight, displayed the signal and he had replied correctly. As the boat came alongside, the smugglers were shocked to receive a blast of cannon shot over their heads and instead of a crew of French and Irish they saw a line of marines with muskets. They had no chance to resist and dropped their weapons immediately when the cheering seamen and marines poured onto the boat's deck.

There had been no casualties on either side and now the smugglers were fastened down in the hold of their own vessel with a guard of marines to keep them there. Jeavons strode to the taffrail to look again at his prize, small though it was. The boat was following astern with Mr.Andrews and a few seamen to sail her. An added bonus to his success was the cargo of casks found in the fishing boat's hold which the smugglers told him were full of graphite. Couldn't be better he told himself, there might be a bit of prize money out of that night's work. And he rubbed his hands with glee. Now all there was to be done was to sail for Dublin and hope to meet the *Aphrodite* on the way, although with the poor visibility they could easily miss one another.

Aboard *Aphrodite*, on deck, bundled up in a scarf and his oilskin coat and with his hat crammed tightly down to his ears

Merriman found the weather to have become worse. It was snowing heavily, but the strong wind blew the snow into flurries which almost totally masked visibility which the feeble light of dawn did little to improve. The snow had formed a blanket over the deck and covered the masts and spars with a coat of white. He could see the figures of men trying to keep the flintlock firing mechanisms of the guns and the tubs of slow match clear of snow and Laing and most of the men he could see looked like snowmen and were looking out to starboard.

"What is it Mr.Laing?"

"Can't say for sure Sir. Man at the maintop said he saw what looked like a ship on the starboard beam but the weather closed in and he didn't see it again ."

"Very well Mr.Laing, have the guns run out quietly, then we'll turn a point or two to starboard, see if we can find her. If it is the French ship we will attack immediately so be prepared to take in the courses."

The courses, the big lower sails, obscured vision and were always susceptible to fire from a glowing wad from the enemy guns. For these reasons they were usually furled before close quarter action.

"Aye - aye Sir, word has gone round the men like lightning and they're ready to fight. They don't want her to escape again."

Silence fell except for the sound of water under the ship's forefoot and the creak of timber but even those sounds were deadened by the snow. Merriman smiled to see Laing vainly waving his hand in front of him trying to clear his vision. The snow seemed to be thinning but still he could see nothing, wait, what was that?, did he see something solid out there? No ---- yes, yes a ship looming up out of the murk, was it the French?

The question was answered immediately by eruption of tongues of flame and smoke from the other ship's side. *Aphrodite* seemed to stagger as shot hit home in the hull, but most of the broadside went high, ripping holes in the sails and cutting ropes and shrouds. A backstay parted with a snap behind Merriman and he saw the topmen already climbing aloft to effect repairs.

"Fire as you bear" yelled Merriman and his little nine pounders and one of the smashers bellowed their reply. The concussion temporarily blew the snow away creating a gap through which Merriman could just see the stern of the other ship as *Aphrodite* closed with her. There was the smashed window from their earlier encounter, as yet un-repaired, the French ship without a doubt, although Merriman had had no doubt about it. The French were as ready for action as *Aphrodite* was and their first broadside had confirmed it.

Both ships were exchanging broadsides as fast as the gun crews could reload but Merriman was pleased to see that his guns were firing three times to the enemy's two, besides which the smasher was doing more damage than half a dozen of the other guns. Even so, the main deck was already a shambles with bodies of the dead lying along the centre line where they had been dragged to leave the deck clear for the handling of the guns. Even as Merriman watched he saw a powder monkey just emerging from the hatchway with more cartridges for the guns, have his head smashed into red ruin together with the marine guarding the hatchway.

"Mr. Laing We'll strike while the iron's hot. We'll be alongside shortly and then we'll board from amidships. Have the boarding parties ready. Mr. Oakley, Mr. Shrigley, run and tell the gun captains to load with grapeshot for the last broadside before we board."

Merriman turned to the men on the wheel. In the increasing [lig]ht he saw that they were not the same two who had been [th]ere when he came on deck and who were lying nearby in the [hu]ddled attitudes of death. The iron discipline of the navy had [en]sured that new men manned the wheel even as the dead [we]re pulled away.

"Bring her alongside, smartly now." Merriman saw the two [mi]dshipmen racing back to their positions near him. "You two [wi]ll stay here; you're not big enough for what's to be done."

He discarded his bulky oilskins as Owen appeared beside [hi]m with his sword. He grasped it firmly as the ships crashed [to]gether. Grapnels were thrown from both ships to hold them [to]gether. The swivel guns blasted their charges of musket balls [ac]ross the enemy deck just before the French swivels did the [sa]me. Fortunately only one of the French guns did any damage [as] the marine marksmen shot the gunners just as they fired.

"Boarders away" shouted Merriman, launching himself [ac]ross the gap between the ships' rails. He knew Laing and [O]wen were to his left and behind them his men eager to get to [gr]ips with the French. Owen was a fearsome sight as he [wi]elded a cutlass in each hand, roaring his hatred of the people [wh]o had been responsible for his brother's death. On his right [Li]eutenant St James was at the head of his depleted party of [m]arines. Although many of the French had been killed by [m]usket balls fired from the swivels they were as eager to fight [as] the English and met them with a fierce determination. Cut [an]d slash, parry and stamp forward, thrust and cut, feet [sli]pping on blood and slush, standing on or tripping over [bo]dies, men screaming in hate and agony. As it continued [M]erriman became aware that Owen had ceased to shout and [ev]en his great strength could not long support the effort needed to fight so many Frenchmen. He also became awa[re] that they were not making any progress.

"We can't hold them Sir," panted the marine Lieutenant [as] he thrust his sword into a man's stomach and immediate[ly] withdrew it to parry a slash at his head. "There are too ma[ny] of them, we're outnumbered." The press of men in front of hi[m] parted and Merriman saw the mysterious scarred Frenchm[an] he had seen before.

"Monsieur Moreau, I believe," he shouted above the noise.

"Oui Capitaine, and I believe you are the man responsib[le] for ruining all my plans," replied Moreau, "On gua[rd] Monsieur."

He immediately attacked Merriman and within the space [of] a few clashes of their blades Merriman knew he was facing [a] superior swordsman and he was pressed further and furth[er] backwards until he felt the ship's rail at his back.

"My bird Captain, if you permit." The voice was St Jame[s] as he smoothly interposed his sword and parried a cut [at] Merriman's head.

Moreau stepped back. "Ha! The redcoat who killed m[y] Lieutenant. I wanted to meet you." The two men met eager[ly,] the movement of the swords faster than the eye could follo[w] until suddenly there was blood on the shoulder of St Jame[s'] coat. Meanwhile around them the fight continued but t[he] English were being forced back by greater numbers. A swirl [of] men separated Moreau and St James who were both forced [to] engage other opponents.

"Back men, back to *Aphrodite*," roared Merriman. The[re] were only a few of his men left aboard *La Sirene* no[w] desperately fighting with backs to the rail to hold back t[he] French, when there was a sudden blast of canister fro[m] *Aphrodite's* swivel guns over their heads and the hail of musk[et]

...lls tore into the French. In the stunned pause Merriman's ...en swiftly regained their own deck, Owen helping the ...ounded marine lieutenant to clamber over the rails.

Merriman looked round to see his two midshipmen each ...ith two seamen hastily reloading the two small guns. The ...ench surged forward to board in their turn but the crack of ...ght cannon fire halted them. More men fell as shot erupted ...rough French ship's deck, striking them as they stood ...omentarily confused.

Lieutenant Laing was bawling orders to the men to reload ...e cannon and to fire when ready and Merriman could see the ...ench frantically hacking loose the cables holding the ships ...gether. They were obviously trying to break off the action.

The snow was still falling, but lighter than before when the ...ash and thunder of cannon fire blew the snow away again and ...erriman turned to see the revenue cutter *Pilote* passing the ...ern of the Frenchman before turning to bring her other ...oadside into action, raking the *Sirene's* stern again. The cutter ...as too low to be able to fire directly along the *Sirene's* upper ...ck, but Merriman could see that her small guns were at full ...evation which was why the balls had come up through the ...emy deck.

Then the *Pilote* turned onto the enemy's disengaged side. A ...istake, as she immediately received a full broadside from the ...ench cannon which had not yet been fired. The small cutter ...aggered under the impact, lethal splinters of wood cutting ...en down on her deck. Her topmast slowly collapsed ...inging down most of the sails in a tangle of canvas and ...ordage, rendering her helpless.

As the ships moved apart both *La Sirene* and *Aphrodite* ...anaged partial broadsides before the French ship drew ahead.

"Mr. Hodges, see what you can do with the chaser," yelled Merriman and to the helmsmen, "Bear away a point so that the starboard bow chaser bears on the French." As the other ship was disappearing into the murk the gun fired. The shot impacted at the base of the French ship's mizzen mast which crashed down alongside.

Unfortunately, the slight change of course brought more wind into *Aphrodite's* sails and the fore topmast, already weakened in the earlier exchange of fire, swayed and then fell across the fo'c'sle, blanketing the guns and striking down the gunner and his gun crew. *La Sirene* disappeared into the darkness and still falling snow.

Merriman dragged his weary mind to the problems of getting his ship back into fighting trim again. Already the bos'n and a party of seamen were swarming over the remains of the topmast and the flash of axes showed where efforts were being made to get rid of it Other men were removing the wounded below and the heap of corpses at the base of the mainmast showed what price had been paid during the engagement. The *Pilote* was in a bad way and would need help as soon as possible. Merriman turned to the men waiting for orders or waiting to report.

"Hull's sound below Sir," this was the carpenter, "Apart from the mast down, there are some shot holes and smashed rails and the like. Soon have those fixed Sir. I spoke with the bos'n Sir and there is a spare mainyard we can rig to replace the topmast but it'll take some time Sir."

"Very well Mr Green, get to it. I know you'll do it as quickly as you can."

Merriman looked at Lieutenant Laing, his uniform coat in tatters and blood splashed over his once white trousers. "Are you hurt Mr. Laing?"

The Lieutenant looked down ruefully at the remains of his uniform. "No Sir, not a scratch, the blood isn't mine."

"Glad to hear it. Now, how soon will we be able to fight?"

"Very soon Sir, or as soon as the foremast is refitted. We had four guns dismounted, but two can be back in use again very soon. The other two need new carriages Sir, so they must wait for the carpenter. Mr. Hodges the gunner is dead and some twenty nine others killed and wounded, maybe more. The Master and Mr. St James are both wounded, Mr. Cuthbert seriously. Here is Mr. McBride Sir, he'll be able to tell you more."

McBride, his face haggard, his shirt and apron covered in blood, approached through the men working on the deck and stood in front of Merriman, absently wiping his hands on a rag already soaked in blood.

"What's the bill Mr. McBride?" asked Merriman gently.

"Of the men Sir, fourteen dead, fifteen wounded of whom three or four are not going to live to see another day. Those who have lost a limb should survive but I can't be certain." His face twisted, "I've done my best, but I have never seen such carnage before Sir, I don't know if I can ------" His voice trailed off miserably.

"Steady Mr. McBride, I'm certain you have done all you can. How about Mr. Cuthbert and Mr. St James? How are they?"

"Mr. St James will recover Sir, he has a clean sword thrust through his shoulder and will be himself again in a few days, but the Master's condition is more serious. A large splinter pierced his side from front to back, I don't think it damaged anything vital but he's an old man and has lost a lot of blood --- I can only depend on his own resources to pull him through. I learned a lot from Doctor Simpson in the short time I was with him but it didn't prepare me for this."

"Carry on Mr. McBride and do your best, I'll come down and see the wounded when I can."

"Thank you Sir, that will please them."

"Mr. Laing, have a boat brought alongside and manned. Mr. Oakley, I want you to take the boat's crew and pull for the *Pilote* still in sight over there. Find out how they are coping with the damage and see if they can manage to bring her nearer so that we can get a line to her to tow if they need it. Stay there with the boat's crew to help."

Aphrodite was lying into the wind with only the spanker set to keep her head to the wind whilst the work went furiously ahead to raise the new fore topmast. The boats had been towed astern to avoid damage and one was quickly ready to go.

"Mr. Oakley, you and Mr. Shrigley did well to prepare the swivels when you did. That was quick thinking. It gave the chance for our men to get back aboard"

Oakley looked down at the deck and then at his captain, drew a deep breath and said, "It wasn't me Sir, it was Mr. Shrigley, he thought of it and got the men to help."

"Nevertheless Mr. Oakley, it was well done."

Oakley disappeared over the side and Merriman took a moment to consider what the lad had said. Oakley was honest enough to credit Shrigley with what they had done without trying to claim the credit for himself and little Shrigley had the makings of a competent officer. He was quick witted and had used his initiative to bring the swivels into use. He watched the boat until it reached the *Pilote*. The snow had stopped, the wind had abated and the clouds were parting to show a few gleams of weak sunlight. There was no sign of the French ship which would have been able to make a fair speed once the smashed mizzen mast and top hamper had been cleared.

"Damn that fellow Moreau, I would have liked to have taken him back to present to Mr. Grahame. As it is we haven't seen the last of him I'll be bound." mused Merriman, "Could I have done more to capture him? Probably not, shorthanded as we were with so many men and marines aboard the cutter. Jeavons did well to find us and his action in putting two broadsides into the Frenchman's stern certainly saved us."

He dragged his mind back. "Mr. Laing, please see to it that the galley fire is relit and the men have some hot food. Also I want every man to have an extra tot of grog including the wounded."

Below, in the cramped orlop deck with low headroom, only lit by a few lanterns, it was a scene from some terrible nightmare. Wounded men were lying where they could, some unconscious, most nursing their wounds in silence, a few moaning in agony and even several corpses with their faces covered with scraps of cloth. The stench was appalling.

"Get these bodies out of here" snarled Merriman to one of the surgeon's assistants, "Immediately."

"Captain's 'ere lads" said a voice from the gloom and there was an instant stirring from the men.

"Rest easy men, Mr. McBride is doing his best for you and there's a tot coming down for each of you. You've done well, I'm proud of you."

"Did we finish those Frogs Sir?"

"No, they got away when the foremast came down, but we hurt them, we hurt them badly."

"Will we get another chance at 'em Sir? We'll finish 'em next time."

"Maybe, but not today. They must be running back to France as fast as they can go with their tails between their legs."

Merriman looked down at a man with a bloodstain bandage round his head and over his eyes, who was shaki the man next to him, saying "Wake up Tom, come on la Captain's come down to see us, come on mate, wake up Merriman bent, touched the man on the shoulder. "It's no u I'm afraid, he's gone."

"But 'e were talking to me but a bit ago Sir, 'e can't be go 'e's me mate Sir." He reached out a shaking hand a Merriman took it in his own.

"I'm sorry, your friend is dead. You were at t smasher with the gunner weren't you. That last shot was good one, sent the Frogs packing and saved this ship."

"Aye Sir, but I wish Tom were alive to see it."

Merriman stood and looked around. What men these we living in awful conditions with poor, often rotten food, with rope's end on the back of a man if he were too slow to obey order and the lash if he dared to answer back. Probably no of them had anything better to look forward to except more the same, but it was pride and loyalty that kept them goir Pride in the ship and loyalty to their mates, not wanting to either down and even now wanting to fight again He turn away, feeling diminished in himself by their sacrifice for whi he alone was responsible.

Back on deck he was surprised to see the *Pilote* appreciab nearer. Somebody over there had managed to raise a scrap two of canvas on the stump of the mast which was helping keep way on her. He looked at his own foremast and w pleased to see that the new spar was already being sway aloft with new shrouds and stays attached. The next step w to guide the butt of the spar into the repaired crosstrees a secure it as the shrouds and stays were taken up to support Then yards and canvas could be sent up.

"Mr. Laing, have a party rig for towing and prepare to pass cable to *Pilote* when she is near enough." It meant grinding il for the already exhausted men but he had to ensure the fety of the other ship and crew.

Eventually all was done. *Pilote* was secured to the tow rope id *Aphrodite's* new foremast was stayed and ready for the paired headsails and square sails to be bent on. Merriman ent forr-ard to where the bos'n and carpenter were overseeing e final part of the work.

"Another hour Sir," reported the weary bos'n, "and she'll be most as good as new."

"I'm pleased Mr. Brockle, Mr. Green, you and your men ive done well."

The boat had returned and the worn-out men climbed owly aboard, Lieutenant Andrews from the cutter among em.

"Welcome back Mr. Andrews, what have you to report?"

"Sir, I'm sorry to report that Mr. Jeavons was severely jured when the French broadside hit us. He was under the pmast when it fell. His plan was to go alongside the enchie and board to take them in the rear while they were ill fighting with you. We didn't expect that they would be ady to fire a full broadside. In addition to Mr. Jeavons being ounded we lost five seamen and three marines dead or ounded including the sergeant Before all that Mr. Jeavons rried out his orders exactly. The fishing boat and the nugglers were taken and we found a cargo of graphite aboard hich is now aboard *Pilote*."

"An excellent report Mr. Andrews. I'm sorry to hear about e First Lieutenant and the others, the surgeon must go across ght away. But tell me, where is the fishing boat and the isoners?"

"When it was realized that *Aphrodite* was in action, M[r] Jeavons took us off and we released the prisoners and left the[m] behind, but not before taking the sails off her. Even if they ca[n] find something to make a sail from, they can't get under wa[y] easily, or get very far, so we should be able to find them agai[n]. There are only ten of them Sir."

"And the condition of the cutter?"

"Not too bad Sir, the hull is sound but I'll need more men [to] effect repairs to the mast and rigging, especially the carpent[er] and bos'n."

"That must wait for now. The first priority is to mak[e] *Aphrodite* seaworthy and ready to fight again. Then the ne[xt] thing to do is to bury our dead. When I've finished that s[ad] duty here I'll go over to the cutter and do the same. Then we'[ll] see about temporary repairs to the cutter. So far as th[e] smugglers are concerned we'll try to recover them when w[e] can."

Merriman smiled briefly, "I don't think they were direct[ly] involved in murdering the Revenue men, so when we hav[e] them aboard I think it will be a fair punishment for them to b[e] pressed into service. We need extra hands now Mr Andrew[s] and they are all prime seamen."

"Aye-aye Sir. I'd like that. One of them is the man callin[g] himself John Trevor that I met on the ship I boarded some tim[e] ago. You remember Sir, he was with the fat man and the sma[ll] wizened little man you were interested in. And there is anoth[er] man aboard, not a seaman, a fat man wearing grey breech[es] and coat. He may be the man you told us of, the card cheat."

"You're right Lieutenant, he is. It seems certain that the ma[n] Trevor is the leader of the smugglers. Owen will be able [to] identify him for sure, so if it is he, we must turn him over to th[e] justices together with the other fellow."

Andrews looked at the state of the ship and the corpses still ing amidships. "Your plans succeeded Sir, the French are feated and we have the fishing boat and the cargo of graphite was carrying. We've been lucky, Sir."

"Lucky, yes I suppose so, but remember David, an ounce of ck is worth a pound of wisdom."

"One other thing Sir, it is perhaps inappropriate at this time, it may I wish you a happy Christmas."

Merriman suddenly realized it was Christmas day morrow.

Trial and execution

A week later *Aphrodite* lay to her anchor off the Point of A under the command of Lieutenant Laing.   Six more of t badly wounded had succumbed but the rest, even tw amputees were recovering well. The Master, old Mr. Cuthbe was still weak but recovering so well that McBride w beginning to boast of his skill. Lieutenant Jeavons, sufferir from the blow to the head when the spar fell on him, w hovering between life and death, sometimes raving ar babbling incoherently, at other times quiet and staring in space not responding to attempts to talk to him.

"I can do no more for him Sir," reported the Surgeon. "T actual wound to his head is healing well but the blow h affected his mind. I can only hope that time will help him."

The *Pilote,* under a temporary rig had been taken to Parkga and moored alongside the fishing boat with a skeleton cre aboard, but until he received orders he could not hand her ov to the Revenue service. The Navy might decide to treat her as prize of war and keep her or even to give her back to t Revenue.

Merriman's report was ready to send to Admiral Edwards the Admiralty, but it was urgent that Merriman first reporte events back to Mr Grahame who was still in nominal commar of Merriman's services. And so, once again he was on the wa back home, driven as before, in the same shabby carriage by t same scruffy individual with the evil breath, but this tin accompanied by Lieutenants Andrews and St James.   Th languid individual had his left arm in a sling but in spite of th was remarkably cheerful.

"Fine view of the Welsh coast and hills Sir," he commented, "minds me of the Northumberland coast near to where I grew ."

"Really, I never realized that you were from the north ward. I'd always assumed that you were from the south newhere."

"Truth is Sir, I was only eleven when my mother died and father decided to sell his property and move to London, ere he set up in business as agent for the coal owners and nufacturers of the north east. Did very well for himself I ist say. Then he concentrated on turning me into a hionable gentleman."

"He provided the best tutors, tailors, fencing instructors that could find, but by the time I was eighteen I was liking the too well. Oh I liked the fine clothes and the company of the ies at parties but in some quarters I was looked down on as ly the son of a tradesman. The drinking and gambling was ting to be compulsive so my father decided he had had ough, paid my debts and bought my commission in the rines. So I could see something of life and the world d'you , beside the gaming tables and bordellos of the city. He told that my future debts were my own and he would provide thing but a reasonable allowance per annum."

"Strange thing is Sir, I took to the life right away and am ppier in the service than I ever was ashore."

"As I am happy to have you in my ship's company ward."

"Thank you Sir, I appreciate that."

As they finished talking, the disreputable carriage turned o the gateway of the Merriman residence, crunched over the ivel driveway and stopped by the front steps. The three icers alighted and entered the house.

There was almost a party atmosphere in the Merriman household. He found that Doctor Simpson and his daughter Helen and Mrs. Prentice were there combining a social visit with the need to attend to Mr. Grahame who was now staying at the Merriman household. Grahame was still weak but recovering well under the doctor's careful ministrations. Even Captain Saville was there.

Merriman introduced his officers to the gathering and after the usual polite courtesies were exchanged Captain Merriman turned to the two lieutenants. "I've heard a lot about you Mr. Andrews, the fight with the corsairs and all that. You did very well."

Before Andrews could reply, the Captain said, "And you Mr. St James, what happened to you?" indicating the sling round the marine's neck.

"A small sword thrust Sir, from a damned Frenchman who was better with his sword than I could believe. I thought I had him but his last riposte was faster than my parry and pierced my shoulder. And of course he had a longer blade than my shorter regulation sword."

Captain Saville who had been listening with interest to the conversation, added, "I'm reminded of our conversation about swords and swordplay the last time we all met here James, I believe you said that a shorter blade was better for shipboard fighting than a rapier."

"That is true, and I still believe that to be the case, but obviously here is the exception that proves the rule."

After more general conversation, Merriman, his father and Grahame retired to a quiet room where Merriman reported everything that had happened since Grahame had been wounded.

271

"So Sir, in short, the Lord Lieutenant and his party are safe d the plot to seize the graphite was foiled, indeed, we found cargo of stolen graphite on the fishing boat. Some Irish bels were caught and will be tried for piracy and murder but ailed to capture the French vessel and I fear that the man oreau, who appears to have been the ringleader, will likely be rouble to us in the future."

"Nevertheless Commander, thanks to you and your men ents have concluded better than we could have hoped and I ve you to thank for saving my life by bringing me to the od Doctor Simpson."

"The ship's doctor did the best he could but I believe you ould have died if left aboard ship Sir."

"Well, I shall be sending a most favourable report to Lord evenage. I am sure that he will be well pleased. If you have mpleted your report for Admiral Edwards, perhaps they uld be despatched together?"

"Thank you Sir. There is one other thing to report. You call that you told us that you believed someone of the Quality uld be involved in treason, well, I believe it to be Sir William rrester." Merriman went on to relate what he knew and spected about Forrester's connection with the smugglers and so the French.

"Doesn't really surprise me," said Grahame, "We've had our spicions about him too. With this information we shall be le to convict him."

"James," asked his father, "what happened to the smugglers ft adrift?"

"When the weather cleared we saw them not too far off and e were able to capture them again very quickly. They were ruggling to make a sail out of fishing net with scraps of old nvas woven into it.. The fishing boat, a handy two masted smack is alongside the *Pilote* at Parkgate and as for the me[n] they are now pressed into my crew in *Aphrodite,* to repla[ce] some of my losses. That will be punishment enough I think."

"Yes James, serves them right, a good move on your pa[rt] and if you mentioned it in your report the Admiralty wo[n't] worry. Always glad to find more good seamen for the navy."

"Father, what of the lawyer, Robinson and his clerk, ha[ve] they been apprehended?"

"No," replied his father, "Mr. Flitwick and some of his m[en] went with myself and the Chester constables to Robinson[']s premises but they weren't there. We went to his house whe[re] we found his wife barely alive, suffering from some fearf[ul] head injuries. A serving girl had also been badly beaten b[ut] she was able to tell us that Robinson had been there with h[is] clerk. They had ransacked the house and beaten the wom[en] until they told where the money and jewellery was hidde[n]. The wife died soon after."

"So, not only are they to be arrested for treason and oth[er] villainy we can only guess at, but they are now wanted f[or] murder as well," said Merriman.

"Indeed so, Mr. Grahame and I have taken steps to infor[m] various authorities, and handbills with their description a[re] being issued round the county. I hope to have news of the[m] soon."

"Surely their only hope is to leave the country, once aboa[rd] a ship they may never be caught. I would think that the[y] would probably head for the ferry across to Liverpool to find [a] ship there to take them to France or even to America. Only t[he] gallows awaits them here and they have money and valuabl[es] enough to bribe a not too fussy captain to take them and kee[p] quiet about it."

"That is so I'm afraid James; we thought of that and sent constables over there but with no luck.. Anyway, it's out of our hands now."

"Mr. Grahame, now that this matter is concluded, do you have any further orders for me Sir?" enquired Merriman.

"Not at present Commander. If we send our reports to London tomorrow by courier we may hear from our superiors within the week. In the meanwhile, you must be in Dublin to give evidence in the trial of the rebels you caught. I expect that the trial will be speedily arranged once you present yourself over there. You should leave for Ireland tomorrow Commander and I will sail with you."

"Yes Sir, but are you sure that you are recovered enough to make the journey."

"Tut man, of course I'm well enough, even though your excellent Doctor Simpson may not agree. I must go and see how many of my people have survived. Certainly two of them were killed and I must know if my network of agents is still capable of sniffing out plots by the King's enemies."

"I suggest that we ask for further orders to be sent to us here, to await our return from Ireland." He turned to Merriman's father. "My apologies Captain, for assuming that you are agreeable to your house being used as a sort of relay station for messages."

"No need to apologize Sir, I'm only too happy to help."

"Thank you. Now, as our business is finished, perhaps we should join your other guests."

When they rejoined the others, Merriman was dismayed to see his two officers paying close attention to Helen, who was laughing at something one of them had said. By the window his sister Emily was deep in conversation with Captain Saville, watched closely by her mother.

"I hope that young man is going to make his intentio clear," she said to Mrs. Prentice, "If he is the right one for h there could soon be a wedding," She looked over at her eld son who was glowering in the direction of Helen and h admirers. Just then Helen caught sight of Merriman and with word of excuse left them and went across to him.

"Do stop frowning James, from what I hear you ha everything to be pleased about. What makes you so gloomy she said coquettishly.

"Nothing Ma'am, it is just that I hoped, I mean, I would li you to, that is – if you could see ---." He stopped, realizing th once again she had reduced him to stammering inadequacy.

She took his hands in hers and the look in her eyes told h all he wanted to know. Mrs. Prentice leaned nearer Merriman's mother with a smile, "There might be tv weddings to plan for."

The Lawyer flees

The trial of the rebels was concluded within a week of Merriman's arrival in Dublin. His clear evidence, supported by an affidavit from Grahame who declined to appear in public, was sufficient for the court to declare the men guilty and pass sentence of death upon them.

The sentence was carried out in public the next day but Merriman did not attend, confiding to Grahame that he had no stomach for that kind of thing. Grahame then disappeared for most of a week about his own mysterious affairs leaving Merriman to his own devices.

The time passed agreeably enough, as there was plenty to do aboard a ship of war. There were still some repairs to be completed and Merriman, with lieutenants Laing and Andrews, had to re-organise the watch bill to include the pressed men, to fill some of the gaps caused by the ship's losses. The new men had tried to object to their situation but after Merriman had offered to put them ashore to be tried for piracy and murder and share the fate of the Irish rebels they had quickly settled down. The fat man was indeed the card cheat. Merriman recognized him immediately and when questioned he confessed to being one the men responsible for the theft of graphite being transported to London.

When Laing was told that the man was to be pressed with the others, his only comment was "Good, we'll soon have some of the fat and tallow off him Sir," rubbing his hands in satisfaction.

Gunner's mate Salmon was promoted to replace the dead Mr. Hodges.

Merriman spent a pleasant evening with Colonel Sir He[r] White and his officers of the garrison telling them all about [the] capture of the cutter and the rebels, and the inconclusive fi[ght] with the French ship.

Dublin society made heroes of Merriman and his offic[ers] when the trial and the circumstances of the Viceroy's esca[pe] from capture became public knowledge. They were invited t[o a] ball at the Viceroy's residence and almost every day there w[ere] invitations to dinners and dances from hostesses determined [to] have the gallant Commander and officers at *their* functi[ons] especially from ladies with unmarried daughters.

It was all pleasant enough at first and Merriman had [to] arrange a sort of roster to give each officer equal chances to [go] ashore, even the two midshipmen. But it soon began to p[all] and a certain reluctance to accept invitations became apparer[t.]

Lieutenant St. James, with his arm in a sling, playing the p[art] of the wounded hero to perfection, had always been the cen[tre] of a group of young ladies wherever they went, but finally ev[en] he had to admit to Merriman that enough was enough.

"Daren't go ashore again Sir, positively daren't. I'll fi[nd] myself up at the altar if I do. I had no idea of the lengths so[me] girls will go to, to trap a fellow. A kiss and a squeeze behi[nd] the drapes seems little enough but one looses interest in ev[en] that when the girl's mother is sighted bearing down under f[ull] sail."

"Same with me Sir, admitted Laing morosely. "Can't wai[t to] get back to sea. I had no idea that women could talk so much[."]

"Well Colin, you've learned the truth of the old dictum [a] woman's chief weapon is her tongue and she won't let it rust[."]

They all laughed. Merriman's officers were well used [to] their captain's use of proverbs and sometimes bets were quie[tly] laid as to which he would use next. Privately Merrim[an] wondered if he should even say things like that, given his feelings and intentions towards Helen.

Fortunately Mr. Grahame soon returned and with his appearance *Aphrodite* was at last able to leave.

Meanwhile, aboard a trading vessel at the dockside in Liverpool, Jeremiah Robinson was negotiating with a ship's captain for passage to America for himself and Beadle. They had tried several ships but this was the first one where the captain was prepared to bargain. The captain, a villainous looking individual, stared at the two men in front of him, thinking hard. They were unshaven and disheveled and it was obvious that they were desperate to leave the country and might be prepared to pay a good price for his help. On the other hand, if there was a sheriff's warrant out for them there might be a good reward for turning them in.

"What will you pay," he asked with a sly look at the bag the first man clutched tightly.

"We are in a hurry to reach America and would normally travel by one of the ships which usually carry passengers. However, there are none sailing for three or four days and as our business is urgent we cannot wait. We will pay the same price as we would normally pay," said Robinson. Beadle nodded his head in agreement.

"Seems fair enough, you can have this cabin of mine but there's nothing fancy on my ship and one of you must sleep in a hammock. You'll have to eat with the rest of us. We'll deal with the money later, I must get under way now or we'll miss the tide."

Left alone, the two fugitives relaxed for the first time in days. Robinson even managed a feeble smile at his companion. "We've done it, we're away free and clear." Little did the fugitives know that their relief was to be short lived. Later that night, with the ship well out to sea, the captain and some of his crew burst into the cabin and overpowered them. Once they were tied hand and foot the captain dismissed his men.

"Now then, let's see what you have in this bag of yours," he said with relish. "O-ho, what's this?" He pulled out a cloth bag and tipped the contents out. "Jewellery eh! I'll wager it's stolen, that's why you had to leave so quickly. And there's more money here than you were going to pay me. Well it's mine now and I have to decide what to do with you two fine specimens."

"What are you going to do," asked a terrified Beadle, "You can't put us ashore in America with no money."

"Oh but we're not going to America, not directly that is. No we're bound for Africa, the Slave Coast to trade for slaves and then we takes them to America for sale to the plantation owners. Until then you can work your passage. You might fetch a good price over there, or maybe I'll drop you over the side first."

Truly they had exchanged the frying pan for the fire.

War with France Now certain

Merriman and Grahame arrived back at the Merriman residence hoping to find new orders for them but it was not until another two days had passed that a bedraggled courier on a lathered, mud splattered horse arrived with letters from the Admiralty for them both.

Grahame read his and looked seriously at Merriman. "My letter is from Lord Stevenage himself. He commends you most highly for your actions over the last few weeks and it now seems that we must continue to work together. Five days ago, on the 21st January, the revolutionaries executed the king of France, Louis XV1 on the guillotine. Beheaded him like a common criminal."

"Good God, I didn't think they would go as far as that. Why would they do it?"

"I imagine it is because the more influential of them decided that if he lived, there would always be plots and schemes afoot to rescue him. If one were to be successful it could mean that the revolution itself could be in jeopardy. I expect that the rest of the French royal family is doomed to the same fate."

"May God help them then," said Merriman sadly, "for it is certain we cannot."

Grahame continued, "His Lordship tells me that war is now certain as both our Government and the National Assembly in Paris have made statements which, unless one side or the other backs down, make war inevitable. Such a retreat will be neither desired or possible for either side and diplomatic communications have ceased."

"Furthermore, I am directed to travel to Antigua in the West Indies and take charge of all intelligence gathering out there.

We must discover what the French intentions are in respect our own West Indian islands and their valuable trad Apparently they have their agents already at work out the trying to stir up the slaves and native peoples into insurrectic I see from my orders that you and your ship are ordered to ta me."

"Yes Sir, that is what my orders say. We are to sail at on for Plymouth for victualling and repair. The port Admiral w have notice of our arrival and is ordered to supply the sh with whatever is needful. Oh, and the *Pilote* is to be released the Revenue. I also have a letter here signed by Mr. Pitt hims no less, requiring all persons in authority to aid us in any w we require."

"Then let us be about it Mr. Merriman."

Merriman broke the news of their imminent departure a the reasons for it to his parents. His mother wept a litt fussing over him as mothers do and enjoining him to be care with his health and not to eat too much foreign food, "Y never can tell what they put in it" she complained. "De James, come back to us safely my son."

"So it is certain to be war is it?" roared old Capta Merriman. "Damned French, if they can murder their ki then they are capable of anything. Thank God we have strong navy to protect us. Well James, it is up to you a young men like you that we look to, to teach the Froggies lesson. It'll mean more chances of promotion eh! I'll see y made post soon."

Merriman asked his father if they might borrow the coa again with Hoskins to drive them to Parkgate from where th could find a boat to take them out to *Aphrodite,* again anchor off the Point of Air. Merriman had sent his boat back to t ship.

"Of course my boy, only wish I could go with you."

The farewells over, Grahame overwhelming Mrs. Merriman [wit]h thanks for the hospitality he had received from her and [her] family, the coach set off for Parkgate.

"Mr. Grahame, I must make a call in Neston on our way, I [nee]d to see Dr Simpson."

"Dr Simpson? I'll wager it's the lovely Miss Simpson you [wis]h to see," replied Grahame with a broad smile on his face. [Co]me, don't try to deny it. I've seen the way you look at each [oth]er, good fortune to you, she is an exceptional lady."

"Thank you Sir, I confess I hope to marry her, but I haven't summoned up the courage to ask her or her father."

"Then do so, at once, or you'll regret it all the while we are [aw]ay. Remember, faint heart ne'er won a lady fair, as some [poe]t has it."

At the Simpson's house, after the usual offer and acceptance [of] refreshment, Merriman broke the news to Helen and her [fath]er about the situation with France and that he was ordered [to t]he West Indies.

At that point Grahame diplomatically asked the Doctor to [giv]e a final look at his wound and they disappeared into [ano]ther room leaving Merriman and Helen alone together. For [a l]ong moment they just looked at one another, then Helen's [n]erve melted and tears trembled in her eyes.

"Oh James, how long will you be away?" she said quietly.

"How long for I cannot say, it could be months or even years [bef]ore I return."

His reply caused the tears to spill over and roll down her [che]eks. He took her hands in his and drew her to him, then [tilt]ed her face up so that he could see her eyes.

"Don't cry my love, I came here to ask you, that is, to see if [you] felt about me as I feel about you," he realized he was floundering again, took a deep breath and said "Helen, [will] you marry me, I haven't asked your father yet and I know [we] can't be married until I come home again, but I love you [you] see and if you would wait ----"

He stopped as she placed her fingers over his mouth. [She] looked up at him with her eyes shining through the tears. "[Of] course I will marry you James, this very minute if I coul[d]." Next moment she was in his arms and they were kiss[ing] passionately.

"Oh James, I never felt like this before, I love you so." [The] time passed swiftly as they murmured endearments to e[ach] other and they only broke apart as the door opened and [the] Doctor followed by Grahame entered.

With Helen's hand in his, Merriman turned to the Doc[tor] and with quiet determination said "Sir, I know I should h[ave] asked you first, but I have just asked Helen to marry me a[nd] she has done me the honour of accepting my proposal."
Doctor Simpson took one look at his daughter's happy f[ace] before grasping Merriman's hand in his.

"My dear James, I couldn't be more pleased. I knew t[his] moment would come. It was obvious the last time we me[t at] your father's house that you two had eyes for no other an[d I] knew something was afoot when Mr. Grahame took me into [the] other room on the pretext of a totally unnecessary look at [my] wound. Helen, my dear, your mother would be as pleased [as I] am."

As the doctor embraced his daughter, Grahame sho[ok] Merriman's hand vigorously and then pounded him on [the] back. "Congratulations Mr. Merriman, I hope you will be v[ery] happy together." He winked, a surprisingly familiar gest[ure] from a man who had always appeared so serious, "See, w[hat] did I tell you about faint heart and fair lady" he whispered.

"I must tell my sister about this," said the Doctor ringing a bell. When the maid answered he said to her "Please be good enough to ask Mrs. Prentice to join us as we have something to celebrate. Gentlemen I trust you will join me in a glass of brandy?"

On hearing the news Jane Prentiss hugged her neice, turned to Merriman, hugged him then kissed him on the cheek before saying "Oh dear, I think I am going to cry. William, I need a drink."

When they were all supplied with a drink of one kind or another the Doctor proposed a toast to the couple, Jane Prentiss shed a few more tears and then Mr. Grahame surprised everybody by saying "Doctor, I know what you think about times but I should like to say more. As a son-in-law you are taking into your family an outstanding young King's officer who, I am sure, will go far in the service of his country. I know he is well thought of at the Admiralty especially after the events of the last weeks and Lord Stevenage himself has taken an interest in James' career."

He raised his glass. "A toast to a future admiral and his lovely bride-to-be."

"Thank you Sir" replied Merriman, "I only hope that what you say is so. Now then, I know we are to leave as soon as possible, but I believe that the tide will allow enough time for me to go with Helen to see my parents. They know nothing of this although I expect that my mother won't be surprised."

"Yes James, you do that," said the doctor. "In the meanwhile I'll write a few notes for your Mr. McBride regarding tropical conditions and diseases which I am sure he will find helpful in keeping your crew healthy. Again my ideas are not accepted by others in my profession but I urge you and

he to consider them closely. I will have them ready for y[
when you return to collect Mr. Grahame."

The Merriman household was reduced to bedlam when t[
news was given to Captain Merriman and his wife. There w[
much hugging, kissing and congratulating, even Annie t[
housekeeper was called in to be told and she, worthy so[
subsided in floods of tears. Merriman's father took Hele[
small hand in his great paw, kissed her gently on the che[
then threw decorum to the winds and gave her a big hug.

"Oh James, can't you stay longer?" asked his mother wh[
Merriman said that they must be going, we've hardly had[
chance to talk about the wedding."

"Now Mary, James is right, he has to go. Anyway, y[
don't need him here when you ladies are discussing t[
wedding, we poor males had best not interfere in such matte[
Besides, Helen and her father will be frequent visitors here a[
you will have ample time for talk."

The journey back to the doctor's home was all too short a[
there was only time for one last embrace before Merriman a[
Grahame climbed into the carriage to be whisked off [
Parkgate. A fishing boat skipper agreed, for a reasonable su[
to take them out to the Point of Air and as darkness f[
Merriman climbed aboard *Aphrodite* and assumed commar[
Dawn found the ship off Anglesey, well on the way [
Plymouth.

A few days later on February 1st 1793, France declared w[
on England.

THE END

Printed in Great Britain
by Amazon